The murder was planned meticulously, confidently and ruth-lessly. Who, after all, would question the death of a can-tankerous seventy-eight-year-old woman in a private nursing home? If it hadn't been for the astute eyes of the pathologist, nobody would have noticed the tiny puncture mark on Mrs Evelyn Norman's body . . .

Despite the cost, both the old woman's daughters were rather glad of the break when their irascible mother was admitted as a short stay patient. And now she's dead, at least it means she won't be coming to live with either of them. If only, however, Mrs Norman had made a will. For what is to become of her prized possession, an extremely valuable set of antiquarian books?

Assigned to the case are Detective Chief Inspector Browne and Detective Constable Benedict Mitchell who must put to one side the urgent problems in their personal lives to concentrate on the hunt for the killer. It doesn't take them long to discover that Evelyn Norman's precious possession is missing. Is the heirloom's disappearance con-nected with the old woman's death? Could it be that Evelyn Norman was murdered by a member of her own family, someone pushed to the limits of endurance? And beyond . . .

The Way of a Serpent

Pauline Bell

MACMILLAN
LONDON

First published 1993 by Macmillan London Limited

a division of Pan Macmillan Publishers Limited
Cavaye Place London SW10 9PG
and Basingstoke

Associated companies throughout the world

ISBN 0–333–60221–8

9 8 7 6 5 4 3 2 1

A CIP catalogue record for this book is available from
the British Library

Phototypeset by Intype, London
Printed by Mackays of Chatham PLC, Chatham, Kent

For John

With grateful thanks for their advice and information to
Craig Deakin, Tony Fothergill, Peter Heaton, and
David and Lesley Lord.

Chapter One

The pale sky was morning clean, still streaked a little on the horizon from its dawn-wind sweeping. Against it, black branches made stark lines just lightly stippled with the yellow of forsythia, the first pink of the cherry and the slightly flushed white almond. Beneath them, the austerity of the purple and white Lenten crocuses had succeeded the cheerful, early yellow ones. A cruel wind turned the normally straight and dapper dwarf conifers lining the path into yielding arcs.

The tall window gave a clear view of this ephemeral beauty but the figure seated at the desk in the bay paid no attention to it. The tip of the tongue made elliptical journeys round dry lips as the hand carefully traced letters only just showing through from the document beneath. The task was almost completed – just a signature, illegible and heavily underlined, to go over now.

The writing looked a bit shaky, didn't flow as easily as in the original. Still, it would be well smudged when it was handed back. It would be all right. Aching fingers allowed the pen to fall back on the desk. There was no need to worry. The old woman wouldn't be a threat for much longer and she wasn't going to feel any pain. She wouldn't realize what was happening and there was no need to stay and watch her die.

The figure in the window rose, stowed the original document safely away and took the forgery into the kitchen for its 'accidental' wetting.

Several miles away, the same wind tossed the branches of the flowering currant bush overlooked by the living-room window

1

of a ground-floor flat in Heath View. The heath was viewed now by Detective Constable Benedict Mitchell from a rather greater distance than when the Victorian terrace had first been built and he could see more council houses than acres of heather as a background to his pink-flowered shrub.

Nevertheless, the proud glow of ownership that he had now enjoyed for almost three days, was undiminished by them. He had spent twenty-seven happy years in his parents' council house and could look on large housing estates with equanimity. He did so for several moments longer before fetching a couple of cans from the fridge in preparation for his afternoon appointment with the rugby semi-final.

He was quite happy to watch it on the black and white set that he had used in his bedroom when he lived with his parents. There were a great many improvements to be made to his new abode before there would be money to spare for a more sophisticated television set. Before Virginia came home from Oxford for the Easter vac, for instance, he would need to acquire something more comfortable to sit on than the lumpy settee on which he was presently slumped. It had been donated by his mother's sister who had bought instead a plump-cushioned collection of insubstantial cane contraptions to which DC Mitchell would certainly have refused house room.

He tuned in to the match. The afternoon stretched on and, as the daylight faded, the room was lit only by the realistic flames of the gas fire. The cosy flickering hid the deficiencies of his furnishings and Mitchell had dispatched the dregs of his first can contentedly by the time the hooter signalling half-time silenced the hysterical screaming of the commentator.

It was succeeded by the soccer half-time scores, read in a public school voice and interspersed with calmly analytical descriptions of the present situation in some of the games. Soccer was not even Mitchell's second love; after rugby he was a cricket man, so the interruption of the telephone at this point was no great annoyance, especially when he recognized his fiancée's voice.

'Hi, Ginny. I'm watching the match. Congratulations on

hitting half time. And don't give me the third degree about how much unpacking I've done. It's all finished and I deserve a couple of hours off.' There was no rejoinder, just a silence for several seconds. 'Are you still there?'

'Yes.' The silence continued.

'What's up, then?' He was puzzled, almost anxious.

'Benny, I'm pregnant.' Then they were both silent.

Virginia was the first to pull herself together. She described her early but growing suspicions and the doctor's confirmation, reliving the events as she described them. The doctor's snooty receptionist had demanded her first name and she had blushed for it. It was just the one not to have in her predicament. She had protested at the verdict, describing the careful precautions they had taken and the doctor had smiled, having heard similar assurances so many times before.

Now Mitchell rallied. 'We'd better get on with some wedding plans, then.' He was adjusting rapidly to the situation. Ever since he'd made the decision to leave home he'd been wondering if Virginia would be willing to risk her parents' disapproval and move in with him during her vacations. He had quite a lot to lose on his own account from antagonizing her father but now, once the old man had got used to this new idea, he'd be on Mitchell's side and want the wedding over and the younger generation to set up house as soon as possible.

'No, Benny, not yet. This changes everything. I'm not sure about it any more.'

His world rocked. 'You mean you don't want to marry me because something we thought we'd taken care to avoid has happened to both of us?' Another silence. He began to panic. It was his child, wasn't it? She hadn't formed an attachment to one of those Oxford namby-pambies who sat up all night discussing abstruse matters that could never have any relevance to real life? He'd met some of them on his various visits and had worried then, not about Virginia's loyalty to himself, but about how he could cater, after she'd taken her degree and married him, for that intellectual, theoretical aspect of her mind that he hardly knew and certainly didn't understand.

'It's not you I'm unsure about, it's me. I'm not the person

3

I thought I was. I've got to get to know myself again before I commit myself irrevocably.'

He felt his anxiety confirmed, justified. 'Well, probably I'm going to change as well, once the news has sunk in – and don't say, "All the more reason to wait." If this had happened two years into marriage it would have altered us both just the same. Extra responsibility does. You wouldn't have demanded a separation to think things over then, would you?'

'Don't badger me, Benny.' Her voice held an element of panic as she replied and he wished she were physically close to him. 'I can't make a decision till I've thought things out. You had a right to know about the existence of your own child as soon as I did, but, now you know, I don't want to discuss it till I get in touch again. It'll give you some thinking time too.'

It was his child then. Thank God for that anyway. 'But what about your parents – your studies?'

'I said don't badger me.' She had herself in hand now. 'I imagine Dad's going to say the same as you, want an immediate wedding, but I'm hoping Mum will see it from my point of view.'

For a few seconds, Mitchell made himself picture his future father-in-law's reaction to the news. And what pleasure and amusement it would afford his colleagues! Half of them considered that his engagement to his Detective Chief Inspector's daughter was an unfair leg up in his career and the only reason he had been temporarily promoted to sergeant during DS Hunter's illness just before Christmas. He shook his head to clear it. 'Are you coming home to tell them? I'll come with you. It's my responsibility as well as yours. In fact, I'll go and tell them for you if you like.'

'No!' The interruption silenced him and he listened, trying not to acknowledge his relief. 'I shan't come home for a week or so. I've written to them and I shall post the letter tonight. If I catch the last collection they'll get it on Monday morning.' There was no reply and she sensed his disapproval. 'No, it isn't that I can't face them. I'd feel better telling them to their faces actually, but I think it'll be easier for them this way. Dad's going to be furious, about it messing up my exams, about our irresponsibility and so on, especially after all the arguments about me coming to Oxford in the first place. And, although he's happy enough to admit to his colleagues when he's wrong about professional matters, I know he'd find it very difficult to apologize to me. This way, all his angry recriminations when I see him will at least be considered ones, not just the result of his going over the top because he was taken by surprise.'

'All right, I can see that.'

'Good. That's all then, for now.'

'No it bloody isn't! Ginny!'

'Yes?'

'This infant of ours is going to make life hellish awkward but – it's very welcome.'

He could hear her smiling. 'Right then. Don't ring me. I'll be in touch.' *Click!*

She hadn't even given him a chance to ask how she was feeling physically. Bother the woman! Mitchell replaced his own receiver, switched off the muted though still frenzied screaming of the rugby commentator and stared, unseeing, for some considerable time at the blank screen.

The wind had raged all day and had almost blown itself out by the time the patients in Ward B7 of the Cloughton Royal Hospital settled down for the night, so that, in spite of the lack of double glazing, so lamented by Whiny in the next cubicle to Pamela Hill, a restful hush soon prevailed.

Pamela did not find it conducive to sleep but was philosophical. After all, she had spent the previous afternoon in the operating theatre under anaesthesia and a considerable part of the intervening time under the soporific influence of morphine so she was already well rested.

She turned instead to a mental consideration of her two fellow sufferers in the ward. Phoebe, whose black face smiled but who conversed in short prim sentences, had seemed unpromising company till Pamela had realized that English was her third language. When her equally black and smiling husband had arrived that evening they had been quietly lively

5

and articulate, obviously arguing amicably with each other in a guttural African dialect with occasional sorties into rapid, excited French that Pamela mostly understood. She had been tempted to make contact in her own French, fairly fluent though badly accented, but she hadn't had the energy. Perhaps she would try tomorrow.

Whiny's attempts to communicate with Phoebe consisted of often repeated phrases in pidgin English and at double volume as if the poor girl were deaf and feeble-minded. Whiny cloaked her lack of sensitivity in a great show of solicitude that failed to stop short of bullying. Phoebe defended herself by spending her nights drugged with painkillers and her days staring at the television screen in the day room, picking up scraps of Australianized English. Doing battle in her weakened state was more than she could manage.

Whiny had Views on coloured immigrants which she expounded during Phoebe's absences. 'These Asians . . . it's as if they're from a different continent.' Pamela pointed out that Phoebe was African. Whiny was undeterred. 'When they have chicken, you know, they slit its throat and let it run round the garden until it drops. Then they eat it. A man who lives near us is like that. He got sent to jail for cutting his father's nose off. That's the sort of thing they do in their country. And all this aid we send them, you know, it doesn't get through; it gets stopped— Course, they must be on earth for some reason, mustn't they? So long as things are clean, that's what I say. That's the important thing.'

She had no idea that her implications were so perniciously offensive and considered her attitude extremely charitable. Pamela had second thoughts about airing her French. Whiny would consider it a deliberate attempt to show off and cut her out. And she really must start thinking of Whiny as Myra before she slipped up and used the apt sobriquet in their half-drugged conversations. She turned over very cautiously. Her wound was sore and no one had told her that the starched sheets would crackle every time she moved, nor that the pillows and mattresses were stuffed with unyielding wood shavings.

On the other hand, she had discovered that the legendary patience and concern of the nurses was real, manifested in a multitude of unnecessary little kindnesses that their superiors would never hear about. Sure enough, she heard the curtain of her cubicle being drawn softly back and untruthfully assured the night sister that she was comfortable.

Myra was not going to be neglected. 'I can't sleep, Sister.' Ever since she had been admitted, Myra had interspersed a welter of unnecessary ringings of the nurse-call bell with protestations of how she hated to disturb them. Once again, she was told that she was no trouble and that that was what the staff were there for. A sleeping pill was offered, accepted with a show of reluctance and imbibed with maximum fuss. 'Goodness, it's a big one . . . I haven't got it down yet . . . it's still not down.' Sister suggested putting it in a spoonful of jam. 'But I've put it in my mouth now. Shall I take it out again? . . . Ooh, it's horrible.'

Pamela reflected that Myra must feel stronger than she did herself if she could manage to create such a disturbance. She hoped the sleeping pill was a strong one. Not that there would be much peace when it eventually worked. Myra's snoring was phenomenal but it was easier to cope with than her comments which almost always ended with a question – 'aren't they? . . . doesn't she? . . . shouldn't we?' A series of insincere and obsequious agreements made Pamela despise herself; silence was rude and only caused the questions to be repeated; argument was beyond her present supply of energy, so that every remark from the next cubicle put Pamela at odds with herself.

She'd made a desperate offer to lend Myra a book. 'I'm not a person that reads books.' Pamela had known it was an abortive attempt before she made it. She'd been surprised when Myra bought a newspaper until she saw her use it, holding it aloft and reading each headline aloud. 'That doesn't cheer you up much, does it? That isn't a very nice thing to have to read about when you're in here.' Still, she'd been quieter since they'd both had their operations and now the blessed snoring was beginning. There was no obligation to answer snores.

Freed from social responsibilities, Pamela fell to wondering about the sinister implications of the questions she'd been asked when she was admitted. Who was her priest, her next of kin, what were her religion, her allergies? Had she remembered them all? It didn't matter. She intensely disliked discussing her own bodily functions – or dysfunctions. She was neither prudish nor squeamish but she fiercely resented the invasion of her privacy.

It would be worse when she was sent home. At least, in hospital, people were being paid for their services. They were doing their job and she could admire them for doing it efficiently. They were clinical, fairly impersonal and she didn't feel, in accepting their ministrations, that she was forfeiting her dignity. At home her care would be due to someone's kindness. She would have to be grateful for other people's offensive attentions, would suffer them with embarrassment, even from Sonia.

Sonia, thank goodness, understood. Pamela had been deeply grateful for her matter-of-fact five-minute stay in the visiting hour and had been amused by Myra's barely veiled opinion that Sonia should be reprimanded for her undaughterliness. Her own immediate family, Myra boasted, had come in force, arriving early, queuing to be admitted and lingering after the bell which commanded them to leave. Pamela thought they looked too cowed to do anything else. She scorned to explain that Sonia was a single parent with a four-year-old to take care of. It occurred to her now that Sonia had been looking particularly well groomed and glamorous tonight. Maybe there was another gentleman friend on the scene.

Perversely, now that Myra was asleep, Pamela wanted to rouse her. She had at least provided a counter-irritation, a distraction from the real problem which was now keeping Pamela awake. Sonia, in her brief visit, had tried to forestall this. 'Gran's fine. Everyone in the place is making a great fuss of her from the matron down, and she's lapping it up. She's well over her flu. She could easily have managed back at her own place if she hadn't been convinced it was someone else's job to look after her.'

Pamela was beginning to fear that, in future, someone would have to. Her mother, an insecure and clinging seventy-eight, had taken more than a month to get over a bout of flu, unnecessarily and deliberately in Sonia's opinion. Pamela had taken her mother into her own house during both the illness and the convalescence and had been glad that her own impending operation had put an end to what looked like being an otherwise indefinite stay. 'You mustn't take her back when you're home again, even when you're completely fit,' Sonia had warned. 'You'll never be rid of her if you do. She had everything nicely as she wanted it when she moved in with you. It brought her up short when she found out you were having this op. She's told Mrs Cunningham that you've just got a few "women's problems" and that everything will soon be back as it was. She knows better than to expect anything from Aunt Stella and she wouldn't sink to accepting hospitality from her immoral and sinful granddaughter, even if I'd have her. She's got you nicely set up.'

Pamela had sighed. Sonia, practical, sometimes ruthless, had never had any patience with her grandmother. At present, Pamela found she could only respond to her daughter's attacks by defending the old lady even while she shared Sonia's fears.

After an hour of wakefulness and of rumblings from Myra, she essayed another turn of her body, being careful not to drag at her stitches nor detach the tube that constantly dripped into the vein in her wrist. Sister appeared again. 'Are you in any pain, Mrs Hill?'

Pamela shook her head. 'Not really. I'm still a bit sore but that's all.'

'You're not worried at all, are you? The operation went very well. It was a fairly big one, of course, but so long as you get plenty of rest you'll be fine.'

Pamela switched on her bedside light. 'I am a bit worried but it's nothing to do with my health.'

'Want to talk about it?'

Pamela was regretting the confidence already. 'That's kind of you but it won't change anything.'

Sister was not to be denied. 'Look, I'm going to send for

some tea. I always have some round about midnight. You'll feel better if you talk about it.'

As Pamela drifted into sleep towards one o'clock, she suspected that she had told Sister a great deal about herself as well as her mother. She hadn't mentioned the problem of Owen, of course, but she and Sister had both been right. She did feel better but talking hadn't changed anything at all.

Chapter Two

Outside the hospital's outer doors, Sonia Hill had paused to open her umbrella. A spiteful gust left over from the earlier storm did battle with it until she abandoned the struggle and dashed, uncovered, through spitting rain, towards the red Fiat at the far end of the visitors' car park. She folded herself thankfully into the driver's seat and twisted the central mirror until she could see herself well enough to check the damage to her face and hair. Her eye make-up had not run and after tucking a few damp strands of black hair back where they belonged and applying perfume to her throat and wrists, she was ready to continue her journey.

It was a short one, the Weavers' Arms being less than a mile away. She wondered whether to park on the cobbled lane that led down, between tall buildings, to the valley bottom, or whether to use the car park that had never been properly surfaced. It had probably become waterlogged in the rain which by now was pouring down. Either plan would mean the ruination of her high heels and muddy splashes on the backs of her calves. She opted for the cobbles, drove as close to the building as she could and welcomed the wall of warmth that hit her as she opened the second of the double doors that led into the public bar.

She glanced briefly at her watch, wondering how long she could trade on Mrs Quentin's good nature, then looked round. She was not one of those women who had qualms about going into public houses on her own. Nevertheless, she was glad to see, as she pushed through the crowd, that Alistair had kept a stool for her by draping his coat over it.

'Thanks. Tish not here yet?'

'Getting them in. How was Pam? You can't have stayed long.'

Sonia removed her cousin's coat from the stool, rolled it neatly and stowed it under the small table. 'Bloody but unbowed. She looked a bit tired, actually, so I left her in peace after a few minutes.'

She looked up and smiled at Tish, accepted her cider from him and drank thirstily. The juke box stopped playing and, picking up his own glass, Tish departed again to feed it. Sonia's eyes followed him as she tried to analyse why she found him so compellingly attractive. He was not handsome, though the dim lighting flattered him, hiding his acne scars and softening the rugged features. His long, square-tipped fingers were feeding coins into a metal slot and she remembered the respect, almost reverence, with which they had held up her tapestries, unfolded the knitted garments made to her own designs, tilted her collage pictures to the light. If only . . . She shook her head at what might have been and returned her attention to her cousin, who was scowling ferociously into his beer.

'What's eating you, then?' He bit his lip but made no reply. She prompted him, impatiently. 'Spit it out, Al.'

He scowled more ferociously. 'The old woman's told Dad he can go ahead and sell the Book.' His tone invested the common noun with a capital letter. 'She says she'll lend him what it fetches till his business really takes off.'

Sonia whistled softly, then shrugged. 'She'll change her mind again. She doesn't know how long it'll be before she's got Mum at her beck and call again, so she's sweetening up your side of the family in case she needs to apply to them. Don't worry about it.'

He pushed his empty glass to the far side of the table. 'But my mother is sure to want to snap it up. They've got rain pouring in through the ceiling of the flat and sod all in the bank for having it repaired. I can see the business being on the line – mine, I mean. I might pop in to see Gran on Monday and find out exactly what the situation is.'

Sonia laughed. 'If you visit her, she'll die from the shock, no one will be able to find the wretched book and everyone will think she's absent-mindedly sent it to a jumble sale. You've thought of the perfect solution.'

They both looked up as Tish came back to the table. 'Take Five' was providing a background to the buzz of conversation. Sonia screwed up her nose. 'Not more fifties jazz?'

Tish looked indignant. 'They haven't got anything earlier and anyway, it's the main reason I come in here. It certainly isn't for the ale or the décor.' He raised a deprecating arm to indicate the opposite wall. The three of them drank, listening companionably as 'Take Five' was succeeded by the quirky rhythm of 'The Unsquare Dance'. Two rounds and a game of dominoes later, the clock crawled towards ten and struck. Tish glanced up at Sonia. 'Shouldn't you be on your way? It's a bit beyond hospital visiting time.'

Sonia grinned. 'Might as well be hung for a sheep as a lamb. Mrs Q. will know where I am, or she'll guess when she smells smoke on my clothes. Anyway, she won't mind. She encourages me to get out and meet plenty of young men. She thinks Thomas needs a father.'

Tish looked alarmed. 'I hope you haven't got me lined up. Can't stand brats, even yours. They stop you getting any work done.'

'But they can be kept out of the way whilst you're working. You don't mean you object to them *per se*?'

Tish grinned. 'I mean exactly what I said. I've no interest in the begetting, the incubating, the producing and particularly in the rearing.'

Alistair appeared amused at both Tish's vehemence and Sonia's obvious distress. 'I wouldn't have thought you were over-fond of the genus yourself.' He leered at his cousin. 'Tom's appearance wasn't exactly planned and rearing isn't proving very convenient.'

'He's no inconvenience to you. Mind your own business.' Seeing Alistair's startled expression, Sonia tried to get a better grip on herself. Alistair had always insulted her with gay abandon and in most contexts she took it in good part. She

13

tried again, however, to convert Tish. 'You might find that observing them gives you inspiration. When I was making that underwater collage for the nursery school I—'

Now Tish looked annoyed. 'I've said what I think. I'm not going to change my mind. Now let's talk about something else.'

Observing his cousin's trembling lip, Alistair chipped in. 'And I'm no good. You're not allowed to marry your first cousin.'

'Yes you are!' Alistair looked alarmed in his turn at Sonia's quick rejoinder. 'Don't worry, though. You aren't my type. Perhaps I had better go.'

Tish rose with her. 'Your shout,' he told Alistair. 'I'll see Sonia to her car.'

Sonia prepared herself for the climax of her evening, the whole point of her visit to the Weavers'. It wasn't a bad sort of pub, after all. Under the plaster and the mushroom paint were blocks of honest to goodness millstone grit. The lintel over the door said sixteen hundred and something undecipherable, and the beams in the ceiling had been there since that date. They had holes in them where huge iron hooks had been removed. Wall lamps twinkled at them from holders made from old shuttles from the eighteenth-century mills. She closed the door on it all and went out into an inviting darkness, grateful for the wind that cooled her flushed face.

Tish took her arm. 'I wanted to get you on your own to ask you if you know what's wrong with Alistair. I haven't had a civil word out of him for days.'

The cold that Sonia had found bracing became enervating in her disappointment. She shrugged. 'It'll be something and nothing. He's always been moody. Tell him to snap out of it. Goodnight.' The rain trickled down her neck. Her fingers, chilled already, refused to insert her key into the ignition. When she eventually managed to start the engine, she drove away without looking to see whether he was waving her off.

Stella Fenton, whose help in the care of her mother was expected with so little confidence by Pamela, her sister, and

14

Sonia, her niece, was at least condescending to assist her husband, albeit grudgingly. At the school, where she taught three days a week, she gave the impression that she was the power behind Tony's business and she sometimes even believed it. Certainly, she had ideas for it that exceeded anything that he had actually achieved. But, when she accompanied him to a book fair, or minded the shop, she was aware that she was merely an inexpert and uncomfortable drudge.

Uncomfortable especially. The temperature of the venue was never right. Early on, it was always cold and draughty, doors open on all sides to admit the trolley-loads of shelving, stock and lighting equipment. Then, when setting up was completed, and the doors, except where the public came in, closed, a stifling fug developed. However, the Guildhall, where they were toiling today, was at least picturesque and imposing. The dark roof rafters were supported by huge wooden pillars, like an old threepenny piece in cross-section, each large enough to have needed a whole tree trunk. They rested on carved stone plinths on the flagged stone floor.

Tony had told her the flags were corallian limestone with polished marble insets in various colours. His sporadic geology lectures bored her, and the insets themselves, which seemed to be coats of arms, were indistinguishable, their designs interrupted by the bookcases that partially obscured them and ruined the soaring dimensions of the hall.

The furniture the dealers used was almost uniform, six-foot-high wooden folding frames with veneered shelves, the pattern laid down not by the rules of the PBFA, but by the DIY chain that produced them for twenty pounds. Stella gave herself a respite from filling them by pretending to admire the stained-glass windows, though the effect of their predominant yellow and purple was not soothing. Taking advantage of her preoccupation, one of the supports spitefully trapped her fingers. A shelf, hitherto firm, suddenly became unhooked and the whole stacked edifice rocked.

Manhandling the shelving pulled the hinges out of true and Tony never had the time for or knack of mending them. She

15

said a quick prayer and everything stayed still until Tony had more or less secured it again. 'Don't worry, I'll finish it off. I shouldn't have left it to you.' Stella, offended, stood aside, watching another dealer take an even more decrepit bookcase and, by dint of kicking and cheerful abuse, manoeuvre it so that the shelves supported not only his books but the frame that was meant to support them.

She turned back to her husband. 'I see we've been pushed to the far end of the room, as usual.'

He answered without turning. 'Don't be silly. It's just the luck of the draw.'

She remained silent but she knew that people she recognized as more assertive seemed always to have the stalls by the door that caught the browsers' attention first. She surveyed the room again. Most people were finished now. The set-up always looked makeshift because the building it was happening in was designed for another purpose. However, most of the exhibiting booksellers were hardly experts in display, though most people's labels and notices were less amateurishly executed than Tony's. She supposed that was something else she'd have to take over. PBFA stalls had to be immaculate. Nothing was allowed to stick out into the aisles, tables had to be covered with cloths that reached the floor and no tacky stock was to be offered.

She thought it was a pity the rules didn't apply to the stallholders themselves, some of whom spoiled the neatness with their longish, unkempt hair and beards, scruffy trousers and faded, matted sweaters. All that remained to do now was to push under the table the various cardboard boxes and crates the books had arrived in. She knelt on the flags to do it. They were dirty and struck cold, in spite of being expensive something-or-other limestone, and, as she got up, she glowered at the dusty, now-baggy knees of her smart, tight leggings. She'd have to watch it if she wasn't to become as dowdy and shapeless as the women who did this work regularly. Their arm and shoulder muscles bulged from loading and unloading their stacks of books, and their hips and stomachs were spread from days of sitting and waiting whilst customers browsed and made their choices.

She knew what was coming next. It did.

'All right if you hold the fort for a bit whilst I have a scout round?'

She gave a grunt that could have been permission or an expression of her resentment. She supposed she did want him to buy from other dealers. He ended up with better quality stock and it wasn't so shaming as having him queue up at jumble sales and hoping no one would see him there. She had watched the aggressive, grabbing women who overtook him on their way to the piles of goods, and was horrified, sometimes, to have recognized the same avid acquisitiveness on her husband's face. She shivered with embarrassment when he poked about in dirty junk shops looking for bargains. Not that her friends shopped there, or at Oxfam, but they sometimes looked round Cloughton's Thursday flea market and might see him, darting from stall to stall, grubbing through boxes on the floor, like a dog rooting through a dustbin for scraps.

The dealer at the next stall was also departing to hunt for his own specialities on his colleagues' stalls. His wife warned him, with cheerful resignation, 'Don't tell me you'll be back in time for the opening because we both know you won't!' Stella felt panic rising. Tony had better be. Always, when he was missing, someone would offer to sell her books and maps. She had no idea of market values and usually either refused to look at them or appealed to the vendor for a valuation, knowing how foolish she was being.

The doors had closed and the room was warming up. At least the surroundings were pleasant today. What she really hated were the university fairs. She remembered the disillusion of her first one. Having expected a Bodleian atmosphere in which crowds of students crept and whispered as they gratefully eked out their grants by buying cut-price texts, she had arrived at the disgusting students' union hall allocated to them. Outside it the gyps had continued, unabashed, their 'cleaning' of the stairs as the bookdealers passed and repassed them, making their efforts totally pointless. Their brief, as far as she could see, seemed to be to transfer the murky contents of their buckets to the surfaces of the stairs and corridors, creating maximum danger underfoot. All the posters seemed to have a background of fluorescent orange, all the doors squeaked as they swung to and fro and the students came chiefly to argue and challenge even the lowest prices.

Tony enjoyed it all and told her she looked for the worst in everything. He'd told her again as they'd driven up from Cloughton this morning. She'd refused to be jollied along. Having slept through the alarm, she'd had barely fifteen minutes to prepare sandwiches and flasks of coffee and then their ancient van had refused to start. Tony had cheerfully coaxed it whilst she fumed. 'How can we hope to run a business when we haven't even got efficient basic equipment?'

He'd grinned. 'We have to have a fairly tatty vehicle. If the punters see you going home in a BMW they think you're making too much out of them.' As he waited for the petrol in the flooded engine to evaporate, he began scraping ice off the windscreen. Stella, who had no intention of climbing out into the bitter wind, had refused to meet his eye until, having scratched a hole in the ice big enough to see through, he resettled himself in the driver's seat.

'There's no way I can incur any more debt if you're hoping to give up school.'

'We can't afford for me to give up teaching, car or no car. Your business is never going to keep us.'

He'd grinned again. 'Not in the style to which you'd like us to become accustomed. Anyway, you say you like teaching, and at least it's an excuse not to have your mother a millstone round your neck as she is round Pam's.'

Stella's face hardened. 'There's no reason why she needs to be round anyone's neck. She's perfectly able-bodied and she isn't all that old.'

'Oh, I grant you her problems aren't physical. I think she's neurotic because she was brought up in a world where it was a man's duty to look after a woman and the woman's chief duty was to let him. Your father did little to disabuse her. You and Pam were sorry for him, but I think her dependence did a lot for his self-esteem and he made her worse.'

Stella sighed, her breath clouding over the inside of the window so that she could no longer see through the hole Tony had made in the ice. 'With a bit of luck she'll decide she likes twenty-four hour a day care and stay where she is. Then I'll not only have her off my back but Pam as well, always complaining that everything's left for her to do. Even that little madam, Sonia, was hinting that I didn't pull my weight when I visited Pam yesterday. The cheek of it! You'd think she'd justify her own existence now and then by doing a hand's turn for her grandmother.' Stella sniffed. 'Not her! She's too busy working out who she can dump young Thomas on next so that she can be off gallivanting.'

Tony wiped the inside of the windscreen and reached for his seatbelt. 'You can hardly expect Sonia to dance attendance on someone who barely speaks to her and ignores her son, grandmother or not. Be fair. Alistair doesn't have much to do with her either.'

Stella allowed no one to criticize her son, least of all his father. She reverted to her former subject. 'If she stays where she is, the problem's solved for everybody.'

The engine gave a stertorous but hopeful cough in response to Tony's continued encouragement but he only frowned. 'It isn't, you know. Even between us we can't afford what St Helen's is costing for more than a week or two, though a place in a council home with the DSS paying the fees is a possibility.'

'There's no chance of her agreeing to that.' Stella realized that her chance had arrived. 'So, why don't we sell the book whilst it's on offer? It would do wonders for your reputation to put it on the market, the money would pay for improving the shop and the stock so that we'd have a chance to get really established. Then we could afford to keep Mother at St Helen's and maybe even do up the flat a bit and make it habitable.'

She saw Tony flinch and could see she was not convincing him. Perhaps he had doubts about his own valuation of the wretched book. She certainly doubted her mother's.

'Look, any gift from your mother has elastic strings. And if I sold it and took a commission, she'd spend the rest of her life making snide suggestions that we hadn't done right by her.'

'My mother would complain that she was ill-used whatever treatment she was given.'

'Besides,' Tony was well launched on his own theme, 'we'd probably find, having disposed of it, that when she dies she's willed it to someone else and we'd be accused of stealing it.'

Stella smiled grimly. 'Can you imagine Mother doing anything so decisive as making a will? I'm just afraid that the mice will be nibbling it up in the loft, or wherever she's stowed it away.'

Tony had had enough. 'Look, the most I'll agree to is a conference with Pam, as soon as she's fit, about the book, about St Helen's and about any other aspect of caring for your mother that you like to include. And, to keep Evelyn sweet, we'll go and see her tomorrow.'

'Well, that's something. She doesn't complain quite so much if you're there.'

The engine was purring sweetly now and Tony had edged the laden van across the waste ground where it was parked, taken the road for Tadcaster and resumed their former topic. 'You just need a more positive attitude. We get to three or four different towns every week and we see dawn in every season.'

She sniffed. 'Is that supposed to be a perk? Anyway, watching the day break doesn't pay the bills.'

He shrugged. 'No, but it compensates us for not eating out or drinking much or travelling abroad.' He turned and smiled at her. 'One day, we'll see it break on the other side of the world and it'll be interesting but not any more beautiful.'

Couldn't he ever discuss things sensibly? She pushed away the hand which had reached across to touch her knee. 'It can break where it likes. It can smash to smithereens for all I care. I wish you'd find a job that pays proper money.'

He'd come to the main road by now and was jolting along in top gear. 'Oh, come on, Stella. We can sample the stock without detriment to it and we couldn't do that if we sold sweets or something. The mortgage gets paid, we eat, we're mobile . . .'

'Just about.'

'No, really, people envy me because I get about such a lot.'

She sniffed again. 'Like the sailors, you mean, during the war?'

20

He understood and grinned, breaking into song.

'We joined the navy to see the world,
And what did we see?
We saw the sea!'

He supposed it wasn't a bad analogy. Then, seeing she was not amused, he gave up trying to placate her. 'Well, I'm grateful when you mind the stall for me and I manage to see quite a lot in my half-hour walk-abouts. It's not my fault if you spend yours looking round chain stores that are the same everywhere.'

The roads were icy and his driving was worse when he was offended. She'd stopped complaining but continued to brood over her grievances. He was so smug and satisfied in his mediocrity. He didn't care about a decent standard of living and just left her to earn for herself anything she wanted beyond food and shelter.

The resentment mounted again now as she watched him across the huge room, chatting easily to a dealer from Oxford whose venerable volumes, bound in softly gleaming old leather, were neatly stacked behind him. To pick up books like that and make some real profit, you needed capital. The sort that would be available to them if he'd only snap up the chance her mother was offering them.

Tony passed on from his Oxford friend, none of whose goods he could afford, even with the ten per cent discount allowed to trade. He stood in front of a shelf of modern first editions, surveying his wife as she sat, shoulders hunched, glowering at a few square inches of the corallian limestone. She didn't exactly encourage customers along. He supposed a book fair was the least exuberant large gathering anyone was likely to experience but Stella wasn't any happier when things were lively.

He remembered their attempt last autumn to sell their books in the open-air flea market. 'Taking literature to the masses', she'd called it, but the crusading spirit had soon evaporated. He'd enjoyed it, though he had to admit it had hardly been a

21

successful business venture. The masses had preferred shapeless jumpers to books and he had soon learned that little could be sold in a market if it couldn't be eaten, worn or put on the mantelpiece.

Stella had come along, determined to be miserable. She had been neither touched nor amused by the child in its rocking baby seat, stuck like a prize bargain amongst the junk on the stall opposite and fascinated by its surroundings. Nor by the chained dog, its forepaws forever on the edge of its owner's stall in an effort to interpret the chaos of feet around him. They had been able to tell the time in the market by the smells, cigarette smoke early as stalls were erected and filled, coffee at ten, when the preparations were complete but custom was still slack. At eleven it was fried onions and hot dogs, and, in the afternoon, sickly sweet candy floss.

Stella said the people were 'common'. Of course they were, and intriguing. He remembered a sweet young thing, painted and polished, buying a three-foot-high pottery leopard. He had wondered how it would look in the box bungalow she was probably taking it home to. And there had been that frumpy, middle-aged lady who had bought almost all his neighbour's stock of T-shirts with their heavy rock motifs. Across the valley he had seen birds flying in and out of the stone tracery of a church spire. It had rained a good deal of the time and water had cascaded from the tarpaulin canopies on to the cobbles below.

Once, above the rattling of crockery, the barking of dogs and the cries of vendors, he'd been amazed to hear the strains of one of the Songs of the Auvergne from the record stall two aisles further down. His life was full of such little pleasures that Stella would never allow herself to enjoy. She had complained long and bitterly about the cold and several times he had spent more than his day's profit buying hot dogs and coffee for her.

A determined-looking lady, obviously more interested in the modern first editions than Tony was, elbowed him aside and broke his train of thought. The customers were arriving; he'd better get back. He surveyed his own stall critically as he

22

walked towards it. He hadn't enough of the right kind of stock to do well at a venue like York but Stella had an eye for attractive display and she had made the best of what there was. She could bring a great deal to the business if he could get her interested in it.

She looked at her watch pointedly as he wriggled behind their erection of tables and shelves to set out the ledger and cash box he hoped they would soon need. Then he concentrated on shrugging off the doomed feeling that always overcame him at the more prestigious fairs. No one would buy from him, the rent had been nearly thirty pounds and the whole enterprise would be a disaster. He fished the previous day's *Guardian* out of a box under the table and began on the crossword. He had to strike a nice balance of preoccupation. He mustn't appear too lost in an article to be disturbed by customers' questions, but nor must he stare at them as they browsed. It put them off if they thought he was willing them to make up their minds quickly and part with their money. In any case, the reading public were not a beautiful sight. Between the shelves, they mostly appeared as slices of distended stomach with buttons straining. If and when they came to the counter part of the stall, they became a study in dandruff, open pores and botched dentistry. Only at student fairs were his customers young, fresh and lithe.

The fair followed its usual course and by six o'clock the packing up was completed and Tony reviewed his day. Stella was making her usual complaints about developing muscles in all the wrong places, though, as far as he could remember, she had done no more than collect the handwritten signs, secure the catches on the bookcases and hold doors open as he wheeled his clanking trolley through. Customers had taken pounds off the value of several volumes by cramming them back on the shelves and tearing the dust jackets. A ranting, evangelical lady had paid ten pence for a religious pamphlet and scared off all his current customers with her proselytizing gushings. A fat woman had read *Lady Chatterley's Lover* almost from cover to cover whilst her bored and naughty offspring poked with sticky fingers. A regular customer had visited him to regale him for the fifteenth time this year with the story of a namesake, the landlord of an inn at Darlington, where Dickens had changed coaches and borrowed the name for one of his characters. 'He was my great-great-grandfather!' And the narrator's one claim to fame! Inevitably, some comedian had toured the stalls enquiring for J. R. Hartley's *Fly Fishing*. 'Sorry, we don't sell porn,' Tony's cheery neighbour had told him. His profit, when he'd deducted the day's expenses, would be in the region of twenty pounds.

Tony locked the back doors of the van and remembered that he had forfeited his day off to visit his mother-in-law.

Sonia Hill was no keener on visiting St Helen's than her uncle Tony. She was squatting on a low stool, her toes toasted by Mrs Quentin's gas fire and her fingers warmed by the mug of tea that the older woman had just presented to her to soften the lecture she was about to deliver. 'You ought to go for your mother's sake if not for your gran's. Pam will recover more quickly if she knows someone's going in each day. You know how the old lady worries about everything.'

Sonia took her nose out of her mug. 'Yes, I know how she worries. Ostentatiously, making a fine art of it, the fine art of blackmail. Actually, although she claims to worry, she never really does. Someone always deals with things for her and she'd be astonished if they didn't.'

Barbara Quentin nodded towards the table with a 'not in front of the child' expression. Thomas was sitting at the table, solemnly constructing banana sandwiches by slitting the fruit lengthwise and wrapping a slice of bread round each of the two pieces. Mrs Quentin joined him and suggested that it would be more polite to slice the fruit across and make a flat sandwich. Thomas watched her demonstration with interest whilst Sonia drained her dregs of tea.

'Have you got a pep talk ready for Alistair and Aunt Stella too?'

Mrs Quentin smiled. 'You'll be happier yourself when you've been. Stella lives further away than you and works more or less full time when you think about what she does for Tony.'

24

Sonia refilled her mug from the fat brown teapot on the hearth. 'That's her defence. Aunt Stella hates teaching and she's no good at it. She'd have given it up long ago if that hadn't made her everyone's first choice for a mother minder.'

'A drastic sort of defence if she really dislikes it.' Mrs Quentin bit into her sandwich and two or three slices of banana slid out on to her plate.

'Mine stays together,' the child remarked without malice. Magnanimous in victory, he fished in his pocket and proffered a couple of jelly babies, covered in fluff.

Conscious of the honour bestowed and of Thomas's expectation of seeing his gift gratefully consumed, Mrs Quentin proppped them against the rim of her plate. 'I don't eat sweets but they're very cheerful colours. I'll leave them here to decorate the table.'

He nodded his approval. 'Are you babysitting me tonight?'

Mrs Quentin glanced across at Sonia who looked faintly embarrassed. 'Didn't I ask you? I just wanted to take some of my tapestries round to Tish. He knows someone who might have an outlet for them.'

'That's quite exciting. By the way, where does the young man get his extraordinary name from?'

'Well, he was christened Stanley after his father and he won't answer to that. He's an artist with red hair.'

Mrs Quentin smiled. 'I see, Titian. But it was his ladies whose hair was red. Yes, I don't mind having Thomas if you get him ready before you go. He rarely stirs, once he's tucked in, do you, young man?'

Sonia, having achieved the object of her visit, rose to leave. 'Put your mug and plate in the kitchen, Tom. Then you can have a long play in the bath. All right, Barbara. I'll visit Gran tomorrow afternoon. By the way, I've left a bag in the hall with your bits of shopping that I got yesterday. I picked up your prescription but I forgot to take it to the chemist. Were you needing it urgently? I'll call tomorrow with it.'

Mrs Quentin shook her head and Sonia, having reminded her that favours were flowing in both directions, escorted her son upstairs.

25

Chapter Three

Detective Constable Mitchell had spent the remainder of his precious weekend off trying to decide how literally Virginia had meant her 'Don't ring me'. Of course she needed an interval in which to sort out her priorities but she surely couldn't object to the casual sort of calls he usually made or to a show of solicitude for her general well-being. In the end, however, he had reluctantly decided to take her at her word, at least until after his first meeting with her father.

He had reported for his briefing the previous morning with some trepidation, but Detective Chief Inspector Browne had treated him throughout the day with his habitual cheerful civility. Mitchell decided that Virginia must have missed the Saturday evening collection. Her letter, therefore, would have arrived first post today. He had woken just after five, and, unable to sleep again, he had got up and polished his shoes to the glassy shine they had not worn since his uniformed days. His breakfast egg had stared him out and been dispatched to the waste bin, but, as he tapped now on Browne's office door, he wondered if he might have felt marginally better if he had persevered with it.

He tried to decide whether the smile with which he was waved to a chair was strained. Browne continued to fill in a lurid pink form while they waited for the rest of the relief to turn up. The briefing was short and Mitchell's first task was to question and possibly apprehend on a charge of joy-riding a youth who lived on his parents' council estate.

'That should give you another chance to prove your manhood.'

Mitchell stiffened, frowned at DS Hunter who had offered the taunt, then glared at Browne before slamming the door. His face burned with humiliation. He had not expected his DCI to make life easy for him when he learned of Virginia's pregnancy, but neither had he thought that he would gossip about it to the rest of the team. He felt disappointed in his future father-in-law as well as angry with him.

Mitchell's dismay was nothing compared with Browne's. He had actually received his daughter's letter the previous day. Not knowing what to say, he had, at least for the moment, accepted his wife's injunction to say nothing. Yesterday had been hectic and it had been easy to be quite professional and talk only about matters in hand. Today, unless something happened quickly, looked like being that rarity in police circles: a slack day with time he didn't want in which to think.

He fully understood his daughter's reasons for putting her news in writing. He had read the letter in silence. Then, in wild fury, he had hurled threats and abuse at the young couple in no one's hearing but his wife's. He was thankful now that neither Ginny nor Benny had heard him, and was pleased with the dignity with which he had conducted himself since then. He was resolved not to discuss the matter with either his daughter or his prospective son-in-law until he had himself completely in hand and until he'd heard what they intended to do.

He wasn't sure whether that was his own decision or his wife's. He was sure though that he was mortified when he compared his own reaction with Hannah's. And now his sergeant had added another dimension to the problem by choosing this particular time and that particular expression to prolong the running battle that had been going on between Mitchell and himself almost since their first meeting. When a telephone call brought the usually unwelcome summons to Superintendent Petty's office, Browne departed with a sigh of relief.

Hunter echoed it. He realized that his last remark had had some kind of unfortunate significance. He had realized too that for more than twenty-four hours, Browne, who usually concentrated fiercely on the task in hand, had been abstracted and unpredictable. The DS shrugged and settled to his paperwork until his superior should return from his visit upstairs with an even darker thundercloud over his head.

But Browne was missing for less than a quarter of an hour and came back looking marginally more cheerful. Encouraged, Hunter showed a polite interest in his CI's news.

'Sudden death at St Helen's House. Suspicious circumstances.' Browne expanded his announcement as Hunter's expression demanded enlightenment. 'Rest home, all female. It's that big place that used to be the nurses' home before the new one was built, up the hill from the hospital. The deceased was a short-stay resident and her GP, a Dr Anne Pedlar, won't sign for her. Ledgard did the PM earlier this morning and he's rung in with a few details that might interest us. The Super's not too impressed but he wants us to go through the motions at least, "with a view to keeping our worthy pathologist sweet". Personally, I'd back Ledgard's nose against Petty's any day.'

Browne had remained in the doorway rather than returning to his desk so Hunter was unsurprised when he went on, 'There doesn't seem to be much on and I could do with a breath of air. I might as well take a look myself.'

Since the hoped-for invitation did not follow, Hunter returned to his files as Browne unhooked his leather jacket from behind the door. He fastened it and gathered up notebook and keys to the accompaniment of gales of laughter rising from the downstairs lobby. Seconds later, DC Bellamy appeared from the top of the staircase, grinning broadly.

'Come in,' Browne invited, 'and share the joke.'

Bellamy perched on the desk corner to explain it. 'A couple of chaps who were on lates yesterday were called to the engineering works behind the railway station. A bloke there, putting in some overtime and in by himself, rang to say someone had put a snake through the letterbox. He'd shut himself into his office to wait for our folk. I gather it's all right for constables to get bitten. Anyway, Taylor and his mate were handy so they went round.

'Meanwhile, someone rang that little private zoo out at Netherholme and got them to say they'd take the snake for now. Taylor had a thick cardboard box in his boot so they put it in – it was only a baby – and taped it up as best they could. They drove off to deliver it but, when they handed the box over, there was nothing in it.'

Hunter had put his pen down and was listening as avidly as Browne.

'They stripped the car down completely but there's been no snake turned up. Now they're all laughing downstairs because someone's been messing about with the board. The hook where Taylor's car key hangs has a green, stuffed-stocking snake hanging with black squiggles down its back. There's a label on it, something about a serpent. Carson says it's a verse from Genesis – the Bible, not the rock group.'

Bellamy departed, still smiling, and Hunter took up his pen again as Browne went downstairs to look at the board for himself on his way out. The text was beautifully written in black italic script. *'Now the serpent was more subtil than any beast of the field. Gen. 3.1.'* Browne chuckled as he walked to his car and set off towards the mortuary. He decided to see Dr Ledgard first and then visit St Helen's armed with the facts that had caused the pathologist's suspicions.

The mortuary was one of a rash of buildings behind the town's main hospital and Browne thought it had the sinister look always achieved by the prettying up of a structure that had a socially unacceptable function. He would have preferred stark concrete to the nervously cheerful forsythia and corpse-pale early jonquils set out in front of the door.

He hoped he would not find Ledgard in the process of another gory dissection and was pleased to see the pathologist come out to meet him in flannels and a sports coat. They hung loosely on him. Off the peg clothes with sleeves and trouser legs sufficiently long were made for a distinctly ampler girth than he possessed.

Ledgard's secretary was making tea in the functional box he called his office. Invited inside, Browne found that the pervasive smell of formalin left as strong a taste on his tongue as the dark liquid in his cup.

'I was due for a break,' Ledgard began, replenishing the

cup he had emptied with two huge swallows. 'We'll have this while it's hot, then I'll show you the body. It's in remarkably good shape, physically, for seventy-eight. I've had a word with Dr Pedlar.' He swallowed the remains of his refill as Browne reached the half-way point with his first cup. 'Deceased was an Evelyn Norman. Apart from a go of flu about a month ago, not a particularly bad one, she was perfectly healthy.'

Ledgard eyed his secretary reproachfully as she drained the dregs in the teapot into her own cup. 'The doctor's talked to the girls on duty at St Helen's when Mrs Norman was found on Monday. They didn't know her very well. She'd only just been admitted and was only staying in the home for a week or two. One of them went to fetch her from her room for a meal or something, and found her unsteady on her feet and shouting. She thought the old woman had been on the bottle and managed to get her to bed.'

Browne could hear a sound of sawing which, in this context he found distressing until he realized that it came from outside. He concentrated hard on what Ledgard was telling him. 'She was afraid to report Mrs Norman's condition at first because she thought she'd be in trouble for not keeping a close enough eye on her and not knowing she had alcohol in her room, but when she still couldn't rouse the woman at about nine o'clock, she fetched the matron. It was too late by then.

'There was a thorough search but no glasses or bottles were found. Dr Pedlar then said the symptoms might equally indicate an overdose of insulin but the woman isn't a diabetic.'

'Did you test Dr Pedlar's theory?'

Ledgard made a noncommittal gesture with his hands. 'There was no point in looking for insulin, it's a natural substance that you'd expect to find in the body, but I did find the blood sugar extremely low and when I examined the skin surface I found an inflamed puncture mark, consistent with an inexpertly given injection. Come and have a look.'

Browne followed him to the huge refrigerated cupboard and waited as he drew out the shrouded form and removed its coverings. He looked with equanimity. The law, both civil and moral, told him he was wrong, but the deliberate or accidental ending of a life that had been lived past seventy affected him far less than the death of a younger person, even in cases where the older victim had suffered pain.

The face of the corpse Ledgard revealed to him showed a supreme indifference to every conceivable human attitude that could be adopted towards it, his own reprehensible one included. Grey hair curled limply round neat features set in an unblemished and, considering her age, surprisingly unwrinkled skin. The pathologist drew Browne's attention from the face to an inflamed mark just below the armpit and he agreed at once with Ledgard's conjecture that someone other than the woman herself had inflicted the small wound.

'The site of it would have been awkward for her to have reached herself,' Ledgard pointed out, 'and it's more susceptible to pain than other areas. It may have been chosen because a mark there was unlikely to be noticed unless it were being deliberately looked for. The puncture's larger than I'd expect. She probably struggled against the needle, causing this small inflamed area.'

Browne nodded. He was already convinced that someone had a charge to answer. The fact that the woman had lived her three score years and ten might have caused him to be less moved than he should have been by her death, but he was none the less determined that her dispatcher should be found and punished. He set off for St Helen's House, debating with himself whether to send for Hunter and proceed overtly with a murder investigation or, as requested by Superintendent Petty, to keep his inquiry very low-key. He couldn't trust himself yet to work in close contact with Mitchell. Of course, he was no more to blame for his daughter's pregnancy than she was herself. Behaving naturally towards her would be more difficult still. Hunter, he knew, had been puzzled by his uncertain temper during the last couple of days. The sergeant knew his place, of course, and Browne was sure he would be safe from inquisitive questions, but he was finding Hunter's reproachful refraining from them very hard to bear. He made his decision and radioed for DC Carson to meet him outside the home.

Arriving first, Browne examined the building with some

31

interest. He had passed it often but little could be seen from the road except its surrounding wall and shrubs. The house was impressive rather than welcoming. The front door was flanked by bays on two floors and sandstone pillars supported an elaborate carved lintel over the door, weathered now so that the scene depicted on it was indistinct.

There were no flowers here, just a large asphalted parking space, surrounded by dripping yews and hollies. It was occupied by only one other car. He noticed, however, that the nets covering the lower half of the windows were crisp and clean and on the doorstep a royal blue plastic milk crate containing several bottles helped to give the place a lived-in look.

Browne got out of the car and walked round the building. Climbing up the side was a structure of ornate, white-painted wrought iron. It looked attractive against the dark wet stone, but, if it constituted the only fire escape, he held out little hope for any of the old or infirm who might have to negotiate it. He looked down and realized he was standing in a puddle. Bending to wipe his shoes clean he smiled to himself as he remembered Mitchell's attempts to regain favour with his glassily shining ones.

Carson appeared at the gate on foot, his expression becoming apologetic as he realized he was keeping his DCI waiting. Browne walked to meet him. The young DC had been out of uniform for only a few months and Browne was anxious to get a better look at him. He explained the circumstances of their visit and gave him an encouraging smile although Carson did not look nervous. 'Don't ask too many questions in there. Let them talk and pick out what you want from what they say.'

Carson nodded. 'I suppose that way they often tell you things you wouldn't think to ask about.'

Browne decided that Carson would probably do. 'What I do want to find out about before we leave is any connection there might be, besides her temporary stay here, between Mrs Norman and any member of the staff. Then I want to know everything about the day she was admitted and the day she died, who's been to visit her and who is in her immediate family. Try and find out whether any of them are diabetic. Oh, and see if a will's turned up yet.'

Carson nodded again. 'If there's no personal connection with any of the staff, sir, I don't suppose anyone here harmed her. Even if we find she was thoroughly obnoxious, she was only a temporary resident, and she wouldn't be worth getting into serious bother for. They wouldn't have had to put up with her for long.'

'True.' They used a well-polished brass knocker and Browne noted as they were admitted that the inside of the house was considerably more cheerful than its exterior suggested. The hall contained good furniture in keeping with its proportions, the carpet was thick, and an overpowering warmth enfolded them. This was not run of the mill council provision for the elderly they were obliged to cater for.

Nevertheless there was the usual confusion of smells over smells, unmentionable ones, disguising ones and incidental ones. Browne had hoped lunch would be over by now, but a gong was sounding and the ladies were obediently crossing the hall to the wide open door of the dining-room, the more mobile of them pushing forward and seating themselves to watch in relative comfort the slower progress of the halt and the lame. The sound of water pouring and the chink of plates mingled with little thuds as the rubber tips on tubular walking-frames struck the linoleum on the dining-room floor. There were grunts and heavy breathing but no conversation, all effort being expended on reaching the tables. An overall-clad young-ster helped where she could, drawing back chairs and easing their occupants on to them.

After the traffic had passed, the two officers awaited the arrival of the matron in the conservatory. By the time she arrived they had made themselves comfortable in the high-seated and straight-backed armchairs that are easy for old people to get in and out of. Before settling herself she opened half a dozen windows and the glass-walled room, which caught the odd gleam of rain-washed sun, became very pleasant. Coffee was offered. Browne had had his fill from Dr Ledgard but, seeing Carson's smile, he accepted.

Whatever the word 'matron' had suggested to the two policemen, neither of them had expected this reed-slim, ash-blonde woman. She wore a black skirt and white blouse but both were brief and close fitting. Realizing that it was impossible for both to be in their original state, Carson tried to decide whether she bleached her hair or darkened her brows and lashes. Browne, who could see that she did both, kept his face deadpan.

Matron grinned at Carson and extended her hand. 'Kay Cunningham,' she announced. 'Were you expecting a nurse's uniform draped round someone frumpy and fat? That wouldn't be very cheerful for everybody. I'd dress smartly if I worked in a city office so I do the same for the residents here.' She included Browne in her glance as she went on, 'Dr Pedlar said not to be surprised if you called.' Browne watched her trying simultaneously to conceal and to satisfy her curiosity. 'We've never had the police before when one of our ladies has died,' she ventured.

Browne gave her points for not saying 'passed away'. 'That's because Mrs Norman's illness was sudden and her death was unexpected. Dr Pedlar is anxious to know if she has missed anything in her patient's condition.' This hardly explained their own visit but Mrs Cunningham nodded.

'She was only a temporary resident here, of course. We hadn't known her very long. How can I be of assistance?' Having exonerated her establishment from any part of the blame due to Dr Pedlar, she was prepared to co-operate.

Carson grinned as Browne became avuncular. 'During the last few days of her life, you saw much more of Mrs Norman than anyone else. You're also knowledgeable about what is normal and to be expected in the habits and general demeanour of a woman of her age. We need your impression of her, in short – unless your role here is purely managerial and the girls we met out there are the ones in daily contact with the residents.'

'Right.' She slid from the creaking arm to the sofa's cushioned seat and crossed neat ankles.

A young girl appeared with a laden tray. The matron beamed at her as she placed the tray on the table after waiting for Carson to remove his notebook. 'Thank you, Debbie.'

Debbie, looking like one of the beautiful people of thirty

years ago, surveyed them with lively interest, then stepped back into the main part of the house and closed the doors on them.

'You may want to speak to her later,' Mrs Cunningham volunteered as she poured from the pot and handed cups. 'You were right in thinking that my post is mainly administrative. Mr Clegg, who employs me, owns two other homes for the elderly, both in Huddersfield. My job is to be responsible for everything that goes on in this one.'

'And that would consist of . . . ?'

'The budget, ordering supplies, including food, medications, cleaning materials and everything else – and the welfare of the ladies, of course.' Browne felt she had listed her duties in their order of importance to her.

She drew attention to shapely knees by pulling down the short skirt in a simulated attempt to cover them. 'I see to staff wages and duty rotas and I book in the temporary guests.'

'And the girls?'

'The staff deal with all the practical routines and problems that occur during their spell of duty but each resident is assigned to one girl in particular, who, hopefully, takes a special interest in her. Evelyn was assigned to Debbie so it was her business to know about any personal problem, although the responsibility to make sure it's dealt with is mine.'

'What sort of problems?'

'Well, the biggest worry for a lot of our ladies is becoming incontinent. They wouldn't confide in me about that because I'm their figure of authority. They'd expect me to be annoyed like a nursery school teacher with a child who wets its pants in class. They're very ashamed so they whisper about it to the girl they know best. She provides protective clothing, swears she won't tell a soul and enters it in the lady's record where I see it. That way, everybody's happy.' Browne reflected on the sad nature of happiness in this establishment as he watched Carson make his unobtrusive notes.

'How many ladies is each girl attached to?'

'It depends. Kerry only has one. Mrs May has senile dementia and needs constant watching. Most of them have three or four. Debbie only has two because she only works part time. She's a student.'

Observing their empty cups, Mrs Cunningham made a gesture towards the coffee pot. It was of Wedgwood china but it contained only instant coffee. Browne shook his head. Carson had seemed thirsty and Browne had thought he would avail himself of the silent offer but the DC was immersed in his notebook and unaware of it.

Browne turned back to Mrs Cunningham. 'Tell me some more about your set-up here. How many residents have you?'

She shook blonde curls back from her face. 'There are twenty-five. They all have a room of their own unless they ask to share. There's one big communal sitting-room with a music centre, television and so on and the conservatory here is available to anybody who just wants to be quiet.'

Browne waited to be told they were like a big happy family and Mrs Cunningham obliged. 'We all use first names here,' she went on. 'We have one lady who's had two strokes and should be in a nursing home but we cope with her here because she doesn't want to leave her friends.'

Browne had looked about him as he was shown in. 'I would have thought a place this size would cater for more than twenty-five.'

She nodded. 'They're just the permanent residents but we offer a short-stay service for people who can normally manage but have been ill or have just come out of hospital, or whose families need a break from looking after them. We keep some rooms available for them.' She abandoned her social worker tone and added, more honestly, 'We have to make a higher weekly charge for them, of course, because of sometimes having the rooms empty. It puts us one up on other homes though, and a lot of the temps eventually become permanent. It gives us a chance to spot trouble-makers and arrange to have no room for them when they apply to be permanent residents.'

Carson was still diligently applying himself to his notebook and Browne wondered what vital evidence he'd missed himself that Carson might have gleaned from Mrs Cunningham's revelations. 'What was the first indication you had of anything untoward with Mrs Norman yesterday?'

She pursed glossy lips. 'A hysterical Debbie, pounding on my door in the middle of the evening, saying she couldn't rouse Evelyn. I hadn't seen much of any of the residents all day. I went to the cash and carry in the morning. It was my afternoon and evening off duty but I live here, on the top floor. I was very cross because Debbie hadn't called me down earlier. I went in to Evelyn and although I could see it was no use I sent for Dr Pedlar.'

'Not an ambulance?'

'For a dead body? There aren't enough to deal with the people who can be helped.'

Browne supposed she had plenty of experience in recognizing death. 'Had there been any symptoms of illness before yesterday afternoon?'

She shook her head and the curls fell in her eyes again. 'No, she was supposed to be weak after flu but I didn't see any signs of it. Most of the temps seem to keep to their rooms. They feel a bit strange here and a lot of them are resentful, thinking they've just been dumped, but she was quite chatty and mixed in with the others. I don't really know why she had to be here.'

Lunch was apparently over now and the sound of the ladies' laboured and halting progress across the hall back to their sitting-room could be heard faintly against the clatter of dishes being cleared. 'Tell me about access to the house,' Browne requested.

Mrs Cunningham wandered to the glass doors and glanced into the dining-room at the girls who were clearing the tables as she complied. 'The main door's kept locked. I told you we had a dementia case and she might wander off – or undesirables might get in. There's no guarantee that one of the ladies won't let someone in when the staff are busy. There aren't enough of us to be watching all the time, but we do our best. The basement rooms at the back have french windows opening on to the garden. They're always used for temporary residents who can lock them but who usually leave them open when it's warm and don't always remember to fasten them properly at night. The girls have to check.'

She eyed him speculatively and risked a second indirect

37

question of her own. 'I suppose you're thinking that someone might have come in with alcohol. It looks as though that's what did it. It would explain the symptoms Debbie described.'

Browne ignored the supposition. 'So it would be easy enough for anyone to get in during the day?' He saw that he had annoyed her.

'The temps are fairly responsible still, most of them anyway. They aren't locked in when they're living alone or with their families.'

Browne admitted this, then asked permission for Carson to explore the ground floor sufficiently to make a plan of it. The constable set off obediently, whilst Browne continued his questions. 'I wonder if you could tell me, just informally, something about Mrs Norman's relations.'

'Well, one daughter's in hospital, having a hysterectomy. Evelyn went to stay with her when she got flu. She likes a lot of attention and she'd said she didn't think she could cope yet on her own, so Mrs Hill approached us, brought her mother to look round and the arrangements were made. The other daughter came as well, on the day Evelyn joined us. She came in Mrs Hill's car and the other daughter, a Mrs Fenton, brought various belongings her mother wanted to have here.'

'And what was your impression of them? Did they seem to get on well with the old lady?'

Mrs Cunningham looked puzzled. 'Are you suggesting that . . .'

'I'm suggesting nothing. This is a sudden death. It's perfectly normal procedure to look at every possibility, however remote. The simplest explanation almost always turns out to be the correct one. You didn't expect Mrs Norman to die during her stay here?'

She shook the curls vigorously. 'Certainly not.'

'So, we're just trying to find out why she did. It's in your best interests too. You don't want it put down to the way she was treated here?' He cut short her indignant denial. 'So, how did Mrs Norman and her daughters get on together?'

Mrs Cunningham gave up the battle with her skirt and let her knees show. She glanced from them to Browne. 'Well, actually, they both seemed to be humouring her, reassuring her. No one showed any concern for Mrs Hill and her operation. They were all three exclusively concerned with whether Evelyn would be all right here. Still, I suppose that is what they had come for. You'll have to ask Debbie if you want any more. I met them all when they first arrived but she settled Evelyn in.'

Browne was thankful to hear Carson returning. 'We're grateful for your time and the coffee. If we could see Debbie before we go . . .'

She stood up. 'You're welcome as far as I'm concerned. She went off duty five minutes ago so she shouldn't have left yet.' She granted permission for Browne to look at anything he liked and ushered him through the dining-room where he found Carson in conversation with Debbie.

The girl broke away from the constable, looking worried. 'DC Carson says you want to talk to me but I've got a tutorial this afternoon and my bus goes in ten minutes.'

Browne smiled at her. On this dank and chilly March day, she was setting off to catch her bus in a thin baggy sweater embroidered with flowers over a white broderie anglaise skirt. She wore no slip beneath it so that the portions of the slim brown legs it covered showed in silhouette through the filmy cotton. He supposed this was quite a sensible uniform for the tropical climate she worked in inside this building. When she had brought in the coffee tray, her feet had been bare, but, as a concession to the weather outside, she now wore a pair of stout and comfortable-looking laced shoes.

'There isn't a problem,' he told her, 'but I'd like to have a chat with you quite soon.'

She agreed readily. 'I could come to the station round about five.'

Thwarted of his interview, Browne decided to content himself with a quick look round the guest room Evelyn Norman had occupied. 'Let's have a look at your ground plan.' He reached out his hand for Carson's notebook but the DC seemed reluctant to part with it. Browne's look of puzzlement obviously intimidated him after a few seconds and he handed over his notes. He refused to meet the CI's eye but wandered to the window to watch Debbie, her skirt blowing wildly, making her way along the road to the bus stop.

Browne glanced at the recently filled pages in the little book, then grinned widely. Carson's account of the interview between himself and Mrs Cunningham seemed virtually fault-less, carefully tabulated and legibly written. A wide margin had been left on each page which he had filled with lightning sketches and clever little cartoons. A picture at the top of the left-hand column showed a very old lady, toothless and tied to her chair, her head falling to one side. A placard, propped on her knee read, 'It's a real home from home'.

Below this was a picture of himself, the cleft chin and the lock of dark hair that fell over his forehead greatly exagger-ated, leaning forward eagerly in his chair. The humour of the little drawings lay chiefly in the clever pencil strokes that made up the expression on the faces.

Resisting the temptation to turn the pages back further, Browne addressed Carson's embarrassed rear view. 'What's your accurate drawing like, Robin? You could end up produc-ing artist's impressions of Cloughton criminals. It's more comfortable than chasing them.' Carson wheeled round, his expression delighted and Browne realized he had uncovered at least some of the DC's plans for the future.

They both transferred their attention to the fresh page where Carson had made his plan of the ground-floor rooms, roughly drawn to scale and unadorned with pictures, amusing or other-wise. 'Mrs Norman's room was the one on the corner.' Carson indicated with his pencil. 'Hers and the five others across the back of the basement all have french windows leading to the garden. The doors open on to a lower corridor and there's a staircase at the end, leading up to the rest of the house.'

Twenty minutes exhausted the room's possibilities at least for the moment. Mrs Norman had only stayed there a couple of weeks. Browne was itching to examine her house and wondered if he dare fly so far in the face of Petty's instructions. Deciding he would, he gave Carson the task of tracking down the keys he would need. The DC departed obligingly, not unwilling to be kept a little longer from his routine duties.

By the time the key arrived, however, Browne was occupied with another aspect of the case. PC Bennett on the desk had drawn his attention to the visitor who awaited him in a comfortable armchair in reception. The young woman who rose to greet him as he went through was taller than he was, slim with a proud carriage. She wore a cotton shirt and slacks and a purple sweatshirt hung behind her, its sleeves loosely knotted at her waist. The thick fair hair seemed to Browne to be coated in glue to keep it looking untidy, but, otherwise, she looked like every middle-aged man's ideal daughter, blue eyed, extravagantly healthy, with an engaging smile.

She extended a thin tanned arm and a ringless hand shook his firmly. 'Anne Pedlar,' she announced. 'I'm Evelyn Norman's GP.' Her voice was deep, her enunciation brisk and precise but retaining the local accent. 'I'd be glad if you could spare me a few minutes.'

He invited her up to his office and punished Constable Bennett's suggestive grin by requesting that he organize a tea tray, but she shook her head, causing huge gold hoop earrings to slap her jaw. 'It's kind of you but I've still got half a dozen visits to make. I really did mean just a few minutes.'

She chose the less accommodating of Browne's armchairs and sat forward in it as though she were not free yet to make herself too comfortable in it. As the fitful sunlight fell on her face, Browne could see that she was much older than her lithe form and unadorned complexion had first suggested.

She made her point without wasting any time. 'I'm afraid I'm quite convinced that Mrs Norman's death was not natural. I'm even more convinced that it wasn't suicide and I don't think it's very likely that it was an accident.'

Browne drew out his notebook. 'Tell me why.'

She established her credentials before offering her evidence. 'Because of the sort of woman she was. I've only attended her for about two years. I joined my present practice four years ago and moved back to Cloughton from Surrey. I met up with Pam Hill again – in a butcher's shop, actually. We'd been at Leeds together. I was a medic and she was reading biology and sometimes we'd find ourselves at the same lectures. We'd been quite friendly, she wasn't happy with her doctor – she felt he'd neglected her husband once it became obvious he wasn't going to make a full recovery – and she transferred to my list.

'She hadn't bothered me much till a couple of months ago when she needed the operation she's recovering from now. Unfortunately though, her mother came to me too. She thought she'd get preferential treatment as the mother of a friend and she found me rather a disappointment. I didn't make the fuss about her trivial complaints that she'd have liked. And trivial complaints were all she did have, haemorrhoids that weren't bad enough to have troubled her as much as she made out, and the occasional chesty cold that she always called flu or bronchitis.

'I suppose she was no worse than a lot of elderly widows but she'd been particularly dependent on her husband who could have done with some support himself. I'm told he was a respiratory cripple for most of his adult life after inadequate treatment for TB. Streptomycin came soon enough to cure his infection but only after it had done its damage. Anyway, when he died, she expected to be looked after by someone else, preferably Pam. And, failing that, anyone else she could lay a claim on.

'I got to know her pretty well. The drink suggestion's a non-starter. The PM will have proved that but, in any case, she was the self-righteous type who got more satisfaction out of condemning the pleasures of the flesh than indulging in them. When Pam had a glass of wine, she always told her she was glad her father wasn't alive to see it. I'm sure you'll find too that Kay Cunningham, for all her paint and polish, runs a very tight ship although she probably exploits those nice girls. I attend several of her ladies and am in and out of St Helen's quite often. There are two insulin-dependent diabetics there but there's no way there could have been any slip-up with their injections. I think Kay gives them herself now, but even when they managed their own, they were always carefully supervised.

'And Mrs Norman would no more have given herself an injection than fly, especially under the arm. She wouldn't have slept for a week for worrying about it, even if I'd been going to do it for her. She was terrified of all physical discomfort. She wouldn't take large pills in case they scratched her throat when she swallowed them. She wouldn't apply an ointment or antiseptic if it made her skin smart a bit. She even wanted liquid medicine changed if it had a bitter taste.'

Browne's pen had had difficulty keeping up with this carefully prepared statement, almost each phrase of which needed recording. He dropped it from his aching fingers and looked up to meet the doctor's belligerent gaze. 'You won't mind signing this, then?' She shook her head vigorously. 'Do you look after the rest of the family? What can you tell me about them? Do you know if any of them are diabetic?'

She sat further back in the chair and relaxed for the first time. 'I don't, I'm afraid – I know a little about the family but only because of being Pam's friend. I don't treat any of them, thank goodness, so that lets me out of any professional difficulties.'

'And what you do know about them doesn't inhibit you?'

She shrugged. 'It doesn't need to. There's nothing discreditable, unless you count her daughter's having an illegitimate son, and that's no secret.'

She saw that he was taking notes again. 'I can't tell you a great deal. Pam's father died five years ago. Pam taught for a while and wrote short stories at weekends. Greg Hill was a partner in a building firm. He died after an accident involving a crane and Pam started writing full time immediately afterwards. Sonia was sixteen then, and doing well at school. She was completely thrown by her father's death, got pregnant and gave up her studies. Soon after young Thomas was born she moved into a flat offered by a friend of Pam's. It was all quite amicable. Pam isn't distracted from her writing and Sonia feels more independent with a place of her own. She works part time now that Thomas is at nursery school.

'The sister, Stella, is much younger than Pam. She's married and living in Leeds with a husband in the second-hand book business. Stella taught juniors and still does a couple of days a week. The rest of the time she helps with the business. They have a son, but I don't even know his name.'

She glanced at her watch. 'I shall have to go. If there's anything else I can help you with you can get in touch.' She handed him a printed card and strode athletically out of the office and down the stairs before Browne could reach the door to open it for her. He called his thanks after her, feeling slightly foolish.

Chapter Four

Knowing that his interview with Debbie and catching up on the day's paperwork would take up most of his evening, Browne decided that he deserved an hour at home with his wife. He informed the desk sergeant and was soon parking in his own drive. He surveyed his garden, sniffing the damp earth appreciatively, his spirits lifted by the ephemeral, burgeoning green that had not as yet sufficient substance to relieve the winter bareness of the branches but still promised the spring that would follow.

Hannah had heard the car engine and a pot of tea was ready brewed by the time her husband arrived in the kitchen. She enquired about his day and they made small talk for a while but, by the time she was pouring the second cups, he had returned to the inevitable subject, in spite of all her efforts.

'I can't believe it. I've lived in dread of Alex getting some girl in the club. We've never seemed to have the knack of making him happy, but not Ginny!'

'I'll pretend you didn't say that.' Hannah was appalled. She took her cup over to an easy chair and reached for a magazine but Browne was well launched and ignored the hint.

'I don't know how you can be so calm. I thought you'd be wringing your hands.' He realized the unfairness of this as he spoke; it was the last thing Hannah would do.

She was indignant. 'Well, I'm not. It's no good crying over spilt semen. We did our best to guide her. She's been of age six months now, they're both consenting adults and they can sort it out for themselves.' She suddenly realized that her husband was not yet capable of taking this attitude. He needed

45

to talk out his dismay for a while longer before he could be fair, uncensorious and practical. She resigned herself to more recriminations.

'There's nothing they can do now that would make things right. If she gets married and looks after the baby she's throwing away the chance of an Oxford degree and a successful career. If she goes on with her course the baby will suffer. I'm not having my grandchild passed round from one minder to another. Why doesn't Benny transfer to the Oxford force and do his share of coping?'

Hannah sighed and looked up from her magazine. 'Because it isn't that easy, and anyway, why should West Yorkshire lose a damned good copper?'

Browne pushed his cup away. 'I can't think what they should do.'

Hannah abandoned her pretence of reading and her last shreds of patience. 'You don't have to think anything. You've no right to express an opinion. As far as we know, it isn't going to affect us at all. They haven't asked us for anything, money, shelter under our roof, prospective child minding, least of all our opinion.'

'Not affect us? Don't be stupid!'

Her tone softened. 'I'm not afraid of being stupid but I am afraid of being wrong.'

'So, you're doing nothing, saying nothing?'

She ran her fingers through her hair, dragging it off her face, and he saw that her own composure was precarious. 'Not necessarily. Doing nothing might be one of the wrong courses I could take . . . I think the first thing we've got to do is listen to them and we can't do that until they're ready to talk to us.'

'I think it's time I gave Benny a piece of my mind. He'll be thirty in three years' time. He should be old enough to have some sense. Ginny's just eighteen!'

Hannah tried to control her temper. Couldn't he say something constructive? Or at least something he hadn't said before. 'Tom, you mustn't discuss it with anyone yet, least of all Benny. They might decide on an abortion and if they do, the less said to anyone the better.'

Browne was silenced. This idea was worse than anything he had so far contemplated.

Watching his face, she reiterated her point. 'They must make their own decision. I'm sure we're anxious to help when they have done but the dilemma isn't ours.' She closed the discussion by going over to the record player.

Browne's spirits sank even lower. Not bloody Shostakovitch again! He departed thankfully for his meeting with Debbie.

In spite of black looks from Hunter, Browne sent for Carson when Deborah Jardine arrived. His DS knew him too well not to see how rattled he was and, anyway, Carson had already met this youngster. Browne did, however, pause long enough to describe briefly his talk to Kay Cunningham and his inspection of the room Evelyn Norman had occupied.

'We didn't find anything very useful. She was obviously a good customer of M&S, drawers full of their underwear, toiletries and so on. She seems to have had an obsession for fancy handkerchiefs. There was a box on the chest beside the bed containing scores of them, all with lace edges and Swiss embroidery. Perhaps she collected them like other people do little ornaments. She wasn't greedy. We found two huge boxes of chocolates with only a couple taken out of each.

'There were some photographs in frames, one of herself and a man, presumably her husband, and two others, each of a young couple and a small child. The clothes were a bit old fashioned, so we decided they must have been taken some time ago.' Browne knew that Hunter was listening hard in spite of his apparent preoccupation with his papers. 'It was an interesting room for what it didn't contain – no knitting or sewing, no letter-writing materials, a few pulp magazines but no radio or other source of music . . .'

Hunter sniffed. 'Fairly ordinary then. Most folk communicate by phone and spend their time glued to the TV these days.'

So, Hunter was in a black mood too. Was he jealous of Carson now as well as Mitchell? Browne ploughed on with his account. 'The most intriguing thing was a collection of four hardbacked books, all written by a P. E. Norman.' He passed Hunter a list of the titles. 'The daughter's work, presumably. Dr Pedlar says she writes. They were prominently displayed and looked quite unused. The old woman wanted the reflected glory but it didn't look as though she had made any great study of them.'

He paused as a flicker of interest crossed Hunter's sulky face. 'You know them?'

'I know of them, sir.' Browne winced at the form of address and knew that his offhand treatment of the sergeant he usually kept in his confidence was responsible. 'My nephew reads this sort of stuff.'

'So, what sort of stuff is it? It looked like some kind of science fiction to me.'

'Yes, it is, but it's a bit out of the ordinary run, according to Martin. I wouldn't have remembered but there was a new one out just a month or so ago and Annette suggested that we bought it for Martin's birthday.'

'That's useful. Bully for Martin and Annette. Ask them about it, will you?' Browne went into his office, tidied his desk and kicked further into the corner the cardboard cartons, purporting to contain margarine, that held his backlog of cases. They were all less interesting than this one for which he had been warned to apply the soft pedal.

As Carson brought the girl in, he came from behind his desk to sit in an armchair and invited her to be seated. Her expression was pensive. Full lips were closed over excellent teeth. The rest of her features were fine drawn, the skin freckled but unblemished and delicate. Her long straight hair was fine and mousy fair, untidy, but held back from her face by a band that looked to Browne like a twisted, pale-coloured nylon stocking.

As he had suspected she would, she ignored the chair he had indicated and chose the stool instead, where she sat hugging her knees. Carson licked his lips and Browne wondered what he would draw in his margins. He enquired about the girl's studies and waited for details of sociology, psychology or possibly politics.

'Nuclear science,' she informed him. He blinked.

48

'You don't carry banners urging people to get rid of it?' he asked, in spite of himself.

'That wouldn't be very sensible.'

Chidden, Browne returned to the point. 'I expect Mrs Norman's death upset you, but I'm sure you realize that I need to know all that happened yesterday.'

'It's not death itself that upsets me.' She regarded him with solemn brown eyes. 'I saw my first dead body when I was sixteen and I just felt very surprised because it was so obvious that there was no one at home in it.' She made sixteen sound like a lifetime away. It must, Browne estimated, have been all of four years. 'But I'm worried that I should have got help sooner and then, perhaps, she wouldn't have died.'

Her face appealed to Browne to contradict her and he did his best to respond. 'We shan't be sure till more tests have been done. I'll let you know about that when I can. I've heard Dr Pedlar's views about what happened and now I'd like to compare them with yours.'

She hesitated, wondering where to begin. 'Tell me everything Mrs Norman did yesterday,' he prompted her.

Once started, she talked easily, one hand playing with a lock of hair that fell forward on to her lap. 'I took her her breakfast in bed at eight o'clock as usual. They think it's to spoil them but it's easier for us that way. If we had to dress them all before breakfast, the kitchen wouldn't be clear in time to get lunch. Evelyn got herself ready, so when she'd finished her meal I went to help Agnes who's blind.

'Evelyn's fairly sociable and watches television in the lounge with the others but she stayed in her room yesterday morning because she knew some of her family were coming to see her. Her younger daughter and son-in-law had promised to call in. They came to the front door to say they'd arrived and then went round the side of the house to Evelyn's window. I think they'd gone by lunchtime. She came into the dining-room by herself, anyway, and said all the usual stuff about having a poor appetite and big meals overfacing her. I didn't see her around after lunch and I thought she was asleep in her room till I heard her shouting and went in to her.'

'When was that?'

She wrinkled her nose, crowding the freckles together, as she calculated. 'About half-past three, probably. Everything was quiet up till then and we'd been making buns for tea. We didn't know who it was at first. We followed the noise. When the others realized that it was downstairs in the basement, they left it to me because I'm responsible for Evelyn.'

'And what did you find when you got to her?'

The girl bit her lip, reconsidering her own conduct as she described it. 'Well, she's usually quiet and sensible enough, even if she's a bit of a fuss pot, but she was shouting to herself and talking a lot of rubbish and when I tried to put her into a chair she shook me off.'

'Can you remember anything she actually said, however little sense it made?'

'Something about someone called Alice. She seemed very annoyed. I can't tell you, really. Her words were slurred and she kept pacing round the room and nearly falling over. In the end, I persuaded her to lie down. She got sleepy after a bit so I left her, fully dressed, on top of the bedclothes. I looked in again a few minutes later and she was hard on by then.'

'And you didn't call Mrs Cunningham?'

She flushed. 'No, it's the worst crime in her book to fetch her down for something she thinks you should have dealt with yourself. She says you're incompetent or lazy or, in my case, afraid of getting my hands dirty. That's because I'm a student and, according to her, not really interested in the work. Besides, I thought that if Evelyn had been drinking, I'd be in trouble for letting her get hold of the stuff.'

She looked suddenly puzzled. 'Now I think about it, I couldn't see any bottles or glasses and I couldn't smell drink.' She added, sadly, 'It would have come out in the end anyway. If she hadn't died, Evelyn would have had a terrific hangover and only Mrs Cunningham is allowed to give paracetamol.'

Browne felt angry that such a young and inexperienced girl should have been put in this position by her employer. 'Presumably you consulted with the other girls on duty. Did any of them help you with her?' he asked.

She shook her head. 'It was Joanne's turn in the dining-room at teatime. I told her Evelyn was sleeping it off. Kerry was there and she said Evelyn looked too respectable to be a dipso. Joanne said a lot of them do when they're sober and that if she had a drink problem we'd have to make sure she didn't move in for good.'

'Anything else?'

She shrugged. 'Kerry said she hoped the bed was all right. She'd had to see to Sally's disgusting sheets yesterday morning, but it had smelt all right in Evelyn's room – as sweet as it ever does when they refuse to have any windows open. I'm sure Evelyn doesn't usually drink. Maybe one of her visitors left her a bottle of something and she didn't realize how much you're supposed to have at once.'

From his corner, Carson asked whether there had been any more visitors during the afternoon. She shook her head as she turned to him. 'I'm not sure. No one else came to the door but she usually got her visitors to come to the french window. The other ladies get jealous if somebody has a lot of people coming and they can be quite bitchy with each other about it.'

'That's quite clear. I've almost finished for now. All I need is a sort of word picture of Mrs Norman as a person by someone less biased than her family. You're in a good position to give it to me.'

She nodded. 'She was quite alert and normal in her manner, not yonderly like a lot of the others.' Browne was familiar with this local term that so well described the mental state of many of the St Helen's ladies. 'But she wasn't independent at all,' the girl went on. 'It seemed as though she didn't want the bother of living her own life. I think she'd stuck out for coming to us so as to be sure of going back to her daughter again as soon as possible.'

'You mean you had to fetch and carry for her, do things for her that she could have done for herself?'

Debbie thought for a minute. 'Not exactly. She was morti-fied when I offered to bath her and she sometimes volunteered to help set the tables and so on – but she didn't seem to want to be responsible for anything. Her daughter made all

51

the financial arrangements for her stay. When I asked her how long she'd be with us, she said she'd have to ask Pamela, and even when I asked what she wanted for her tea, she said, "You help me choose." She wanted somebody else to make all her decisions for her. She soon grumbled though, if she didn't like the ones you made. She wanted other people to take charge but to do things the way that suited her.'

She was silent for a few moments. Browne made no attempt to prompt her till she spoke again. 'I don't know what to tell you – what this is all about. She had some nice jewellery, quite pretty, and a gold necklace that's probably quite valuable. She didn't seem interested in what it looked like, just who gave it to her and how much it cost them. And she was always boasting about her dutiful relations. She'd say, "I'm always driven by Pamela or Tony. I never have to walk anywhere or catch a bus." She seemed to think it was a good thing to be dependent on other people, sort of measured how important she was by how much she was waited on by her family.'

Browne was pleased. 'That's just the kind of thing I meant. Did you mention a Pamela?'

She nodded. 'That's her elder daughter, the one in hospital. She's a writer and Evelyn was very proud of her, had all her books on the chest of drawers for everyone to see. Her married name is Hill, but she writes under her maiden name.'

'Mrs Norman had a very valuable book that she'd inherited. Did she mention it to you at all?'

'No, she didn't.'

Browne could see that the girl looked weary and was not surprised. She'd done a full shift at St Helen's, an afternoon of academic work and now he was keeping her from her evening meal. 'What else did she talk about?' he asked.

There was another pause. 'Her photographs,' the girl said, eventually. 'She kept showing me one of herself and Mr Norman and telling me what a good husband he was. Then she'd got some more of her daughters and their families and she talked about how good it was in the old days when the photos were taken. I got the impression she didn't get on with them lately as well as she used to. Mrs Hill's husband is dead now I gather and her daughter's grown up and has a little boy but there wasn't any picture of him. Evelyn never said much about him. Her other daughter, Stella is a teacher. Evelyn thought that was a very good job.' She shuddered. 'It wouldn't do for me. I can't think of anything else to tell you.'

Browne assured her that she had given him plenty of food for thought and let her go, asking as she reached the door, 'How does caring for old ladies fit in with studying nuclear science?'

She replied with a curious dignity, 'It helps me to keep in mind what science is for.' Browne kept Carson happy by allowing him to drive her home and cheered up Sergeant Hunter by taking him to the canteen for steak pie, pints of coffee and a description of his day's activities.

The two of them were on their usual good terms by the time they were ready to continue their evening's work. As they stood up to go Hunter caught sight of Superintendent Petty who had been sitting behind them, consuming a hot dog. Hunter spoke out of the side of his mouth. 'What's he after in here? He only comes slumming with a purpose.'

Browne frowned a warning, met his superintendent's eye and resignedly accepted a summons to his office. His two superiors disappeared together whilst Hunter went off to mull over what he had just heard and to read for himself, at his CI's invitation, the reports he had left on his desk. Now he was in Browne's confidence again, his ill humour was quite dissipated. As he waited, he tried to make his own assessment of the matter. Did they have a case? Was it a case of murder? The evidence seemed to him pretty slim but he had learned to trust Browne's judgement. When, after ten minutes, the CI had not returned, Hunter went back to his own desk and the report he was writing.

Ten minutes later still, Browne quietly opened then closed his office door, determined not to advertise his black mood by either kicking or slamming it. Petty's recriminations were ringing in his ears. 'Don't you understand plain English, man? Does low-key have some fancy new meaning that I haven't cottoned on to yet? I meant you to send some alert but lowly PC to have a look around. What the hell are they going to make of a DCI poking around the place and dragging a nubile young lass of theirs into his office?'

Browne's fury was mostly with himself for not having anticipated this attack. His chief motive in spending his day out of the station had been to immerse himself in a new bit of business and to keep away from both Mitchell and Hunter. The certainty he'd felt that the corpse he'd been shown had been murdered had almost evaporated. The evidence he'd found so convincing this morning seemed tenuous now. He couldn't face a discussion about it even with Jerry. He would sit at his desk doing soulless paperwork till it was time to crawl home and collapse into bed.

There was a knock at the door. He called out and it opened to admit Mitchell, perky with success, his hangdog expression of the last couple of days abandoned in his triumph. He dropped his report on Browne's desk and, uninvited, arranged his substantial person in the more comfortable of the two armchairs. 'It's my lucky day. When I nobbled that joy-rider he had his mate with him. It only took a bit of bluff to get them to lead me to another car that hasn't even been reported stolen yet.'

Browne's resolutions and Hannah's warnings flew out of the window he had just opened. Mitchell's unaccustomed sheepish expression and quiet demeanour over the last forty-eight hours had convinced him that at least the lad was thoroughly ashamed of himself. To see him now, flushed with success, all thoughts of Virginia banished, was the last straw.

Doors opened down the corridor as Browne's voice, his words indistinct behind his own heavy closed one, roared and echoed. It was established that Mitchell was the recipient of this unprecedented onslaught, and Hunter's was not the only spirit to be solaced by the thought that the clever but self-opinionated and abrasive DC was getting his desserts.

Some minutes later the doors along the corridor were smartly and tactfully closed again as Browne's opened. Mitchell shut it as carefully as Browne had done, walked down the empty corridor and made himself scarce.

Browne, spent and incapable of paperwork, drove home. Switching on the light, he found the hall cluttered with a nylon travel bag in glaring primary colours and a French horn in a black case. His daughter had come home.

Chapter Five

Sitting at his desk the next morning, Browne glared at his pot of hyacinths and felt that his own existence, like theirs, was turning brown at the edges. His heart had lifted the previous evening at the sight of his daughter's possessions, then dropped again when he realized that only his wife was in the kitchen waiting to serve his supper.

Ginny had arrived soon after Browne had left, Hannah admitted. What had she said to the girl, Browne wondered, to persuade her to go up to bed without waiting to speak to him? And so he had had to spend the night with his loss of temper and his unplanned interference unconfessed.

Virginia had been tired, Hannah insisted, and unsure of her reception. She'd obviously decided to tackle her parents one at a time. 'I listened to her. She talked through her various difficulties. She was grateful that I didn't press her for any decisions. We kept the conversation light. She seemed well.' Hannah had reached over his shoulder and banged his well-filled plate in front of him, then relented and nuzzled the back of his neck. 'Don't be heavy handed, Tom. Give her some space.'

He'd tried to be reasonable, given the required promise, even complimented his wife on the meal. Nor had an almost sleepless night shaken his intention. At least Ginny had made the effort to get up before he had to leave and he realized that the early morning was, temporarily, not her favourite time of day. He'd forgo his fried bacon on her account and he'd greet her with a joke.

He forced a grin. 'I knew you had reservations about taking

up a place at Oxford that other people would give their right arm for but this step was a bit drastic, wasn't it?'

Ginny's lips had set in a straight line. 'I'm not a drop-out. I've started this and I'll go through with it.' Whether she was referring to her pregnancy or her course of study, she didn't wait to be asked. As the door slammed, Browne cast his eyes heavenward and waited for his wife, too, to accuse him of making cheap jibes.

Hannah, however, had perfectly understood his good intention. 'Go to work, Tom. I'll sort it. Come home for lunch if you can. She'll feel human again by then.'

At least one good thing had come out of the fracas with Mitchell last night. He'd been able to make it clear to him that Hunter's jibe about proving his manhood had been purely coincidental. Now, as he waited for his team to report for their briefing, he glared again at the inoffensive hyacinth that had sweetened and brightened his office for the last four weeks before succumbing to its current death throes. He could not decide whether the trail of a murderer was going cold because of the super's obstinacy, or if his domestic problems were making him eager to invent a case in which to submerge himself.

He was perfectly able to deal with a crisis at home or at work, but he liked to get things done. Having to hold back from decisive action in both areas at once was more than he could stomach. Petty, of course, had not suggested that Dr Pedlar's suspicions should be ignored – he wouldn't dare – but the resources and manpower Browne was being allowed said more clearly than words that, in Petty's opinion, if someone had helped a tiresome old woman into a better world, he wasn't likely to repeat his offence. Joy-riders and burglars would.

There was a tap on the door. It wouldn't be Mitchell. It was his day off, which was probably why Virginia was home. DCs Carson and Bellamy came in, both laughing.

'It's the joker on the board again.' Bellamy appropriated the visitor's armchair. 'There's a kid's jack-in-the-box hanging up, with a green sock pulled over the jack with snake markings

57

on it. What's written on it, Robin? You should remember, you go to church.'

' "*And he laid hold on the dragon*",' Carson recited, obediently, ' "*that old serpent . . . and shut him up and set a seal upon him.*" It's a bit from Revelation today. It's quite clever, isn't it? Bennett's on reception this week. He's going to keep his eyes open in the morning to find out who's doing it.'

Browne grinned and pulled his file towards him as the rest of his team trooped in. Bellamy nudged Carson. 'Now we'll get the whole story.' Browne followed his gaze to a blushing Constable Smith who was endeavouring to hide herself. He looked puzzled.

'Jennie's just got herself engaged,' Carson explained, 'to Paul Taylor – Sergeant Taylor of traffic division. It was his car the snake took refuge in.'

Browne offered his congratulations. 'Has it turned up yet?' She shook her head and he began to bring his team up to date with developments in their various inquiries. He made much of Mitchell's success with the stolen cars and the other constables exchanged disappointed glances. They were evidently not going to learn the reason for the CI's wrath the previous evening.

He distracted them by outlining briefly the facts surrounding Evelyn Norman's death. 'Neither Ledgard nor her GP will go along with natural causes. We haven't ruled out either accident or suicide yet, but both doctors think there's a case to answer. It obviously isn't top priority with the powers that be though. We've had no one drafted in to give us a hand with it so it's down to us.'

Browne affected not to hear an aside from DC Dean to the effect that Petty was a prime example of a man promoted to the level of his incompetence. 'I've given you all I have,' he went on smoothly, 'from Doctors Ledgard and Pedlar, including what they've said unofficially. In writing, Ledgard will only say that his mark is "consistent with an injection given against the recipient's will", but it's significant, together with the low blood sugar and the untypical behaviour.'

Carson's fidgeting had become irritating. 'Did anything strike you that I've missed out, Robin?'

'Not at the time, sir, but Debbie Jardine was chattering about the home when I was driving her back to her flat. I thought I might pick up something useful while she was in the mood so I invited her for a drink at the Cross Keys.'

'Purely in the line of duty, of course.'

He blushed. 'Of course, sir.'

'So, what did you find out?'

'Well, first that there are two diabetics at St Helen's. She doesn't know whether either of them were insulin-dependent but she was warned about giving them food other than at their meal times. Then I managed to get her on to medication in general. She says it's strictly in Mrs Cunningham's hands. Pills are given out in egg cups on the breakfast trays and then at other meals if necessary. The girls have to stay and watch till all the pills have been swallowed and till all hot liquids have been drunk in case somebody scalds herself. She said that Mrs Norman wasn't specially friendly with anyone – she hadn't been there long enough – but they didn't seem to take to her much. She was always trying to help people who'd rather manage on their own and she was a bit self-righteous – "a great sniffer", Debbie called her.'

'Come on, what else?'

Carson had an air of excitement not accounted for by the merely confirmatory evidence he had offered.

'Well, Debbie was hesitant to make much of it. The old ladies often invent stories to make themselves seem important. She said she often wondered when one of them said something – usually something nasty about one of the other residents – that obviously wasn't true, whether it was best to humour her or to try to argue logically. It's not possible to distract them with another idea. They cling to their grievances, real or imaginery.'

Dean at least had run out of patience. 'Get to the point, man!'

When Browne added a confirming nod, Carson hastily obliged. 'Several times, Mrs Norman told Debbie that she had a very valuable set of books, "worth thousands" she kept repeating. They used to belong to her father-in-law. She said they were about whales. She also said, on a couple of occasions, that since the family obviously didn't want to do what was right by her, she was going to sell them and then pay a live-in companion who'd look after her properly.'

'And Debbie thought she was making it up?'

Carson shrugged. 'She didn't know but she said Evelyn didn't seem to be the sort of woman who'd know about books. The nearest she got to reading at St Helen's was sitting up in bed in the evening with sloppy magazines.'

Browne considered the question. The woman described to him by the three witnesses he had so far seen had not come across to him as a reader and scholar. 'Her daughter went to Leeds University and became friendly with Dr Pedlar there,' he offered. 'She read biology so that might explain books on whales being in the house, but I shouldn't imagine they're valuable.'

'I suppose Mrs Hill might know if a textbook was worth something,' Hunter put in. 'Maybe it's a former standard work, gone out of print. It could have a certain value that Mrs Norman has either exaggerated or misunderstood.'

Dean was unimpressed. 'Are we seriously considering that she was killed off so that a few old books shouldn't go out of the family?'

Carson glared at Dean. 'I didn't suggest anything of the sort. I'm just passing on what I was told.'

Browne's glance quelled them both. 'And everything we're told, we'll follow up. Right then, what do we all think?'

At most briefings, Mitchell waited impatiently for Browne's invitation to speak. In his absence there was a slightly longer pause than usual before contributions were offered.

'The book's the only interesting lead so far.' Bellamy's offering came first. 'We need to know if it's really valuable, or, at least, if the family thinks so. And we'll have to find out who's got it at the moment.'

'If the son-in-law's a dealer, we'd better see what he's got to say about it.'

'Are you volunteering, Richard?'

Dean grinned. 'Yes, sir. They visited Mrs Norman on Monday morning, you said?'

He subsided to write in his notebook as Carson and Hunter spoke together. Carson deferred to the sergeant.

'You've searched her room and sealed it?' Browne nodded. 'No book about whales there?' Browne shook his head. 'I could have a look around her house, then.'

'We'll do it together later this morning.' Hunter looked put out and Browne felt irritated. 'I'm not doubting your efficiency but getting to know the victim has to be the chief concern of whoever's leading the inquiry. After lunch, Jerry, you can practise your bedside manner on the writer daughter. She might go in for revealing nightdresses so you'd better take Jennie with you to guard your reputation.'

Jennie looked amused at the idea of being Hunter's chaperone, then, struck by another aspect of the inquiry, asked, 'How many girls are on duty at a time at St Helen's?'

Browne shrugged. 'There seemed to be just three or four on Tuesday afternoon.'

'Not enough to watch twenty-five old people constantly as well as cleaning and cooking. Mrs Cunningham says medicines are locked away and her old people supervised constantly, but then, she'd have to say that. It might not always be so.'

Browne considered the comment. 'Dr Pedlar is impressed by her efficiency. Said she ran a very tight ship. Anyway, you could spend your morning finding out, and checking as far as you can whether any of the family besides the Fentons were seen around the place on Monday. Any more great thoughts? Nigel?'

Bellamy looked up from his notes. 'I was wondering who the book has actually been left to, and whether there's anybody in urgent need of the money it would fetch. And nobody's considered the grandchildren, Sonia and the young chap who designs the jewellery.'

'I suppose you're volunteering to see the young lady?'

'I'll see them both, if you like, sir.'

'Creep!' muttered Dean, audibly.

Browne glared at him, then turned to Carson who had remained silent since he had interrupted Hunter. 'And where do you fancy spending your day, Robin?'

Carson blinked, then smiled. 'I could ask Debbie Jardine if there's anything she'd like to add to her statement, sir.' There was general laughter.

'You can begin by ringing Dr Pedlar. There's one St Helen's resident with senile dementia. Ask her for an assessment with respect to all the circumstances of this case. And then get on to the family solicitor and see what you can discover about who the book – and any other property – has been willed to. Jerry, have the car outside at eleven. I've another errand to see to before that.' He waved them away, but caught Carson's eye as he trailed out last. 'Cool it with the girl, Robin, until this matter's sewn up.'

The errand that prevented Browne's imminent departure to search Mrs Norman's house was a visit to Mitchell's flat to make his peace with him. Since he could remember very little of what, in the heat of the moment, he had said, he was not sure in what terms his apology should be couched. Perhaps, in the circumstances, it should be very humble.

He had rung the bell to the flat before it occurred to him that his daughter might be inside and he prayed that her morning sickness would keep her at home just long enough for him to speak his lines and depart. When Mitchell appeared at the door, in sweatshirt and jeans, beamed at him and stood back to let him in, Browne felt that family harmony would not be furthered by a churlish refusal.

Mitchell seemed unabashed. 'Thanks for last night,' he offered, airily, as Browne followed him to the kitchen. 'Waiting for it was worse than getting it. Now the air's a bit clearer we can work together again. Want a coffee?'

Speechless, Browne nodded and sat down at the new pine table. What he could see of the flat was spotless, rather bare but not unwelcoming and the coffee smelt good. 'I came to apologize,' he announced, stiffly.

'What for?'

'For what I said last night.' Browne disliked putting what was obvious into words.

Mitchell turned his back on the filter machine and opened

the refrigerator in search of milk. 'I don't see why you should. Most of it was true and deserved. Ginny and I are equally responsible for what's happened but, as you rightly pointed out, she is much younger, though she wouldn't consider that relevant, and she has much more to lose. You're concerned about her reputation though, and I'm not.'

He forestalled Browne's angry protest. 'That's because it isn't in any danger. We may have flouted an outworn code of respectability but neither of us has any intention of behaving irresponsibly towards our infant. Thinking people will respect Virginia for the way she copes. Unthinking ones won't worry either of us – but she does have a difficult choice to make that shouldn't have been necessary. If we'd been a bit more careful she could have completed her degree course with no other responsibilities to distract her. As for getting married, I'd have done it already if she'd been willing. You were unjust about that.' His tone revealed that he was anxious to get the facts right rather than air a grievance. 'But it wouldn't be to avoid the disapproval of self-appointed judges.'

'She's home,' Browne announced, baldly.

Mitchell nodded. 'Yes, she rang me last night to say she was coming, then hung up before I could comment. She doesn't trust either of us not to rush her, not to take away her right to choose.' He placed a steaming cup in front of Browne. 'I don't trust us either. She's going to be very angry with both of us before it all gets sorted out. Thank goodness for Hannah.'

The coffee was wonderful. Browne was pleased that someone in his daughter's future household would be able to produce a less poisonous brew than her own. Perversely, although he had not wanted to make an apology, he now felt balked because Mitchell had prevented it. The man's self-possession infuriated him. However he had imagined Mitchell would behave, he had not expected this calm admission that he had acted merely unwisely. Only cringing self-abasement would have satisfied Browne's desire for vengeance when he first arrived, but he supposed it was not a quality he should seek in his daughter's husband.

At a loss for something else to say whilst he finished his

coffee, he gave Mitchell the information the rest of his team were presently following up on the Norman case. Mitchell reached for his notebook and scribbled as he listened. His CI, his mind recalled to his work, hurriedly departed to continue it.

Mitchell poured himself more coffee and reached for the phone. He was pleased to hear his fiancée's voice giving her number. 'Lunch?' he enquired, laconically. 'And, unless you decree otherwise, we shall talk about the weather, your college work and the state of the nation.'

'Thanks, Benny, but I want to take Dad out to lunch. I blew my top at him over breakfast.'

'Dinner, then?'

'Fine.'

He arranged to pick her up, then restored his kitchen to perfect order as he worked out how to occupy himself on his free day. He knew quite well what he wanted to do but for a few minutes he hesitated. He had been in trouble before for taking off on his own initiative without reference to Browne as leader of the current investigation. He argued the pros and cons of his plan: he was in quite enough disfavour with his CI at the moment. On the other hand, he had to fling himself into some sort of absorbing activity to get through the hours before his half dreaded, half longed-for dinner date with Virginia. He knew, however, as his hands replaced crockery and his mind went through the motions of debate that he was going to carry it out. If he achieved nothing, Browne need never know and if he learned something useful, it would be worth having his knuckles rapped. It was a free country. He could browse in a second-hand bookshop if he liked.

It would be advisable, he decided, to visit the library to prepare himself. He grabbed his newish denim jacket that emphasized the disreputable state of his jeans and scooped up his car keys from the hall table. He parked in the Pay and Display down the hill from the shopping precinct and walked over sun-baked flags to feed his money into the ticket dispenser. After the squalls of the previous days it was incredibly warm. Tar was melting on a recently mended patch of road and it could have been July if a vindictive breeze had not wrought havoc with female shoppers' hairstyles and the flapping polythene wrappings over the load of a passing truck.

The library was surprisingly busy. He stood, slightly disorientated, just inside the door. It was not a place where he felt at home. He was made uncomfortable by the muffled footsteps and hushed voices. The huge notice-board in the entrance looked more interesting to him than the shelves of volumes. He never seemed to have much time to spare from making his own observations on what interested him to compare them with those of people who had got into print and he had never had much truck with fiction. It was not only middle-aged ladies heading for the romance section who were trying to lose themselves in a dream world. Real life was quite fascinating enough for him.

He could see the point of the reference section, though. He climbed the wide, glass-walled staircase to the top floor and grinned at the girl he had consulted a couple of times before. She grinned back. 'More poisons?'

He shook his head. 'Not this time. Have you got a section on marine biology?' He was annoyed to discover he had joined the conspiracy of silence and was whispering in spite of himself. She showed him the relevant shelves and he lifted down several volumes.

Twenty minutes later, he had become interested in spite of himself. He soon abandoned a tome that informed him that a whale was 'a cetaceous mammal of the larger pelagic species whose two main subdivisions are mysticeti and odontoceti'. He became mesmerized by another that had huge pictures of sperm, bottlenose and sulphur-bottom whales. They cast a spell from which he had difficulty freeing himself and he put the books back reluctantly, reminding himself that he had to be in and out of Fenton's shop well before Dean's afternoon visit.

He had copied into his notebook several titles from the bibliography at the end of one of the books and now he tore out the sheet and folded it carefully inside his wallet. Half an hour's drive took him to his destination on the outskirts of Leeds.

Anthony Fenton's shop was one of a row of rundown cottages that had had its window slightly enlarged for display purposes.

Two huge chunks of stone made steps leading up to the door with a wrought-iron railing, newly painted black. A sign at right-angles to the door advertised books and prints in block capitals whilst a large, dog-eared card in the bottom of the window announced *Antiquarian Bookseller* in Gothic script.

A stool stood on the top step in front of the open door. Mitchell wondered whether it was for customers who had found the two steps exhausting or whether a lack of them left Anthony Fenton free to sit on his step in the sun. The window space was shelved across and filled with books but only on the middle row did the spines face outwards. Perhaps curiosity was supposed to draw the clients in.

They would need to be intrepid. Piles of dog-eared volumes in the doorway repelled them and barricaded Fenton in. The shop, being a converted house, opened into what had been the entrance lobby. A staircase went up straight ahead and another door on the right led into the main downstairs room. The stairs had worn lino on the treads and risers, painted white but badly scuffed. There was a double pile of books on each step and those on the fifth one up had collapsed to form a barrier.

Mitchell's plan was to prowl and get the feel of the place before addressing himself to the proprietor. He was agile in spite of his bulk and managed to make his way safely to the narrow landing. Books were piled three feet high on each side, mostly with their titles to the wall, presumably waiting to be shelved.

There was just room for Mitchell to squeeze along to the first doorway. It led into a white-painted room but here the walls, particularly the chimney breast, were damp and huge white flakes had fallen to reveal parchment-coloured paper and a faded flowered border which also threatened to come adrift. A flex came through a rough hole in the ceiling, the double socket attached to it holding two fly-specked, unshaded bulbs. A huge solid table with bulbous legs was the only other furniture. There was just sufficient room to walk round it and the number of books, maps, prints and pictures heaped on top of it doubled its height.

When he had gazed his fill, Mitchell carefully edged his

way to the other first-floor room where a start had been made on uniform shelving. The windows were clean and the floor covered in dark coloured cord carpet. The light fittings were of the same primitive nature as in the neighbouring room. Mitchell thought it a pity that the work had progressed so far when the damp had not been cured.

The journey down the steep stairs made him glad of the stout handrail. He reached the bottom unscathed and looked into the main part of the shop. Fenton sat at a desk with his back to a kitchen range he had not removed. From the doorway, Mitchell could see only his head, the rest of him being hidden behind yet another free-standing bookcase in the middle of the floor. Pictures hung from hooks on the ceiling, circling on lengths of string and threatening the unwary.

The DC guessed that the till would consist of two plastic boxes to separate the silver from the copper. He felt a contemptuous pity, for the proprietor of this establishment revealed to Mitchell's eyes not as lazy but as totally impractical, pathetic. The building was doomed, though it had character and potential if there was money available to spend on it. He suspected that there was not and that both the building and the stock would gradually disintegrate round their owner. A set of books 'worth thousands' would certainly make a difference to this place!

With difficulty, Mitchell made his way to the desk and presented his list of books, taking stock of Fenton as he scrutinized it. His thick checked shirt and sleeveless padded jacket were unconventional garments for business hours though they would provide practical protection against the lack of heating. The fine fair hair, cut short and brushed back, was both thinning and receding but the face was tanned and alert.

Fenton appeared not to be depressed by his circumstances and showed a lively interest in Mitchell's spurious requirements. 'I can probably help you with some of these. You'll need to be determined to plough through all of them.' His voice was clipped, academic, what Mitchell categorized, derogatively, as 'middle class'. He regarded his customer quizzically, as though he doubted that Mitchell's powers of concentration would be equal to the intention that the booklist represented.

Then, with a red biro, he began to decorate the list with various crosses, ticks and asterisks. 'I've had a copy of the Fowler but I sold it a couple of weeks ago. I've got Cheriton on the beluga.' He crossed to the door, mounted unerringly to the eighth step of the staircase and, without hesitation, extracted a thin black volume from near the bottom of the inner pile.

Mitchell was astonished. The apparent chaos represented a system! He accepted the proffered book in some confusion and turned the pages. They struck him as less than compelling and he hoped Fenton would be unable to supply him with any of the other volumes on the list. He was pleased to see the red pen make crosses against all the rest but one.

'I do have a copy of Massey's *Marine Biology*. It's lost its dust jacket and the spine's a bit rubbed but it's a good reading copy.' Mitchell was puzzled. What else would he be likely to do with it? 'The problem is it's in a box somewhere on the table in the room upstairs that you've just been exploring. It would take a while to move everything off but if you're not in a hurry . . .'

In devotion to duty, Mitchell trusted his substantial person to a flimsy-looking stool and confided that he'd come over from Cloughton. It was his day off but his girlfriend had stood him up in favour of lunch with her father.

Fenton grinned. 'Students, are you?'

'She is.'

'Oh, the books are for her? I thought you looked a bit lost in this set-up.'

He admitted he was and cast around frantically for a way of initiating a more general conversation. He was pleased when an elderly man appeared in the doorway, a banana box in his arms. Mitchell obligingly gave place to the newcomer, announcing that he would browse a while longer until Fenton was free to dig out the jacketless Massey.

Hidden in a metal shelved bay, he listened carefully to the transaction that followed. Fenton was being offered history books to which he gave polite consideration but a firm refusal to buy. 'You're right. They're in good condition, but a series of histories with a couple missing is practically valueless. People don't ask for odd copies.' The old man embarked on a tear-jerking hard-luck story. Fenton was mild mannered, sympathetic in a detached way and still firm in his refusal. After a few minutes, he gently but adroitly sent the old man on his way.

Mitchell revised his opinion of Fenton as a businessman and came to reseat himself on the stool. 'Is that how you get your stock, people coming in with stuff to sell to you?'

Fenton shrugged. 'That's one of the ways. I buy them from other dealers, charity shops, car boot sales, remainder shops, anywhere I can find them.'

Mitchell was becoming genuinely interested. 'How do you know what to charge for them?'

'You learn what the market will offer but I usually work on a times-three mark up to cover costs and feed us.'

'Is it a good living then?' Mitchell was impressed. He began to wonder if the crumbling building was one of the props in a huge con of the customer. Maybe Fenton went home to a solidly built mansion on which he lavished his two hundred per cent profit.

Again, Fenton favoured him with the quizzical smile. 'With the shop and fairs and postal sales, I get by.'

'Fairs?'

'Big indoor sales. They're held in hotel reception rooms or church halls or theatres.' A buzzer sounded somewhere at the back of the shop. He ignored it. 'There are two main organizations that do the administration and individual dealers rent stalls there. There's one every couple of months at the parish church hall in Cloughton. You've probably seen them advertised.'

Mitchell vaguely remembered Traffic Division once complaining about their parking arrangements. 'Do you have to close the shop then, when you go to those?'

Fenton shook his head. 'Not usually. We live in the flat on the top floor so my wife sometimes comes down and takes over.' If he minded the catechism he didn't show it.

Mitchell beamed at him. 'Oh, I see. A family business.' He let his grin broaden. 'I'm sorry. Because I'm at a loose end, I'm giving you the third degree. You've probably got plenty to do.'

As he had hoped, Fenton expanded a little further to prove that he was not offended. 'Don't worry about it. It's usually quiet on a Wednesday. As a matter of fact, I did think at one time that my boy was getting interested. He spent most of his adolescence avoiding getting landed with minding the shop. I suppose that's only natural. But, about eighteen months ago, he got interested in various very rare books and how auctions were organized. I sent him off to talk to the well-established businesses in Manchester and York. I've had no experience with that kind of stock. I deal in good standard academic works and follow up a few of my own special interests, old maps and books on athletics in particular.

'I didn't push Alistair, just waited to see how things went. Then, suddenly, he lost interest and decided to go into partnership with an old school friend and they have a nice little business of their own now.'

'Were you disappointed?'

He paused, as though he'd never really considered his own feelings. 'I suppose I was a bit, but I'm glad the lad's making a living and is happy.'

A young woman appeared from a door at the back of the shop. She wore a purple velour track suit and high boots. Fenton began stacking papers on his desk to avoid her eye but she came forward, uttering complaints about the disregarded buzzer. As she stood in front of the window, Mitchell saw that although she was only slightly built and her hair hung in a youthfully tangled curtain to the middle of her back, she was probably in her middle forties. She described graphically the congealing contents of his plate upstairs in the flat as Fenton flipped over the open/closed notice on the door, grinning and winking at his customer as he passed him.

Mitchell placed his Cheriton on the desk and prepared to depart. 'Enjoy your lunch, both of you. I'm getting peckish myself. I'll pay for this and call back later. Perhaps by then you'll have had time to dig out the other one.' He was reasonably pleased with his morning. It had been too much to hope that Fenton would discuss a priceless annd soon-to-be-acquired volume on whales with a casual buyer. If the book really was valuable, he would not be selling it over the counter to someone who was not sufficiently well off to buy new. Nevertheless, he had got the feel of the place and an impression of the man, and, if he called back towards closing time, he might even be able to steer the conversation in a direction that would persuade Fenton to mention, even talk about, his visit from DC Dean.

Chapter Six

The key Carson had acquired fitted Evelyn Norman's back door which Browne and Hunter reached by walking through a tunnel passage between her house and the end one in the block.

The houses were of red brick, their fronts stone faced, their back gardens narrow but quite long. Mrs Norman's was neat and colourful, consisting almost entirely of a well-trimmed lawn. Below it was a rose bed with tidily pruned bushes, whilst the end nearest the house sloped up to it by way of a small rockery, bright with bulbs and tiny conifers. Its planning was not imaginative and had obviously aimed at easy management but nevertheless it was cheerful and attractive.

The neighbouring plot covered a similar area but a very different effect had been achieved. A path across its grass wound round two raised flower beds towards a boundary wall covered in climbers with vivid foliage. The neighbour, carrying a bulging black plastic bag in the direction of the dustbin, intercepted their appreciative gaze. She smiled as they expressed admiration. 'It's all my husband's work. He spends every spare minute out here.' Her expression changed. 'You weren't wanting to see Mrs Norman, were you?'

Browne introduced himself and Hunter and showed her his warrant. 'We'd be grateful for a word with you in a little while but there are one or two things we need to check in the house first.' She looked puzzled but asked no questions and proceeded to the dustbin with her bag of waste.

Browne unlocked the back door which opened straight into a kitchen–dining-room. He had worked with Hunter for several years now and they began a methodical search of it with no need of preliminary speech.

72

Everything was neat, matching and cheap. The dining-room suite was Formica-faced in a woodgrain pattern. Even the pottery ornaments on the mantelpiece must have been bought as a matching set, rather than being collected one by one.

A door from the kitchen led into a sitting-room. Here the furniture was teak-veneered, the sideboard holding table linen, good cutlery and glasses, all carefully boxed or wrapped. On top were photographs, two of young children, smooth and sleek and smartly dressed, one seated at a piano keyboard and the other being presented with a small shield. There were no school photographs showing them untidy and casual.

On the mantelpiece was a studio portrait of a wedding group, the garments rather old fashioned but not sufficiently so for the wedding to be Mrs Norman's own. Obviously one of the daughters. Hunter picked it up and studied the faces. Yes, here was Mrs Norman, the gracious bride's mother in suit and hat.

He moved over to the music centre and opened the doors of the cabinet on which it stood. He was surprised to find that the tapes and records it contained were packed into two cardboard cartons so that only the titles of the top ones were visible. Mrs Norman had obviously preferred watching the large-screened television set.

Browne was busy with the top section of a writing desk in the corner. It must have contained every letter Mrs Norman had received in the last seven or eight years. He clipped back the flap front over the shelves and bent to examine the cupboards below. His indrawn breath caused Hunter to look round at him. 'Have a look at this.'

Over the CI's shoulder, Hunter gazed at a huge collection of pill bottles, ointments and liquid medicine. Browne turned them gingerly, reading the chemists' labels. 'Antacids, blood-pressure pills . . .' He whistled. 'There's a bottle of diamorphine as well. They're all prescribed for her husband and dated '87 and '88.'

He closed the cupboard and they moved upstairs to scrutinize a bathroom in blues that didn't quite match and two bedrooms. The one Mrs Norman had used contained the usual furniture, a large oil-filled electric heater, a bedside table with a Teasmaid and a Bible. On the dressing-table a cut-glass tray with matching candlesticks held matching silver-backed hairbrushes. As well as a fitted carpet, there was a sheepskin rug beside the bed. There were no books in the house besides the Bible, nor any magazines, nor even newspapers.

'There's no more flavour of the woman here than in her room at St Helen's,' Browne observed.

Hunter's nose wrinkled. 'I think there is.' Browne waited politely. 'Well, the photographs, for instance, the children both shown bringing credit to the family in their Sunday best. No snaps of them being just themselves, scruffy and natural. And the wedding picture, everything present and correct. I wonder which daughter it was and how the other one's wedding fell short.'

Browne shook his head. 'I think the "special occasion" photographs of the children are just a matter of her generation and possibly her social class. And perhaps one daughter gave her a wedding picture and the other didn't.'

'Perhaps. Or maybe she displays them according to which one is currently in favour.' He sighed. 'It's taken a long time to work our way through such a small house.'

Browne grinned. 'It's because she keeps everything double wrapped in every drawer and cupboard, polythene covers over all the clothes in the wardrobe, hats and underwear in bags in the drawers, shoes in the boxes they were bought in and everything loose wrapped in tissue paper. It's as though life had stopped happening for her and everything was put away because it wouldn't be needed again. I've met this in old ladies before. But, having unwrapped every blessed object, we haven't turned up the mysterious books. We'd better find out who's had a chance to get in while the house was empty and remove it. Let's go next door. If you're as dry as I am, we can perhaps jointly will the prize gardener's wife to put the kettle on.'

Mrs Barnes had anticipated their thirst, pouring boiled water into the warmed pot as she heard her back gate click. She proved, too, to be a useful witness, having taken a responsible interest in her elderly neighbour. 'It was no trouble doing her shopping when we did ours, easier than Pam trailing over.'

'She couldn't get about much, then?'

Mrs Barnes looked nonplussed. 'Well, physically she was quite sprightly but she always behaved as if she couldn't. She never went anywhere by herself. If you suggested she did something, she'd always say it wasn't worth it on your own. She went to church with us on Sunday mornings but, if ever I missed, she didn't go either, although you'll have seen it's only just down the road and everybody made her welcome there. It made you feel guilty for not going on her account as well as your own.

'It was the same with the garden. Mr Norman laid it out so it wasn't much trouble to look after, so when he died, she could have done it. She was fitter than he was anyway. But she just watched it go wild and in the end my husband couldn't bear looking at it so he started doing it for her. The only thanks he got was the odd snide comment on the difference between ours and hers.' She sounded amused rather than condemnatory. Obviously a generous soul, Browne thought.

'They get odd when they get older, don't they? Do you know, she never opened a letter, not even a personal one. She always shoved them into that writing desk thing until Pam came to deal with them. She said official letters frightened her and she'd lie awake worrying if one was typewritten and official looking and might need dealing with promptly. She'd ring Pam up and ask her to come the next day to sort it out.'

Browne put his empty cup down hopefully. 'Was Pam the only member of the family who visited?'

She shrugged as she took the hint and reached for the teapot. 'Stella came occasionally but I think it was more because she was afraid of Pam's tongue than because of concern for her mother. Tony was quite good to her, took her out in the car now and then, cut the lawn when we were on holiday.

'Sonia, that's Pam's daughter, never came, although they sometimes met at Pam's house. That was Mrs Norman's own fault, though. She looked down her nose at Sonia because of the little boy and refused to recognize that Thomas existed. I mean, we all hope that our daughters will have more sense but it's no good standing in judgement when it's happened and it certainly wasn't the child's fault.'

Browne bit his lip and stayed silent. Hunter, wondering what Mrs Barnes had said that was so thought-provoking, took over the questions. 'What about the Fentons' son?'

She shook her head. 'Hardly ever saw him, though Mrs Norman talked about him occasionally. She's got an old picture of him getting a prize for a painting competition that the newspaper ran. She used not to be too impressed with him. Sonia was the clever one that she boasted about until she blotted her copybook. She's very artistic. Made her own clothes from about twelve and now she designs them as well. I'm surprised she doesn't make it her career, but I suppose it's awkward with the little boy. Anyway, Alistair's in business now, designing jewellery. Mrs Norman thought it was a funny job for a man but now he's quite well known, at least locally, and she'd changed her tune.'

Third cups of tea were refused and, since Browne seemed to have no more to say, Hunter turned back to Mrs Barnes. 'Have you seen Mrs Norman since she went to stay with Pamela or at St Helen's?'

She shook her head. 'No, as a matter of fact we were wondering if we'd ever see her again. My husband said Pamela had made a bad move. He said Mrs Norman would get her feet well under the table and Pam would have a job to get her to come back here again. He may have been right if she'd lived.'

'You weren't expecting her to die though?'

She shook her head again, her eyes widening. 'Not at all. It was quite a shock when Sonia came round to tell us. She had the little boy with her. He's really sweet. It was silly of Mrs Norman to cut herself off from them.'

Suddenly Browne broke in again. 'Whatever did she do with herself all day? We looked all round and we didn't see any of the things old ladies usually occupy themselves with, no knitting or sewing, no novels or newspapers, all her tapes and records packed away. It looks as though she sat and did nothing.'

Mrs Barnes looked impressed. 'Fancy you working that out just from looking at the house. You're right, though. We took her out occasionally and she'd always thank us politely and say she'd thoroughly enjoyed it but she obviously hadn't. She'd just passively let the trip happen round her. She didn't seem to have a sense of taste – I don't mean food – although she wasn't any more interested in that than in books or world affairs or music or anything. She never really . . . well, "tasted" them is the only way I can explain it. She got nothing out of anything for its own sake.

'My Sarah plays the piano. Mrs Norman gave her a pound every time she passed another exam. It was good of her and she meant to encourage the child, but Sarah would rather have been asked to play something for her.' Mrs Barnes began to clear away the tea things. 'And the music centre hasn't been used since Mr Norman died. She said it was too complicated and she was too scared of breaking it and she wasn't bothered much about music anyway. She not only had no enthusiasm about anything herself, she rather scorned anybody who had. When my husband roared on his football team on the box for instance, she'd give a derisive sort of smile and she told Val on the other side of her that he's no better than a child.

'There's no harm in her though. Perhaps we should have tried a bit harder. I used to go in quite often but I was careful not to stay long in case she started expecting me to spend all evening there. When I left, she always used to look crestfallen. She only wanted company. We aren't very kind to old people who expect things of us, are we? Her husband wasn't like her though. Even at the end, when he was very ill, he was independent and cheerful.'

'You never thought'— Browne's tone had changed and she turned to him warily – 'that she might be so switched off because she was taking some kind of drug?'

'Apart from what she got from the doctor, you mean? Is that what all the police interest is about?'

'It's a question we'd like you to answer if you could.'

She was silent for some moments, giving the matter consideration. 'I can only say I don't think so. I wouldn't know what signs to look for and she did behave a bit strangely, as I've been trying to explain. But she got into a terrible panic if she had the slightest thing wrong with her. She was terrified of being ill. I don't think she'd have dared do anything to harm herself.'

Browne smiled at her earnest expression. 'Thank you for taking so much trouble with your answers. Did you know that the drugs prescribed for Mr Norman are still in a cupboard in the sitting-room?'

She smiled ruefully. 'No, or I'd have done something about it. But it doesn't surprise me. She'd have expected somebody to dispose of them for her.'

'Did her husband have any of his drugs by injection?'

'Not as far as I know, and I think I would have known. I was in there a lot just at the end.'

'He wasn't diabetic?'

'No, I'm sure he wasn't.'

She glanced at her watch and Browne realized that she was anxious to prepare the midday meal. Promising to convey her condolences and wishes for a speedy recovery to Mrs Hill, they took their leave. 'Doesn't sound as if the next Pamela Norman would have met its publishing deadline if Mrs Norman had lived,' Hunter remarked as their footsteps echoed in the passageway.

Virginia had chosen to entertain her father in the restaurant of the Shepherd's Rest because, in March, its flowers were real, cut from the shrubs of its back garden. Fresh flowers always lightened her mood. The table where she sat held two narcissi with shortened stems and a sprig of forsythia. The one behind had a couple of twigs of flowering currant and a fresh, almost peppery smell drifted across from them each time the door opened.

The cloths were crisp and white, the cutlery scratched but silver. The windows were high in the thick walls, letting in some cheerful sunlight but none of its unseasonable warmth. There was a small fire blazing in the hearth. Virginia suspected that the flaming coals were a clever invention of the gas board but was reluctant to go near enough to find out. She preferred to enjoy the small illusion. There was going to be quite enough reality to face up to soon.

She sipped her orange juice and tried to decide whether her father would be more pleased by her willingness to sacrifice her limited resources on buying him a good meal or by the opportunity to spoil her at his own expense. She had planned to preface many of her remarks over lunch with 'Do you remember . . .' to recall many of the pleasurable moments in the history of their very good relationship, but she was beginning now to think that this would not do. It would entrench him more firmly in his disapproval of her present situation, remind him of the plans he'd made on her behalf that she was not now prepared to fulfil.

She wondered if there would come a time when the little creature growing inside her would grieve her and Benny and would sit as she sat now, wondering how best to soothe and placate them. She was growing tired of being expected to apologize for him and herself. It seemed to her quite in the right order of things that this child, conceived on Christmas Day and busy preparing himself to face the world, should become a member of the family in September. He couldn't go on being a mistake! She had established a relationship with him already. She felt rather guilty about the problems caused by her carelessly snatched pleasure but she was certainly not ashamed of him.

So, over lunch, for which she must pay, she would take the initiative in the conversation, make her father look forward to a future which included his grandchild. What she really had to decide about was Benny. Not about whether she loved him, that hadn't changed. She'd promised to marry him and one day she'd be glad to, but, somehow, it was desperately important to her that it shouldn't be because she couldn't cope without him. Her father was going to say that it was Benny's child too, that he had responsibilities, and also the right, to make a home for his own son or daughter. She knew that she wouldn't be able to make him understand. It was only important that he should accept it. But, by eight tonight, she had to find a way of explaining it all to Benny.

Browne felt he was achieving little over lunch with his

79

daughter. No plans of even the vaguest kind for a wedding had so far been mooted. She had cleverly steered him away whenever his remarks had half turned the conversation in that direction. She had at least assured him that the doctor was pleased with her, that she was swallowing her vitamins and drinking her milk. She had talked about her college work with an obviously genuine enthusiasm that would, in other circumstances, have delighted him. She was drinking fresh orange juice with her meal and had refused even to taste the half bottle of St Émilion that she had ordered for him.

They were tempted by the unseasonably warm sun to take their coffee at a plank table in the garden, which, tucked into the right-angle of the building, was sheltered from the prevailing winds. It would be a particularly beautiful spring, Browne decided. Virginia had confided in him at least the few decisions she had so far made. Apart from Hannah's single reference to it as a possibility, there had been no talk of an abortion. He supposed matters might be worse. Virginia seemed to have enjoyed entertaining him and he congratulated himself on having had sufficient tact not to order all the least expensive dishes on the menu. When he arrived back at his desk he found that his bowl of jaded hyacinths had been replaced by the fat-leaved promise of budding tulips.

Chapter Seven

Pamela Hill too, in the much prized 'single' to which she had been moved, was eating lunch. The infection which had set back her recovery was clearing now and she was unlikely to need to summon urgent help. Her reward had been banishment to one of the three little rooms at the end of the corridor beyond the series of four-bed wards and furthest away from the nurses' station.

Her pleasure had not been much marred by hearing that Myra had also been granted this privilege. Myra was not similarly grateful. 'We might still need someone; we aren't out of the woods yet. And the food's cold when it gets right up here.' Pamela's meal had not been cold at all and, having eaten as much as her appetite allowed, she put her plate back on the tray. Like Browne's, served at almost the same moment, the dish had been called chicken casserole, and, like his, it had consisted of a chicken leg, chopped tomato, celery and onions, but there the similarity had ended. Nevertheless, it had contained a number of basic nutrients, had not been entirely unpalatable and she had managed to dispose of at least two-thirds of it. Now she would get down to the letter to her editor that she had been putting off for some days.

This was the first time she had failed to meet the deadline she had previously arranged with him and she felt irritated with herself. Her manuscript being unfinished had little to do with her stay in hospital. She had anticipated this and made allowances. What had put her behind had been having her mother to stay, and now making the funeral arrangements would interfere with catching up. There was no help for it. She would have to make her excuses.

She rather despised herself for not using the telephone but, with a pen in her hand, she could apologize at one remove and thereby avoid hearing the reproach which would be betrayed in his tone even though it was unexpressed in words. After all, it wasn't her fault that her mother had been ill so she wasn't to blame for her manuscript being late.

She wondered whether she should write to Owen too, now that she'd had time to think their relationship through. It was a great relief to have made a decision. A clean break was the only way and she'd make it as soon as she got home. A letter wasn't fair, though. She felt justified in avoiding the wrath of her editor, but she had positively encouraged Owen at times. She owed it to him to see him and explain exactly why it all had to end. She'd be glad to get it all over.

She headed her letter merely 'Ward 9. Wednesday.' That way she would receive no reply until she was back at home and working again. 'Dear Ken, Thank you for the mass of lovely freesias and what an extravagance in March! Their perfume even triumphs over the aura of antiseptic . . .'

Myra appeared at the open door. 'Are you writing another book?' Pamela explained that she was writing an urgent letter and Myra hesitated, trying to work out whether she had been repulsed and whether to be offended. 'I'm on my way to the loo,' she confided, and disappeared.

Pamela went on writing, realizing how much, over the last few weeks, she'd missed arranging words, even feeling the pen in her hand. She had scarcely finished her first paragraph when Myra reappeared, looking disappointed. 'It was a waste of time going.' She waited for sympathy, obviously having given Pamela the benefit of the doubt and accepted that her letter was important.

Pamela grinned and, hoping to stave off the details of Myra's failure, wrote another sentence.

'I'm a right fresh-air fiend,' Myra offered, 'but there is a draught from that window.' She waited hopefully. When Pamela glanced at it but otherwise did not move, she transferred her attention to the freesias. 'These flowers do cheer a ward up, don't they? My mother used to like flowers.' Her tone suggested that this was a highly unusual preference. 'She was like me.'

Pamela did not trust herself to describe Myra in her presence. Instead, she wrote, 'There's a ward orderly here who might appear in a story soon. She has dyed white hair, straw-textured, high heels under fat calves that taper to non-existent ankles and a substantial bottom to bustle with. Her painted face smiles. I'm not sure about the one underneath.'

Myra had somehow moved to the subject of cats. 'I couldn't have animals in the house.' Since the implication was that those who did were feckless and unclean, Pamela was tempted to defend her own. She desisted, since she had learned to cope with Myra by volunteering nothing and shutting out most of the inconsequential chatter from her consciousness. 'They go out in the grass and come in covered in fleas.' Her expression lent the assertion several exclamation marks.

Pamela nodded and returned to her letter. 'We've all been similarly mutilated on this corridor and I'm constantly amused when a geriatric shuffle in the corridor precedes the appearance of quite a young-looking female.' She wrote another paragraph before surfacing to find that Myra had changed her subject again.

'She grows all her own stuff. She loves gardening. She uses it to make all her own stuff. She makes her own soup, her own wine, her own dresses . . .' Pamela hastily repressed the image that arose and kept her lips straight. 'I think I'll lie down for a bit. I think I had too much dinner. I keep thinking I'm back to normal but my tummy can't cope properly yet.'

This time Pamela answered. She must accept the reprieve before it was withdrawn. 'Good idea, and I must do some work. Close the door as you go, would you? Then the nurses will know I'm busy.' She brought her letter quickly to a close, explaining that she must ring the undertaker and see a policeman because her mother's death had been so sudden.

It occurred to her that Ken might think it odd that she'd written a four-page letter to explain why she hadn't had time to finish her book. He'd think it strange too that she had written so cheerfully, referring to her mother's death only in the last couple of lines. She leaned back against the pillows. She'd enjoyed writing the letter and was surprised to find herself exhausted. Ken would have to think whatever he liked. It had finally got itself written and she would send it. It wasn't full of grief and regrets because she didn't feel any, just a profound relief that she could now get on with her own life, without the frightful shadow over it of the possibility, no, probability, of her mother's moving in with her permanently. It would not have been a matter of doing 'anything' for Mother, but of doing everything. Of course, she had been ill when she had last visited but a pattern had been established, taking her tea, filling the house with a stifling heat before helping her out of bed and fastening her buttons as though she were a small child.

Pamela had found the withered flesh revolting, the pathetic dependence abhorrent and the future frightening. It was not the puckering of the skin itself that repelled her, or the slowness of her mother's movements that made her impatient. She had never shrunk from Greg's mother who was older, whose disabilities were more severe but whose spirit was unbroken. Her mother's helplessness caused impotent rage because it was unnecessary, self-induced, until it had become genuine and her abilities, physical and mental, had atrophied.

She had made the possibility of having to take in her mother the excuse, both to herself and her daughter, for not offering a home to Sonia and Thomas. She wasn't sure, even now, whether she was relieved or annoyed that Sonia seemed to have settled so well into the flat Mrs Quentin had offered her and to be coping so efficiently with no help from her mother. She supposed it was best for them to have their own place and a child, even more than an old woman, would have made writing impossible. Pamela sighed. She, her mother and her daughter had had each their different set of values and priorities and the only sort of co-operation they had managed was to humour one another from time to time. Suddenly, her repulsion and contempt frightened her, causing physical tremor and nausea. Why now? The woman was dead.

Pamela had confided in her fellow patients neither the fact

nor the circumstances of her mother's death. Even if she had felt the unqualified sorrow that Myra would have expected, Pamela would have shrunk from the hectoring commiserations she would have been offered. The mixture of pity, guilt and relief she was actually experiencing could be borne only as long as it was concealed.

Myra's snores, dulled by a hardboard partition and a closed door, were now providing comforting reassurance of an hour or so free from her commentary on the world as she saw it. Unable to sleep herself, Pamela reached for her headset and fiddled with the radio controls until she found some therapeutic music. She was struggling to assign it to a composer when a tap at the door heralded the arrival of a man and a woman, shepherded by Sister.

If they constituted the scheduled invasion of police, they didn't look like it. The man, extremely tall and spare, introduced himself and his companion and brought a plastic-moulded chair from the corner of the room for her before wandering over to the window. He was neatly and conventionally dressed in sports jacket and flannels with a haircut that the uniformed branch would have approved of and yet there was something arty about him. If Myra woke in time to ask inquisitive questions, she would pass him off as a fellow writer. Not that Myra was the sort who read character in faces.

Returning her scrutiny, Hunter saw a woman in her early fifties who showed no embarrassment at being clad in only a brief but unrevealing cotton nightdress. The thick fair hair was uncompromisingly short and straight and the fair skin was rather blotched, due, possibly, to her present state of health. Her mouth was mobile and, somehow vulnerable, whilst the light blue eyes, short-lashed, alert and watchful, indicated that she intended to learn as much from him as he did from her.

Whilst DC Jennie Smith made friendly overtures and enquiries about her recovery, Hunter considered what he was hoping to learn from Mrs Hill. Having been incarcerated in the hospital on Monday, she was not, officially, a suspect, though she would not necessarily answer his questions truthfully on that account. Nor was she in a position to know the details of her mother's last day. What he was hoping for was some information about family relationships.

As Jennie paused and turned to him, Hunter, planning an oblique approach, drew a newspaper clipping from his pocket. He came forward and handed it over. '*The Times* reviewed you this morning. Very complimentary.'

Pamela read it and smiled at him. 'It was kind of you to bring it.'

'Is it exciting to get a good review in a reputable national paper?'

She smiled again. 'Initially it pleases me – and it helps to confirm my own judgement. I live in dread, not of running out of ideas but of becoming a bad judge of what I've written.' She frowned as she groped for the words to pin down and analyse her reaction. 'A critical faculty is the most important of a writer's gifts so it's good to be reassured by someone you respect that you haven't presented the public with something contemptible.'

Hunter took another chair and came to sit beside Jennie. 'I suppose this stay in hospital is holding up the next book.'

She nodded. 'It's holding up the current one, yes, but the preliminary stages of the one after are coming along well.' Hunter looked puzzled till she went on, 'I have to have one book going that I'm actually writing, with all the raw material ready collected. I can work to a deadline with that. At the same time I have to be collecting ideas and information for a future story for which there is as yet no deadline. Once I'm given one, the ideas dry up.'

Hunter noticed that her complexion was improving as she became animated. 'Dreaming up ideas is easy. Under no pressure they pour out sometimes more quickly than my pen can keep up. Arranging them into a narrative is easy too. What's difficult is trying to produce a chapter in a hurry, finding the ideas as I go. It demands that your brain should produce them in a logical sequence and usually it won't.'

Jennie was interested. 'Is that why children hate writing essays?'

Pamela nodded, sharing Jennie's unhappy memories. 'Could

86

be. I hated English at school. I did sciences in the sixth form and read for a biology degree.'

A junior nurse came in with a tea tray and went back to report to Sister that her patient looked bright-eyed and relaxed. Pamela watched Jennie wield the teapot and accepted her cup before asking Hunter. 'You didn't come here because you're a fan of mine, did you?'

Jennie took out her notebook, then, seeing that Hunter seemed rather at a loss as to how to open the interview proper, helped him out. 'You must have been wondering about the cause of your mother's death, maybe blaming yourself because she had to be moved before she was fully recovered.'

Pamela did not consider it expedient to announce that she had been harbouring none of these altruistic thoughts, that she had, on the contrary, been justifying her inability to feel much sorrow in connection with her mother's death. She did feel, though, an almost unbearable grief for the sterility of her mother's life. She said nothing, waiting for the interview to continue.

'Dr Pedlar tells us that she expected your mother to live for another ten years or so, in reasonably good health. Naturally, she is unwilling to sign the death certificate until the pathologist has discovered what she has missed.'

Still Pamela asked no questions, made no comment.

Hunter continued, desperately, 'That process will delay the funeral, of course.' He caught Jennie's eye and again appealed to her.

She responded by closing her notebook. 'There was a mark on your mother's body, Mrs Hill, that we can't explain. It looks as though she had been given an injection and neither Doctor Pedlar nor Mrs Cunningham knows anything about it. Can you offer any explanation?'

Pamela's lips formed a mirthless smile. 'You want to know which of the family had most reason to administer a fatal dose of something?' When Hunter failed to reply, she sat up suddenly, wincing as her healing muscles protested. 'My God, you really do!'

Chapter Eight

Fate in the shape of a careless driver prevented a meeting between Mitchell and Dean in Anthony Fenton's shop. Dean was irritated by the carelessness of the driving public, horrified by the dent in his passenger door and incensed at the tardy appearance and lengthy procedures of the Traffic Division. When he eventually arrived to make his inquiries, Fenton had consumed the dried-up remains of his lunch and was unlocking the door for his afternoon's business.

Dean, who created and therefore could tolerate a certain amount of untidiness around him, was less put out by Fenton's arrangements than Mitchell had been. 'Open as usual, in spite of your bereavement?' he enquired brusquely as Fenton replaced his stool on the step and turned the card on his door from closed to open.

Fenton shrugged. 'I suppose she was a great one for marks of respect but she wouldn't know about it now and I need the custom. Are you . . . were you a friend of my mother-in-law's?'

Dean was already several hours behind schedule and wasted no time on polite preliminaries. He described the precise nature of his inquiry and shot his questions.

Fenton blinked but then answered the first one crisply. 'Evelyn didn't have a solicitor and never made an official will – at least as far as I know. She didn't have much to leave. She lived on her state pension, a pittance from her late husband's firm and whatever Pamela and Stella could spare her. She was comfortable but she had no capital. The house was rented and the landlord was panting to get her out so that he could refurbish and sell.'

88

'We've heard there was an extremely valuable book to dispose of. What can you tell me about it?'

Fenton smiled tightly and settled himself behind his desk, waving Dean to the flimsy stool that Mitchell had occupied. Though considerably lighter than his colleague, Dean was equally unwilling to trust it and sat gingerly, resting his notebook awkwardly on his knees as Fenton gave authoritative details.

'A set of three books, actually, published in 1851 and entitled *The Whale*. Unfortunately for its backers, the circulating libraries refused to take it in that form and it was a flop. A few years later it was reissued with the title page cancelled, in just the one volume and with a new date. Examples of that edition are worth having but would only fetch two or three thousand.'

'So it isn't one of those?'

Fenton shook his head. 'Exactly a month later an American edition was produced, again as a single volume and with a new title which you'll have heard of.' Dean raised his eyebrows. '*Moby Dick*. The American edition's not really valuable at all, but an original three-volume set like Evelyn's, rubbed and stained, not in such good condition as hers, fetched twenty-two thousand pounds in 1989.' He extracted a dusty reference book from a shelf behind him. 'Here we are. "Sotheby's, February 7th '89, lot 841".'

Dean was impressed. 'What does it look like, this expensive version?'

'About so big.' Fenton measured with his fingers. 'Blue cloth boards, cream cloth on the spine and corners and gold lettering. Evelyn's is still bright and clean.'

Dean fidgeted, uncomfortable on his stool, whilst Fenton, at home behind his desk and expounding his own specialist knowledge, seemed to grow in stature. 'I suppose you expect to inherit it.'

Fenton was not at all put out. 'No, but I expect to be given the task of disposing of it.'

'So you have it on your premises?'

'No, it's in Evelyn's house.'

'Aren't you concerned for its safety?'

He smiled. 'Yes, but not enough to risk a tongue-lashing from Sonia for interfering. I just warned Evelyn but she took no notice of me. She was used to having it around. Her husband's father had a huge collection of books that came to Stella's father when the old man died. Evelyn nagged him into getting rid of them. She didn't think much of them as furnishings and it wouldn't occur to her that they had any other purpose. He wasn't the strongest-minded person I've ever met and he wasn't a great reader either, but he did insist on hanging on to his favourites, the ones he'd looked at as a child. The rest went in job lots to charity sales. God knows what priceless things were amongst them. I wish they'd hung on till I'd met Stella.'

Dean saw frustration in his face. 'Where exactly is it now?'

Fenton grinned. 'I explained to her that if the cover was exposed to sunlight it would fade and the value would decrease. Her reaction was to wrap it in tissue paper, then put it in a plastic bag, in a suitcase in the wardrobe of the spare bedroom. It's been there since she showed it to me about ten years ago. I think she thought it would fade visibly if she so much as opened the wardrobe door.'

Dean shook his head. 'According to my CI's message, it isn't.'

There was a silence as Fenton worked out some of the implications of this news. Before he had time to reach any conclusions, Dean changed tack. 'I gather you don't get on with your niece.'

He grinned, cheerfully. 'I often squabble with her if that's what you mean, but I don't really dislike her. She's a talented girl who's had a pretty rough deal. Her father spoilt her dreadfully and then died suddenly. She couldn't cope and must have fallen for this chap. The only thing we know about him is that he shirked his responsibilities. At just short of seventeen she was saddled with Thomas. He's a bright child and we're all fond of him, but he has prevented Sonia from having the same chance to exploit her artistic gifts as Alistair had.'

'Alistair's your son, the one who designs the jewellery?'

He nodded. 'Yes, it came as a bit of a surprise to us that

someone on our side of the family was creative too. It didn't show much when he was younger – I mean, he didn't show much interest in art at school. I suppose it's easy to teach it rigidly and frustrate the children who want to do their own thing. I must confess he always made a mess of setting up a bookstall display but I expect he didn't want me to find him too useful.'

Seeing that Fenton was prepared to extol his son's talent at length, Dean brought him back to the inquiry. 'Where were you last Monday?'

For a few seconds, Fenton looked indignant. Dean could not decide whether he was offended by the interruption or by the nature of the question. Then he answered quietly. 'Stella and I visited St Helen's in the morning. Stella was going shopping and I waited whilst she asked Evelyn if she needed anything. Whilst she did her rounds of the market and super-market I checked the junk shops and Oxfam for books. We were going to call back and take Evelyn out to lunch but when we stopped off at Sonia's flat to drop off a book she wanted, Mrs Quentin said there had been a call from the hospital and Pamela was allowed to come home.'

'Get on with it,' Dean interrupted, less than politely. 'It's the afternoon we want to hear about.'

'Sonia wasn't due back from work till later so I volunteered to fetch her.' Fenton kept to his own chronology, undeterred. 'We rang to let her know and to offer to have her to stay for a day or two until she was fit to manage on her own.' He stopped as he noticed Dean's hard stare.

'Are you telling me that Mrs Hill was out of hospital the day Mrs Norman was killed?'

'I'm trying to. Pamela came to the phone herself. She had to have a final check with the consultant and she wouldn't be ready to leave until after lunch. She refused our offer to stay with us and told us she'd turned down a similar one from Sonia. She was annoyed with herself because she was behind schedule with her book and she said she'd recover more quickly if she could catch up and not have to worry about it. She was sure she could look after herself.'

Dean interrupted this account with a wave of his hand.

'Right. We'll check with her about that. Go on about your own movements.' He hoped his acerbic tone would shake the calm assurance of his witness, but Fenton showed neither dismay nor indignation at Dean's implied suspicion. He answered levelly: 'Pam had said she'd be ready by two o'clock. Mrs Quentin kindly offered us lunch so we ate with her and then Stella took Thomas to nursery school whilst Mrs Quentin and Sonia washed up and I went to the hospital.'

'Times?' demanded Dean, rudely.

Still Fenton displayed no resentment. 'The only one I'm sure about is that I left at one forty.'

'It was a twenty-minute drive?'

Fenton shrugged and grinned. 'It should only have been about ten but I passed a car boot sale on the edge of the town moor. I can never resist them. This was a good one. I got several children's books and a nice volume with illustrations by Tunnicliffe and several interesting old maps and . . .'

Again Dean interrupted. 'So you eventually arrived at . . . ?'

Fenton bit his lip. 'About two thirty. Pamela wasn't put out or even surprised. She knows me.'

'You said your niece helped with the washing up.'

'That's right. Sonia came in just as lunch was ready, about one o'clock. When I left she was about to go over to Pamela's house to put some heating on and to be there to meet her.'

'And was she?'

Fenton tilted his chair backwards and eyed Dean with amusement. 'Actually, no. She went into town to get Pamela some flowers, which meant she had to come through that complicated junction at Royds Cross. The lights had packed up and there were queues in all directions. We'd made our own tea by the time she staggered in with her daffs and irises.'

As he recorded Fenton's reply in his rapid, neat shorthand Dean could hear sounds on the staircase above. Fenton's wife had better not be going out. He noted quickly her son-in-law's impression that Pamela Hill was anxious to be left alone and that he had departed to pick up his wife, leaving Sonia pouring tea.

'I need to speak to Mrs Fenton. Is she upstairs?' Dean got

up thankfully from the rickety stool and Fenton, too, got to his feet, looking disconcerted for the first time.

'Please treat my wife gently. She's still very upset at the news of her mother's death without these distressing circumstances.'

Dean put his notebook in his pocket. 'They were very close, were they?' He smiled to himself at Fenton's rueful expression.

'Well, no, not exactly, but she's rather a nervous woman – easily frightened.'

'We all find murder a bit frightening, sir.' Dean made for the stairs. 'I dare say you do yourself. Two floors up, did you say?'

Fenton nodded and let him reach the bend before asking, 'Constable, do you have a colleague, shorter than you and heavily built? Thick, brown hair, cut short, army fashion.'

Dean turned. 'Sounds like DC Mitchell. Why?'

Fenton was grinning widely. 'I think I met him once. And, just one more question? Did you know the title of Evelyn's book before you came to ask me about it?'

'She'd apparently mentioned a book about whales to someone at St Helen's.' Dean's manner was stiff. He wasn't here to answer questions.

As he disappeared round the bend of the stairs, Fenton smiled more widely. He moved back to his desk, lifted the front cover of a venerable-looking volume, crossed out a pencilled figure and wrote in another one.

Stella Fenton was sitting on a kitchen chair, regarding her left leg anxiously. Walking about hadn't caused the tingling in her thigh to subside. It was a year now since that benign cyst had been removed. Could there, after all that time, be a clot in a main artery? She was sure the rest of her leg felt a bit numb. She touched it with her finger and relief rushed over her as she felt the contact. But was it a leg or a finger sensation that had registered in her brain?

She wouldn't be happy until she'd seen the doctor – though she knew he wouldn't even listen to her. He'd decided she had a nervous temperament and put all her complaints down to that. It was sheer neglect really. She knew that she did tend to worry about things that turned out to be not too serious but she was really concerned this time.

She drained her cup and reached again for the jar of instant coffee. She supposed, at the time, she'd been just as worried about the lump that had turned out to be an infected spot, but that reflection didn't calm her now. What if the clot moved during the day whilst she was telling herself to forget it and caused a heart attack?

She made her usual pact with herself. She'd make a note in her diary to check the leg out in seven days' time and then try to forget it. If she was making too much of her symptoms, they'd be gone by then, but, if the situation was as she feared, a week was not so long to wait. And the fact that she'd waited should impress Dr Clarke. Knowing that she'd have the hot tap on again next time she had the kitchen to herself, she reached into her handbag for her diary.

When DC Dean rapped on the door, she had opened it before realizing that she had reached it with no difficulty and with no untoward sensations in her lower limbs. She disliked the young constable on sight. She supposed he was not to blame for the dreadful news he brought but at least he could have broken it gently!

Dean settled himself in the chair she had cleared for him and considered her. Probably, a few years ago, she had been a very alluring lady. Not that her blonde good looks had faded to any important degree, he decided. It was just that she spoiled the effect by refusing to accept maturity. The tight leggings revealed very shapely legs but the amusingly printed sweatshirt was a few years too young for her and she had got past the age when the thick blonde hair could be left to hang free round her shoulders without drawing attention to the encroaching lines on her pretty face.

She began a lengthy apology for the state of the flat, though Dean found it a considerable improvement on the arrangements downstairs. 'It's the best I can do when, sometimes twice a day, he arrives with yet more cartons of dusty books and maps.'

Dean told her her domestic arrangements were not his affair and asked about her relationship with her mother. After a pause to show she was offended by his brusque manner, she became garrulous again. 'A sweet old lady, getting a bit frail recently, of course. I always felt guilty at not spending as much time with her as Pam did but I could only do my best. Tony's business has never flourished. I helped with that on top of my teaching. I've done all kinds of teaching, different age groups and types of school. I'm working part time now with nine-year-olds.' She smiled deprecatingly. 'I thought, considering all my other commitments, that I'd find them easier but it proved not to be so . . .'

Dean asked for her version of the events of the previous Monday.

She sighed, gustily. 'Well, it wasn't one of my school days. I should have spent it catching up with the housework. I'd had to help Tony at a book fair in York at the weekend, and we thought that, as Mother was in a strange place and hadn't had a visit from Pam for a while, she might be feeling miserable. I had to fit the shopping in, of course. Tony was too busy prowling round grubby second-hand shops to have time for the supermarket. We called to see if Mother needed any shopping and promised to call back and take her out for lunch. We had to ring and cancel that, though, because Pam was discharged from hospital.'

Dean wondered why his witness continually rubbed her left leg.

'We had lunch with Mrs Quentin and Thomas, then Tony went to fetch Pam and Sonia went to Pam's house to make sure that everything was ready for her. I was going to help, but, by the time I'd got back from taking Thomas to school, I had such a dreadful headache that I could only spend the afternoon lying down. Mrs Quentin must have thought I looked ill because she apologized for having to go out and leave me.'

'When did she go?'

Stella pondered. 'About a quarter of an hour after Sonia left. She still hadn't got back when Tony came to fetch me just after three.'

Dean moved on to the subject of her son.

'The school never understood Alistair – treated him very unsympathetically. In fact, he was so unhappy we took him away at sixteen although he would have done well at A-level. Not that his teachers agreed. They thought he had no particular talent, though they had to admit that he was quite intelligent. They just failed to channel it. It was their failure not the child's because they never bothered to know him well enough. I always knew, though. I wish they could see him now with his flourishing business and his lovely house.'

'Yes, I've heard he's doing well.'

Dean's prompt was unnecessary.

'All he needed was a lucky break, and, thank goodness, he got it. He was offered this chance by a former school friend who saw his potential. Now they're partners. Alistair supplies the talent and his friend a bit of capital that he was lucky enough to inherit.'

As soon as Dean managed to stem the flow, he rose to leave. Reaching the door, he stopped and asked her abruptly, 'Where would we look for the valuable books your mother is supposed to have owned?'

Stella's peevish expression intensified. 'Why ask me? Tony said that, considering what they were worth, the less people who knew where they were the better. I'm only his wife, of course. I'm going to gossip all over town if he tells me, I suppose. Or, perhaps, he thinks I'll steal them.'

Dean negotiated a way downstairs between the stacks and boxes. Her voice floated after him down the stairs. 'If she'd only made a will we'd know what to do with the blessed thing . . .' Stella filled the kettle for more coffee, feeling angry all over again at Tony's refusal to disclose the whereabouts of her mother's rare first edition. And what an insolent young constable had been sent to interview her. She should have answered him in a curt, off-hand manner like his own.

She sighed as she realized that wasn't in her nature. She only knew how to be ingratiating. She needed people to like her and approve of her, even her pupils. She hardly ever punished them, even when they behaved atrociously. She would feel an impotent fury against the ringleaders. She wanted them to be punished by somebody but, when she opened her mouth, it was only to placate them. She couldn't believe they would obey her so she tried to persuade them, rather than issuing commands.

Tomorrow morning, Mark, from his desk at the back, would be watching her, picking his moment to attack, overstepping the bounds of good manners, but always staying just on the right side of the written rules, leading even the more timid of his classmates into noisy and disrespectful behaviour. He looked at her with just such an expression as that unpleasant young Constable Dean had worn.

Stella sighed. She'd been ingratiating to her mother too. That's why she'd hated visiting her. Tony could refuse the less reasonable of her demands, giving no reason, but Stella had felt she always had to explain why she couldn't oblige, offering excuses that her mother had no problem in demolishing. Well, that was all over now, thank goodness. As she poured boiling water on instant coffee, the malevolent cat, left behind for her to look after when Alistair left home, leapt on to the worktop where Tony did not allow him to sit. He watched the dark liquid rise in her cup, then settled down on the cream Formica and began to wash himself, a symbol of her inability to assert her will.

Chapter Nine

Bellamy decided that he would interview Sonia Hill before he looked up Alistair Fenton and, by half-past nine, he was driving along Hepple Lane.

It was not his idea of a lane, with its wide pavements edged with strips of grass. The grass was left uncut so as not to interfere with the growth of the crocuses, now a riot of purple, gold and white to which his eyes kept returning. The colour scheme was spoilt by the red wooden panels of the bus shelter at the end, the choice of a crass council. The residents' paint rarely varied from white, and then only to tactful green. Even the parked cars toned with their surroundings.

The people in this area had culture and money. Their winter gardens had a subdued cheerfulness from foliage in interesting colours, beech hedges, glossy holly and speckled laurels. Some contained trees, tall and massy, that did not allow street lamps or telegraph poles to rival them.

Bellamy rang the brass bell on the white door of number twelve and it was promptly opened by just the sort of resident he had imagined, elderly, small and slight but brisk, with faded tweed skirt and clipped version of the local accent. Sonia, she informed him, was out at her work in the office of the local school, where she did mornings. After his identification had been carefully examined, she agreed to answer a few questions and offered him coffee.

She showed him into a warm and comfortable sitting-room where a dark-haired, round-faced youngster sat on a stool, his bare feet extended towards the fire. 'This is Thomas, Sonia's son. Tom, this gentleman is Mr Bellamy. He's trying to find out what made Granny Evelyn die so suddenly.' She departed to the kitchen, leaving them to get acquainted.

Bellamy approved of treating children as intelligent beings and telling them the truth. Nevertheless, he thought it safer to distract the child rather than have to parry awkward questions. 'I work for someone called Thomas.'

Enormous eyes were raised to Bellamy's face. 'He can't be. Thomas is a little boy's name.'

Bellamy thought quickly. 'Yes, you're right. He was a little boy when his name was chosen. Now he's a man, he's just called Tom. When you're grown up, that's what people will call you.'

'Mum calls me Tom sometimes.'

'That's because you're starting to grow up already. She's practising for when she has to call you Tom all the time.'

The boy was silent, examining this novel and attractive idea as Mrs Quentin returned with a tray. She placed it on a low table by Bellamy's chair and glared at Thomas, who seemed now to be absorbed in contemplation of his feet, his brow puckered and his breathing laboured. 'I told you to put your shoes on. Why is it taking you so long?'

The huge eyes were raised again. 'I can't decide which one to put on first.' He made an extremely hasty selection as she took a step towards him but Bellamy could see that there was no fear in his attitude, just a healthy respect for her authority. It occurred to him that she probably filled the role of mother to the child more adequately than Sonia.

'I can tie them now, Aunt Barbara, and I used to couldn't,' he told her, proudly and proceeded to demonstrate. 'Which shoe do you put on first?' he enquired of the visitor, politely drawing him into the conversation.

Bellamy had to give the matter some thought and only realized as he saw Mrs Quentin bite back an amused smile that he had gone through a pantomime before being able to answer Thomas, solemnly, 'Always the left.'

Bellamy dispatched three cups of excellent filtered coffee whilst Mrs Quentin explained her household arrangements. 'I like children and enjoy Tom's company, so I'm pleased to

99

mind him and give Sonia a chance to establish some sort of career and meet a few people. I also love living here and there's no way I could maintain this place without the extra money that her rent brings me. Besides, it's something I can do for Pam.'

Bellamy enquired, as tactfully as possible, about her movements on the previous Monday.

'That was the day Pam was sent home – too soon, in my opinion, and now she's back in hospital with an infection. Anyway, Sonia was still at work when the call came from the hospital so Tony organized things, bless him. His useless wife spent the afternoon in my bed. Migraine my foot! She was jealous of all the fuss that was being made over Pam. Tony went to fetch her and Sonia went to switch the heating on at Pam's place, check the bed was made up and make a pot of tea. Stella did at least take Thomas to school. I went to meet him later on.'

'What time would that have been?'

Bellamy watched her trying to decide whether she was a suspect or whether her evidence was merely required to check the family's statements.

'School ends at three fifteen. I left at about a quarter to and brought Thomas home by bus. He was quite excited. He doesn't go on public transport very often.'

The child looked up from a final adjustment to his shoelace. 'We went past where Granny Evelyn was staying, didn't we?' He reached into a box behind him and extracted a red model bus which he steered with realistic engine noises across the room and under the table. Safely out of sight, he sat quietly, running the rubber wheels up and down his thighs. When he sat here and listened to Mum and Aunt Barbara talking they sometimes forgot he was there and he heard things he wasn't supposed to know, but Aunt Barbara was only telling the man about Granny Evelyn and he wasn't interested.

He thought instead about his bus journey. Aunt Barbara had said they could go up to the top deck but when they got there people were sitting in both front seats. He had put his special power over one of them and made him get off the bus and they'd moved to the front to take his place. From there the bus always looked as though it was taking up the whole width of the street, so that all the cars coming up on the other side were being mowed down. Then, just on All Saints' Avenue, the branches of the trees bashed against the window with a really loud noise. It was exciting but he hoped the birds weren't being knocked out of their nests and their eggs broken.

Granny Evelyn's place was round the corner. From the top deck, he could see over the wall into the car park. 'I can see a special yellow car,' he'd told Aunt Barbara.

'Whose is it?'

'You've got to guess.'

She usually played games with him but, on Monday, she was too busy thinking about Granny Pam and had only said, 'Don't tell me, then, if you don't want to, and don't poke your finger into that hole. You'll have all the stuffing out.' He listened to her telling the man all about it and debated with himself whether he dared make his red bus crash into the man's shoe. Before he'd decided, the man got up to go.

Mrs Quentin had scribbled Alistair Fenton's address on a scrap of paper and given Bellamy detailed instructions that led him with no problems to the substantial and prosperous-looking house overlooking the town moor. A couple of rose bushes grew by its front door but there had been no real attempt to make a garden. Instead there was an asphalted area that would take a dozen or so cars. The house front featured an abundance of white paint and an imposing plank door with great iron hinges, black-enamelled.

Mrs Quentin had told him that Fenton Junior and his partner worked from home, so he supposed a place this size was necessary. There were two brass bells, labelled Fenton and Sykes. When two pressings of the upper one had failed to summon his quarry, Bellamy rang for Sykes, who appeared promptly. He was tall and thin, red haired and scowling, though, after a few seconds, Bellamy decided that the scowl was the result of the way his features were arranged rather than an indication of his mood.

Energetic, jazzy music could be heard somewhere in the

background. Bellamy displayed his credentials and raised his eyebrows. ' "The Red Flag"?'

Sykes grinned and shook his head. ' "Maryland", interpreted by the great Kid Ory.'

Bellamy blinked, no wiser. 'Do I gather Mr Fenton is out?' Sykes nodded. 'Perhaps you could spare me a few minutes yourself.'

He nodded again, gestured to Bellamy to follow him upstairs and ascended further into the noise. Half-way up and shouting above the music, he explained, 'There are only the offices and workrooms down here. Our flats are on the first floor. Sonia! Take the CD off, will you?'

He led Bellamy into a large room, elegantly proportioned and sparsely furnished, and the constable watched Sonia, slim and graceful, lifting the disc from the machine in the corner and stowing it away in a rack on the wall. Her behaviour seemed to him deliberately proprietorial as she moved about the room, adjusting the position of various objects as though she were responsible for the impression they gave.

Bellamy wanted to know why she was here when she was supposed to be at work and how exactly she fitted into this ménage. He realized that, the less he asked, the more he was likely to learn about both questions. Instead, he professed a raging thirst, shuddering at the idea of adding to his consumption of the three coffees from Mrs Quentin, but reflecting that if his stomach could cope with four pints of beer, it could presumably manage the same volume of any other liquid.

Sykes's offering was strong tea, served, even to Sonia, in pint mugs. She made no offer of help but her eyes followed him to the kitchen door. She sat, after he had disappeared, in rapt contemplation of a collage picture propped up on a table, whilst Sykes pottered.

Passing Bellamy his mug, Sykes promised that Alistair Fenton would return within the half hour, then the two of them returned to the conversation that Bellamy's arrival had interrupted. The discussion was chiefly about a woodland scene in water colours that had been acquired, or at least hung, since Sonia's last visit. Bellamy understood few of the points that either of them made, but thought Sonia's contributions gave the impression of a prize pupil, showing off her cleverness when prompted to do so. He was surprised to hear Sykes speaking about a painting with such feeling. Sonia was disagreeing with him whilst obviously respecting his authority. Bellamy had understood from the case notes that Alistair's partner was merely a rich Philistine who had recognized good commercial potential and profited from exploiting someone else's talent.

As the discussion became increasingly technical he lost the thread of the argument but it was clear from Sonia's expression that Sykes was her hero and mentor. He decided there was much to be gained from his own point of view by throwing a spanner in the works. 'I can't see a lot of point, these days,' he volunteered, 'in painting bluebell woods. In another month you'll be able to go out and take a photo that's much more realistic than that picture you're arguing about.' He buried his nose deep in his mug and waited.

Sonia smiled at him and called his bluff by refusing to be drawn. Sykes, however, took the picture from its hook and brought it across to him. 'But absolute realism isn't a good feature of a painting. You're right that that can be achieved more accurately, and more easily, with a camera, but a painting is a subjective treatment. It contains something of the object, of course, but something of the artist too. It's not worth his trouble otherwise.'

He gestured to Sonia, inviting her to back him up and she did so, eagerly. 'It's an artist's vision that makes him special, not his technique. Most people would agree with that. Otherwise, why do we consider someone who can do a convincing fake as a bit of a charlatan at best, and a criminal at worst?'

Bellamy was pleased with himself and continued his needling. Draining his mug he sat back complacently. 'Vision and technique are all Greek to me. I'd rather be out and about seeing things for myself than looking at pictures of them.'

Sonia grinned at him amiably. Sykes, although aware by now that he was being deliberately provoked, took a step backwards, pulling the picture away from his visitor as though

103

he suspected him of intended vandalism. His voice became hoarse. 'But outside there's so much to see that you're confused. A picture of something confines your experience of it to something you can cope with, hope to comprehend, something that makes the object itself less threatening.'

Sonia shook her head. 'The only important thing about a picture is whether it provides a place for the imagination to inhabit. It should help you to slide into another world. One moment you're just looking and the next you're transported into it.'

'What about abstracts?'

Sonia, deadly serious, admitted, 'Getting into them takes more practice.'

'That's right!' She basked in his approval as Sykes laid the water-colour on the table and picked up the collage. 'This is Sonia's work. What can you see?'

Bellamy peered. 'Two women in a street.'

'Go on!'

Bellamy looked again. 'They're talking to one another.'

'Yes.'

He thrust the collage closer and Bellamy became interested in spite of himself. 'One figure's made up of scraps of rich fabrics, silk and velvet and such. It looks as if she's rich. The other's made of bits of thin cotton and stuff, in the same sort of colours though. That makes the thin material look cheap and tattier, because the contrast is only in the quality.'

'What do you think they are talking about?'

Sykes's grip on Bellamy's shoulder was painful. He wriggled free but continued to look at the collage. 'I don't know but they're standing close and seem very intimate. Whatever it is, it's made them forget their social differences.' He shook himself and turned from the picture to Sykes. 'But, what if she didn't intend it to mean that, what if I've imagined something totally different, on my own?'

Sonia beamed at him. 'That would be all the better.'

Bellamy whirled round on her. 'What are you doing here when Mrs Quentin thinks you're at work?'

She was surprised into honesty. 'You don't throw away a free morning to do what you like with. I've been given it in exchange for an afternoon I did last week. The head had to teach in the place of a colleague who was absent so she asked me to stay on to listen for the phone and to hold the fort if any visitors arrived. I'm doing it again tomorrow. Tom's in school in the afternoons so it's no extra work for Barbara.' She stared harder. 'You must have been to my place.'

He nodded. 'If you'd answer a few questions here, it would save me having to go again.' She grimaced, then settled into an armchair resignedly. Sykes tactfully gathered cups and disappeared with them to the kitchen.

Sonia's answers were methodical and succinct. She rented the first floor of Mrs Quentin's house which had been turned into a self-contained flat for her and Thomas. From nine to twelve thirty on weekdays she did office work at St Mary's, a fairly local Church primary school. She got on well with the headmistress, with whom she chiefly worked, and the hours were sometimes adjusted to their mutual advantage.

There was a nursery playgroup run by local parents in St Mary's church hall. She had only been able to enrol Thomas for the afternoon sessions so Mrs Quentin minded him during the mornings and took him to the church hall by bus on the few occasions when she wasn't home in time to take him herself. She made no payment for this service, except in kind. Mrs Quentin wasn't strong and had some eye trouble. Sonia did most of her shopping and some of the heavier housework.

Bellamy looked at her well-kept hands. They were not work-roughened but they did look capable, the nails short and unlacquered. 'Mrs Quentin takes Thomas about by bus? I take it she doesn't drive.'

Sonia shook her immaculate dark head. 'No, that's something else I can do for her, provide a lift if she needs to go out, especially at night, not that she does very often.'

At Bellamy's request she described her movements on the day of her grandmother's death. 'Barbara rang to say Mum was being discharged so I left school promptly at twelve thirty. Tony had already volunteered to fetch her, so after lunch I went to check her place was ready for her. It's a good job it was because I didn't get there till after Tony.'

'Why not?'

'I stopped off to buy flowers. Town was unusually crowded for a Monday and then the lights at Royds Cross were off again. Queues often build up there even when the lights are working. You could get through much quicker before they were put there and there was just that big roundabout to negotiate. You knew who to give way to and it worked quite well. On Monday with everything kaput and nothing to indicate who had right of way, everybody was trying to edge in. There was the inevitable bump and the long delays that always follow the slightest accident.'

'You didn't visit your grandmother on Monday?'

She shook her head vigorously again. Bellamy noticed that the hair was so well cut that it flew in all directions, then settled exactly as it had been before. 'I was going to. I'd promised Barbara but Mum's being sent home let me off the hook.'

'You weren't fond of her?'

She shrugged slim shoulders. 'She wasn't fond of me. I'd wasted my talent, disgraced the family and let her down.'

'Did you resent her criticism and disapproval?'

She sniffed. 'Of course I did, but not enough to kill her because of it. I didn't see enough of her to be very irritated because she avoided me.'

'Can you think of anyone who might have found her intolerable?'

She got up and began to pace the room. 'You don't want a flippant answer, do you? She was pretty harmless but she wanted somebody to look after her all the time and no one wanted to do it. Mum wanted to get her book finished, Tony had his business to run . . .'

'And Stella?'

She stood still to consider. 'Stella's the same sort of person as Gran was. She's always denigrating Tony's work and ambitions – or lack of them. She doesn't think of him as a person, just as an extension of herself.'

'The provider of the comforts she deserves?'

'No, it's more than that. Tony has to be a success because that justifies Stella in a supporting role and frees her from having to make anything of her own life.'

106

'And she didn't want to be responsible for Mrs Norman?'

Sonia laughed. 'No fear! But I shouldn't think Stella dispatched her to be rid of the responsibility. Tony always jollied Gran along so she called him insensitive and unfeeling. Stella always stressed that they didn't get on, said no house was big enough for the two of them.' She sat down again in her armchair.

'What do you know about the book on whales that belonged to your grandmother?'

She frowned. 'Not a lot. You'd do better to ask Tony. She boasted about it from time to time but I shouldn't think it has anything like the value she imagined.'

Sykes reappeared, hesitating in the doorway. 'Is it all right to come back?'

Bellamy nodded as Sonia demanded, 'It's your flat, isn't it? Anyway, I'll have to go. Barbara likes lunch dead on time and Tom's school begins at one thirty. If you've anything else to ask me you'll have to come back later.'

She rose to leave and Sykes helped her into her coat, addressing Bellamy over his shoulder. 'I'm sorry Alistair's still missing. He should have been back ages ago. He must have been held up.'

Bellamy, anxious to stay his rumbling, liquid-filled stomach with something solid, prepared to depart himself, but Sykes held him back with a gesture. 'Just let me see Sonia out.' He returned and took the place she'd vacated opposite the DC. He looked, Bellamy thought, like a third former about to explain how the cigarettes got into his pocket. 'It's just that our business set-up isn't quite as people think. Oh, nothing illegal and nothing that's anyone's affair but mine and Alistair's, but, when the police find they haven't been given the right tale, they might suspect more than there is to find out. You're on a murder inquiry but this is nothing to do with that.'

Bellamy was intrigued. 'Let's hear it then.'

Now he'd begun, Sykes looked more relaxed. 'Look, I'm starving and your stomach's rumbling fit to drown all my revelations. Come into the kitchen and I'll do us some cheese on toast.' Bellamy hesitated only seconds before following

107

him with enthusiasm and being put to slicing cheese. 'Alistair's family thinks that he designs jewellery and I put up the money. Actually, it's the other way round.'

Bellamy had realized more than an hour ago that Sykes was more artist than businessman. 'So, why the deception?'

Sykes grinned ruefully. 'Alistair and I were thrown together in the first place because we took it in turns to get the bottom marks in the bottom maths set. We both left school at sixteen. Alistair was on the dole, though he helped his father from time to time. I worked for a scrap-metal dealer and hated the actual paid work. At school I'd not been any good at anything except art and in my spare time I began to mess about with small bits of various metals, making trinkets and ornaments and using some of the firm's equipment.'

The toaster on the spotless worktop shot four nicely done slices into the air and Sykes, evidently used to its ways, caught them deftly. 'I spent all my spare money on semi-precious stones and, after a while, I took some of my things to a jeweller in Leeds who sold some of them for a percentage.

'Alistair and I used to have a drink together quite often. One week, over two years ago now, he came into the pub and said he'd had this big pools win. He didn't tell any of his family about it because they disapprove of gambling. I'm surprised he cared that much because he didn't mind upsetting them in other ways. I think he didn't want the hassle of being badgered to invest it in his father's business. Anyway, possibly because we both celebrated with a few too many jars, we decided that he'd invest in me, but explain things the way we have done to his family.'

Having spread the toast liberally with butter, he piled it with Bellamy's cheese slices and popped it under the grill. 'I didn't mind using his name so long as he kept me constantly supplied with the raw materials I wanted. After all, "Alistair Fenton" sounds more in keeping with filigree metal and semi-precious stones than Stanley Sykes.

'We got a good accountant and he introduced us to some other useful people and we really took off. We're making enough to think about moving over to gold and diamonds now in a small way, but I love lapis and amethyst and silver and I'm getting known for it. Maybe later I'll give the expensive stuff a try. Anyway, now I've set the record straight – and I know that the police usually keep confidences that aren't directly related to their particular inquiries.'

Bellamy, forbearing to comment on this last observation, accepted his toasted sandwich and asked, instead, 'What if you and Alistair decide to part?'

Sykes shrugged. 'Well, he won't be able to produce the goods, will he? If I did want to alter our arrangements, people who would be useful contacts know who I really am and that I use Alistair's name because it has more commercial potential than mine.'

'How does Sonia come into all this?'

He laughed. 'Ah, now you're asking. She and Alistair are in league to persuade me to take her in and diversify, but I won't. I think Alistair would like us to become producers of the sort of high-class, up-market tat that people buy as presents for other people who've already got two of everything. I think he has visions of a string of "tasteful Gyfte Shoppes" in all the touristy places in Yorkshire. I only want to work with jewels and fine metals.'

The food disposed of, the two men began to wash up companionably. 'So, Sonia's annoyed with you,' Bellamy observed.

Sykes wrinkled his nose. 'She's still hoping I'll have her. It hasn't come to a confrontation yet but she shouldn't be annoyed. She's also too good for the tat trade. If it weren't for the child, she'd have enough work completed already to exhibit and then she'd be offered commissions for original work of any kind she wanted. She still might make it. He'll be at school next year.'

The telephone rang. As Bellamy dried the last clean knife, Sykes called him from the hall, 'It's Alistair. Do you want to speak to him?' Bellamy arranged to meet the younger Fenton at the station late that afternoon and departed, well pleased with his morning's work.

Chapter Ten

At six thirty that evening, Browne collected a weary team for coffee in his office. 'Not pints at the pub?' Hunter had enquired, hopefully, but Browne had refused.

'That's for when we've found out all that unrelenting routine can tell us and we're searching for inspiration, following up mad ideas because the sensible theories have been disproved. Coffee is what's needed to get the routine finished.'

His men had little in common but their glum expressions and he tried to rally them. 'Look, without minimizing the tragedy of the deaths of three young girls, you all found the last murder hunt on this patch exciting in a sordid sort of way. This one won't be. Someone got rid of an old woman who was becoming a bit too much hassle. She can't give us her version and she possibly bears some responsibility for what happened to her.

'Someone clever did this murder – clever enough to keep it simple. The forensic evidence isn't conclusive enough for Ledgard to commit himself to much in writing and the means were to hand for the x per cent of the population who're diabetic, all the people who have access to their belongings and all medics and chemists. It's more of a challenge, not less, and there's plenty more humdrum footwork to be done when you've compared notes on today's exploits.'

'You'd better make that coffee black,' Carson remarked, dolefully.

Browne handed it round and gave Bellamy first turn to report. Bellamy described his meeting with Sonia and Sykes and the team listened dutifully, showing a glimmer of genuine

110

interest at Sykes's disclosures concerning his business.

'What did you make of them as people?'

Bellamy considered. 'The chap seemed a decent sort, sir. The girl was a bit waspish. She seems to have the family all sussed out. Very forthright.'

'I take it young Fenton showed up.'

Bellamy nodded. 'He was none too pleased that Sykes had spilt the beans. Tried to tell me at first that he'd spent all day Monday in the library studying medieval ornaments, but, when I said I was sure Sykes did all his own research, and he realized what we knew, he admitted to spending the afternoon at Ladbroke's, placing bets and watching the races on the big screen in the back room. Says he allows himself one afternoon a month and a limit of a ten-pound loss before jacking it in for the day. "I'm fond of a flutter but certainly not a compulsive gambler, Constable." '

Bellamy gave place to Dean, who reported efficiently his morning with the Fentons. Browne's eyes travelled round. 'You next, Jerry. What progress with the great writer?'

Hunter's expression was the bleakest in the room. 'Absolutely none. We didn't realize that she'd left hospital on Monday, so we only asked general questions about family relationships. She was as discreet and noncommittal as possible without actually refusing to answer us.'

'I don't think,' Jennie added, 'that she intended to conceal the fact that she'd been at home. We just didn't ask about the details of the day because we didn't realize that she could tell us anything useful about it.'

'Do you fancy going back, or do you think she'd respond more to a new approach?'

'I'll go.' Hunter's face now wore an enigmatic smile.

'Any joy at St Helen's, Jennie?'

She grimaced. 'I'm not sure, sir. Several of the old ladies had plenty to say but I'm not sure how much we can rely on any of it. One of them said Evelyn had at least two visitors that afternoon. She explained, quite sensibly, that she can't bear the constant, moronic television in the lounge, and that she passes the time chatting to and watching the temporary residents who bring a breath of the outside world in with them.'

Jennie smiled at her memory of Sadie with her thick-set waistless body, caved-in chest and rounded back. Parts of her face had deep furrows, like an old-fashioned ruched swimsuit, but there were smooth, shiny patches over her cheekbones that were not wrinkled at all. She'd had hardly any eyelashes and filmed eyes, surrounded by a prominent tracery of veins and her breathing was a high whine as she sought the words to finish her sentences.

Jennie looked back at Browne. 'I'd just written down her rather vague description of these extra visitors, when she asked me to tell her mother that she'd call round in the morning as usual and clean through the house for her. Kay Cunningham said she was sometimes quite lucid, but you could never tell whether she was describing something that happened yesterday or fifty years ago.'

Browne nodded his understanding. 'Anything else from anybody?'

Carson raised a hand. 'Dr Pedlar was quite adamant that the dementia patient was constantly and closely supervised and that all medication at St Helen's is under lock and key. The key is always in Mrs Cunningham's possession except when she's off duty. Then the girl, Kerry, has it.'

'So.' Browne refilled everyone's cup. 'What do we make of all that?'

Jennie was the first to break the silence. 'I think we were right to discount Mrs Hill, even if she was sent home. She'd very recently had a fairly serious op and, as it turned out, wasn't fit to be out of hospital anyway.'

Dean disagreed. 'The hospital wouldn't risk its reputation by sending her home before she was ready. Anthony Fenton said he didn't stay very long at her house because she seemed anxious to be alone – and there'd be nothing like dashing across town to give your mother a fatal jab for causing a spectacular relapse.'

Hunter was indignant as several of them nodded in agreement. 'What's her motive?' he demanded. 'Her mother was no more of a trouble to her last Monday than she'd been for the years since Mr Norman died.'

112

'The longer a frustration continues,' Carson announced, pompously, 'the higher its demands become.' Hunter favoured him with the glare he usually reserved for Mitchell. Carson continued unabashed. 'Most old people are a burden to someone . . .'

'No, they aren't!' Browne got on very well with his own fiercely independent parents and found the lifestyle of Hannah's mother exhausted him.

'This one was apparently more of a burden than most,' Carson ploughed on relentlessly, 'and only one suspect was carrying it.'

'How astute was she?' Bellamy wondered aloud. 'Alistair talked as if she was feeble-minded and thought she'd probably sent the famous book to a jumble sale in a fit of absentmindedness. But, then, Mrs Hill and Fenton senior thought she was quite wick enough to manipulate the family easily to get what she wanted.'

They looked at each other uncertainly till Browne gathered their attention again. 'Let's sum up. There's a lost book, three volumes of it, in fact, worth approximately twenty-five thousand pounds. Stella and Anthony Fenton admit to visiting St Helen's on Monday but in the morning. In the afternoon, a good many interested people could have been there. Mrs Hill could have gone after Fenton and Sonia had left her to her writing. Fenton himself could have called on the way to pick up his wife or before going to the hospital. We'd better check on that car boot sale. Stella Fenton was alone after Mrs Quentin had gone to collect the little boy and Mrs Quentin herself could have called in on her way to the school. Sonia took a very long time to make a very short journey – we'd better check out her tale with Traffic Division – and no one was keeping an eye on Alistair Fenton between horse races. Go on, Jerry.'

Hunter looked startled, then he slid into gear and took over. 'The Fentons' business badly needs a cash transfusion. Mrs Hill is a writer who needs to be alone to work and was having trouble keeping her mother out. Sonia Hill, formerly a favourite with her grandmother, was now considered a disgrace . . .'

113

'It didn't seem to be getting to her much,' Bellamy put in.

'And the grandson, who'd been disapproved of, was becoming the blue-eyed boy . . .'

'By false pretences!' Bellamy interrupted again, but Hunter seemed to have finished his summary.

Browne invited comments but none followed and he went on, 'Robin's established that no will's been left with any Cloughton solicitor. We've got to go on looking for one, of course, but I think it's going to be a vain search. Meanwhile, where's the book? If someone in the family is hanging on to it he won't be able to sell it – or, at least, he can't be seen spending the proceeds. Could Mrs Norman have disposed of it herself?'

Jennie shook her head. 'I think not. Everybody keeps stressing how irresolute she was. Besides, it was her hold over at least some of the family.'

'When does someone last admit to seeing it?'

'Fenton has handled it but he didn't say when.' Dean chuckled. 'Stella Fenton's long list of complaints included his refusal to tell her where it was kept. I'll check the actual time. Was anyone else in financial difficulties?'

'Not exactly, but . . .' They turned to Bellamy. 'Sonia Hill is doing part-time secretarial work in a school when she really wants to be free to do her art work.'

Browne nodded. 'Any other ideas?'

'Could we,' Jennie asked, 'persuade Doctors Pedlar and Ledgard to give us more exact times for the death and the administration of the injection? Then there'd be more point in pushing these people for more precise accounts with times of their movements on Monday.'

'I'll try, Jennie.'

'And, sir!'

'Yes, Robin?'

'Didn't Debbie Jardine say that while Mrs Norman was shouting she mentioned someone called Alice? What if she was saying Alistair?'

'Good point, but it wouldn't necessarily mean that he'd been there. Perhaps she was angry with him because he hadn't.'

Carson accepted this, adding, more hesitantly, 'Sir . . . I've been reading a book about ways of thinking.'

'Oh, God,' breathed Dean, 'not another one!'

'This writer says that in his kind of thinking, high intelligence is a disadvantage.'

'You should be brilliant at it.'

Browne quelled Dean but looked puzzled himself. Carson hastened to explain. 'It says that all people have preconceived ideas, but that very clever people, who are good at justifying theirs and answering the people who challenge them, tend to have closed minds. Those who are less good at arguing have more open minds, can see more options, even though they might not be able to decide between them.'

'I gather you're going to apply this idea to our case in some way.'

Carson nodded. 'What if Mrs Norman never possessed the book?'

'Fenton says he's seen it. He described it in great detail,' Dean objected.

'All right, what if she'd given it to someone outside the family?'

'Or hidden it somewhere else because she'd stopped trusting Fenton,' suggested Jennie, catching the mood, 'or that this killing has nothing whatever to do with the book.'

'Or someone has it hidden away to sell later, when it's safe.'

'Or,' finished Carson, triumphantly, 'what if it was stolen and sold ages ago and Mrs Norman killed now because she was going to give it to Fenton and would discover it was missing.'

Browne was watching his team, pleased that Carson's idea had restored some of their usual animation. 'If that's right, Robin, we'd have to believe that she'd never opened the suitcase to look at the book, check on it or gloat over it or show it to anyone.'

'Sounds totally in character, though it doesn't let Fenton off the hook. If he'd embezzled the proceeds from it already, he wouldn't be able to produce the cash it would fetch now.'

Dean was leafing through his notebook. 'Fenton says he

bought his shop about eighteen months ago. Before that he kept all his stock in the bedrooms of his council house and just traded by post and at book fairs.' He closed the notebook and laughed. 'His premises look as though they cost something less than thirty thousand!'

Browne made a note to provide himself with the authorization necessary for investigating Fenton's bank account, then dismissed his team to their long-anticipated beer.

Having slept for an hour after she arrived home in a taxi, Pamela Hill was running out of excuses for not beginning a solid evening's work on her current book. There were no urgent odd jobs to do and she'd already made and drunk a pot of tea. It was not laziness that deterred her but a dread that it wouldn't come right, that what she wrote would be pedestrian, that the spark would be missing. She couldn't control it and, therefore, she didn't trust it. She was afraid, not of wrestling with her medium, but of losing sight of what she was trying to do with it. Afraid, most of all, of the possibility that she wouldn't realize when she'd failed.

After a few minutes, she capitulated and switched the radio on, hoping the music would not be anything she particularly liked. She used most music as food for her imagination when her hands were busy, but her favourite composers claimed her full attention and seduced her from her work. The radio emitted a repetitive pattern of semiquavers, satisfactory for her purpose because, to her at least, it was unsatisfying.

She was musical, but not a musician. She reacted to music by opening up her repressed feelings. She got drunk on it, could marvel at the imagination that could pluck a melody out of silence or out of chaotic noise, but she never wanted to make music, accept the discipline of learning an instrument, have the worry of singing something and getting it right. She had little interest in the laws by which it worked.

She was beginning to experience the hoped-for calming effect when the doorbell rang. She heard a key being inserted in the door and knowing that her visitor was her daughter she remained in her chair till Sonia entered the sitting-room. 'I'm glad you've come. I've been trying to ring you.'

116

The girl refused a seat and glared down at her mother. 'You've rung me! The hospital beat you to it, asked if I knew you'd discharged yourself. Sister says they aren't responsible for you any more and letting me know what you'd done was over and above what was due. They can't understand why you've done it. I told them I couldn't either.'

Pamela began to feel like an irresponsible schoolgirl who'd come home too late. 'I've done nothing foolhardy. They said all I need now is rest. I've brought the antibiotics home with me and I can rest better here.'

'You aren't usually so unreasonable.'

The silence between them was filled by the radio announcer. What they had not been listening to was a Bach arrangement of music originally by Vivaldi. Pamela waved her daughter into the chair opposite, remarking conversationally, 'That sort of legal plagiarism has never extended to the other arts. How would it work out, I wonder, if Pope or Dryden had expressed the sentiments of Donne's Holy sonnets in rhyming couplets? Or what about the story of Emma Woodhouse and Mr Knightley told in the style of Lawrence – or, to move into your field, if Rembrandt had painted that peculiar light he loved reflecting from figures he'd borrowed from a busy Breughel canvas?'

Sonia's face was deadpan. 'You're not going to distract me from what I came to find out.'

Pamela ignored her. 'Crossing media is quite different, of course. You know, setting poems to music, making films from novels and so on.'

Sonia decided to let her mother have her head. She'd have to run down some time. She sat back in her chair and surveyed the room. The coffee-table held the file of the current manuscript and notes on scraps of paper, a copy of *Castles of Europe*, two theatre programmes, a biography of Peter Pears and a three-week-old copy of the *Independent* with the crossword half done. The telephone table held a pile of books and papers in which you would find the directories if you looked hard. A carrier bag leaned against its legs. Sonia knew it contained wool and pieces of a knitted jacket that Thomas just might receive before he'd grown out of it.

The wooden box by the hearth contained the correspondence, bills, building society and bank books that Gran had dumped, expecting Mum to deal with them. An antique clock shared a shelf with an unopened tin of biscuits and below it was the box of toys that Thomas played with on his visits. They were stowed tidily inside. She never allowed Tom to add to her mother's chaos.

She couldn't bear to turn and survey the bookcase and music centre behind her but her fingers itched to straighten the leaning books and collapsed piles of tapes and discs that she knew would be there. The cat, deprived of an empty chair, sprawled in the window box to the great detriment of whatever was trying to grow there. She realized that her mother had fallen silent.

'Have you finished pronouncing on the state of the arts?' She sighed and shook her head. 'I don't understand how you can create whole imaginary worlds where everything is beautifully organized, but you can't sort your possessions into order and keep them tidy.'

Pamela got on well with her daughter, enjoying her company and her acerbic tongue. She explained, without offence, 'Every time I begin to straighten the place up I'm overcome by a strange panic. It's partly the fear of what I'm missing whilst I'm occupied with such unimportant matters, and partly a fear of being told I'm not capable of doing even the simplest thing properly – and it's so boring!'

'That's all down to Gran.'

Pamela shrugged. 'Maybe, though the criticism was more often in my mind than on her lips.'

'She put it there.'

'She couldn't help it. She was afraid of life, of other people, but she was organized within her own home. She had to feel that that was all-important. She criticized out of weakness.'

Sonia snorted. 'It's the weak that inherit the earth. More damage is done by their fumbling inadequacy than can be assessed and people like you go on making excuses for them and easing their path.' Pamela was staring ahead, unseeing. 'What are you thinking?'

'I'm thinking that you're only twenty and that you'll grow more tolerant.'

Sonia was shocked. 'You've never talked down to me before.'

Pamela smiled. 'I'm not doing it now. You're going through a black and white, critical, uncharitable stage. I'm going through some other kind that comes later in life, and that I can't see so sharply because I'm still in the middle of it.'

'You mean, no one ever reaches a static state of maturity?'

'Not unless they're brain-dead.'

They seemed to have got back to their usual condition of uneasy intimacy and Sonia wondered if this would be a good time to speak to her mother about her relationship with Tish and her plans for their future together. Somehow, though, the atmosphere was not quite right. She returned instead to her original enquiry. 'So why have you come home this afternoon?'

Pamela shrugged. 'To organize a bit of family solidarity. I realized when the police came to see me this afternoon, that they're making a serious inquiry into all our affairs.'

Half an hour exhausted what they could find to say about their experiences with the police and, at half-past seven, Sonia rose to go. 'It's Tom's bedtime. Barbara thinks I should always be there to settle him down but . . . before I go, there's something I want to ask you.'

'You don't usually hesitate.'

Sonia fiddled with her handbag, then raised her eyes to her mother's face. 'All right, then. When I got back from here last Monday I hadn't got my gloves. They were the leather ones that Barbara helped Thomas choose for my Christmas present so I rang to check that they were safe with you and that I hadn't dropped them in the street.'

Pamela looked startled. 'I don't remember.'

'No, you didn't answer.'

Pamela bent to adjust the gas fire so that her face was hidden. 'I'd probably fallen asleep. The antiobiotics made me feel so tired that I was willing both you and Tony to go, I'm afraid.'

'But you don't sleep heavily.'

The uneasy silence between them was broken by the

particularly loud and strident peal of Pamela's telephone bouncing off the walls.

Before retiring to bed, Mitchell walked through the six small rooms of his flat, checking that they were in immaculate order and reviewing his day.

His wallet was considerably lighter than it had been that morning. Massey, without a dust jacket, had been solemnly presented to him when he called back at Fenton's shop. 'The crossed-out price is what I was going to charge a hard-up student,' Fenton had explained, 'but a detective constable can well afford to pay the going rate. In fact, in the circumstances, he can hardly afford not to.' The accompanying smile had been sardonic and Mitchell had paid up thankfully, sure that Fenton would make no further reference to his unauthorized visit.

He had collected Virginia more than an hour before their meal was booked, intending to relax with her over a couple of drinks. Finding that she had given up alcohol for the duration of her pregnancy, he had suggested a walk in the park instead. They had wandered along straight paths under sodium lights that turned the close-cut turf to a murky brown and scorned the designer of the uncompromisingly square flower beds, each with its two regimented rows of well-pruned, well-mulched rose bushes.

In the more flattering light from the candles on their table and the shaded wall lamps, Mitchell had noticed that three months of pregnancy had added to the lustre of Virginia's dark curly hair and healthy complexion whilst not detracting from the taut lines of the figure hugged by the silk dress. Perhaps the rather grand and formal attire was meant as a compliment, but Mitchell had felt that it was a message to him to keep his distance.

Whatever her clothes had meant, she had made short work of three generous courses. During the first one they had made general conversation but, well before the meal was over, she had tired of this. 'We've never play-acted before, Benny. Let's say what we're thinking and quit the party games.'

Before the liberally sauced duckling was disposed of, they had come dangerously close to quarrelling. 'I'm sure there'll be no shortage of crèches in Oxford, and having to stay in in the evenings will mean time for extra study.'

'I thought,' he'd replied, through gritted teeth, 'we'd agreed to do what was best for the child.'

Virginia had chewed thoughtfully for a moment. 'Fulfilling our long-term ambitions will be best for him. He'll suffer badly if he has resentful, frustrated parents. I'm not just being selfish. I really believe that.'

He'd laid down his fork and reached for her hand. 'If we were married . . .'

She'd withdrawn it, quickly. 'I'm not getting married till after he's born at the earliest – and you can stop looking like a striker who's had his goal disallowed. I'll get married after I've proved that I could cope if we didn't. That way, neither of us will ever wonder if we were pressured into it.'

'Will you have proved enough by the time he goes to school?'

Mitchell's angry tones had attracted the attention of several other diners. Virginia had smiled at them, serenely, before remarking, casually, 'I'm going to get fat anyway so I might as well have sticky toffee pudding.'

Mitchell had sighed and ordered it. Ginny was living in Cloud-cuckoo-land if she thought the infant would fit nicely into a student ménage. She didn't seem to be seeing him beyond the carrycot stage. The abundance of children in his own Irish Catholic background had taught him that Junior would be at the tearing-up, muddling-up, scribbling-on stage, just when Ginny needed peace and quiet and all her notes conveniently to hand to revise for finals.

He wasn't sure how attached she was to her particular Oxford course and her friends there, but the solution to their problems seemed to him to be, whether or not they married, for Ginny to transfer to whichever of the universities near by, Bradford, Manchester, Leeds or Huddersfield, that supplied the best continuation of the work she had already begun. Then they could both live here in his flat and would only need to abandon Junior to a child minder when Ginny's lectures clashed with his own shifts. Even then, Browne and Hannah and the hordes of his own family would be queuing up to help. When she decided to lift her ban on all discussions about her future, at least his arguments would be ready marshalled. He wondered how long his patience was going to last out.

He had thought about little else in his free time for more than a week, and now he felt profoundly thankful for his ability to divide his life into compartments and to concentrate wholly on the currently relevant one. He had been glad to be free today to sort out some of his ideas and to spend the evening with Virginia, but he was sorry that a murder case had been blowing up in his absence and he looked forward keenly to making his contribution next day.

Chapter Eleven

Browne's heart sank as he stopped in the station foyer on Thursday morning to read the new additions to the car key board. Hook twelve was adorned with a cardboard replica of the registration plate of the car Paul Taylor had driven on his notorious journey to Netherholme zoo. Round it was twined a plastic snake in garish black and yellow with a venomous-looking red tongue.

The accompanying white ticket read: *There be three things which are too wonderful for me, yea, four, which I know not: The way of an eagle in the air; the way of a serpent upon a rock; the way of a ship in the midst of the sea; and the way of a man with a maid.* How was he going to convince Mitchell that this was not a carping allusion to his predicament? And anyway, who was to say it wasn't? Someone in the station might have found out, and Mitchell, although acknowledged as a good copper, rubbed many of his colleagues up the wrong way. Mitchell might even think Browne had put the card there himself!

His carelessly light manner as he approached Bennett at the desk cost him considerable effort. 'Snakes don't have red tongues, do they?' Bennett communicated his ignorance with a shrug. 'You haven't tracked down the joker yet?'

Bennett seemed amused. 'I took over the desk at seven o'clock, sir. You're the only one who's been near the board whilst I've been sitting here.'

Browne nodded and ran upstairs to his office where he opened windows and turned off his radiator as he waited for his team to arrive for their briefing. He was relieved, though

123

not surprised, when Mitchell turned up first. After his day off, he could seldom wait to get started on the job again. Browne was thankful to see his lips were twitching.

'I suppose that ticket downstairs is another coincidence? It's all right, I believe you. Bennett's been telling me all about it.'

Browne waved him to a chair. 'Never mind the man and the maid. Let's concentrate on the way our serpent managed his trickery.'

'Quite an appropriate name for him, considering the method he used.' Mitchell lowered his substantial frame into Browne's chair and wondered how much inane conversation about the wretched text was necessary to convince his CI that he was not offended by it. The arrival of the rest of the team in quick succession rescued them both.

Browne's remarks to them were brief. 'Hunter's gone straight to reinterview Mrs Hill. We said all that was necessary last night. The action sheets are ready.' He began to distribute them. 'Most of you are on house to house in the neighbourhoods of all the family. Back here at one thirty.' They trooped out, thankful for the mild weather.

Thomas Hill heard Mrs Quentin go into the kitchen to begin preparing lunch. He listened for the bustling sounds that meant she was well started before creeping to the living-room and shutting the door quietly. Mrs Quentin waited to hear the living-room door shut quietly before concentrating on her cooking.

Thomas carefully lifted the telephone from its table to the padded chair arm, climbed into the comfortable chair and picked up the receiver, trying to decide who to ring today. Making his choice, he carefully punched out the numbers, wriggling with pleasure as the satisfying burr-burr was succeeded by a voice. He began the game. 'You've got to guess who it is.'

There was a pause for consideration before the reply. 'Father Christmas?'

Thomas gave the crow of laughter that was expected of him. 'No, have another guess.'

'I haven't time today, Tom. I'm going out.'

'You went out on Monday, didn't you? You went to that morbid place to see Granny Evelyn.'

'That what?'

'Where she was staying. I wanted to go but Aunt Barbara said she wouldn't take me to that morbid place. I was on the bus and I could see you over the wall, getting into the special yellow car. I told Aunt Barbara I'd had a ride in it.' He paused, suggestively.

The tone had become long-suffering. 'Would you like a ride in it, Tom?'

He agreed, with delight. As he replaced the receiver, he listened hard. Was Aunt Barbara still busy? With satisfaction, he heard the voice of Mrs Vickers from next door. He'd have time for more calls now. What about Mrs Shaw? His fingers punched again and he pictured her coming to answer him. She had a funny plastic thing behind her ear and a mole on her cheek. He was careful to listen out for Aunt Barbara as he talked and laughed. 'Not Prince William, no. I'm not Prince Harry either. It's Thomas. I've got a secret.' He was overcome by sudden panic. Would saying even so much cancel his ride? 'It's not really much of a secret. Anyway, I can't tell you.'

'Of course not. You must never tell secrets. Is your mummy there?'

Twice more Thomas dialled a number before he heard the kitchen door squeak and he replaced the receiver hastily. By the time Aunt Barbara appeared he was carefully parking a model car under the telephone table. They grinned at each other, neither of them deceived.

DS Hunter tried to analyse the mixed feelings with which he anticipated his second interview with Pamela Hill and had to admit to himself that he was very attracted to the woman. He was anxious to see her again but unwilling to enter into a policeman–witness relationship with her. It was not a physical attraction. Annette was totally satisfactory in that department. Even if she had not been, Hunter knew he was not a man who could be comfortable seeking the pleasures of the flesh outside his marriage.

He just liked Mrs Hill. She'd done no whingeing about her

operation. In middle age she made the best of her remaining attractions without giving her appearance too much attention – although, in different circumstances, he supposed she might. He felt, somehow, that she had a great deal to tell him but he wasn't sure whether it was about the current case, literature or life in general. If Browne had known he felt as he did, would he have encouraged him to visit the woman again? Hunter decided he probably would. He always encouraged a show of initiative and understood that other members of his team had a right to follow up their hunches – except when someone like Mitchell tried to run the show on his own, trampling all over the carefully laid ruses of the rest of them.

Hunter felt a little less kindly disposed to his witness when he discovered she was not at the hospital and he had to recross the town during the second half of the morning rush hour to reach her home. She led him into the untidy sitting-room where she had been sorting through a box of photographs. When he had settled himself in the cat's chair and the cat had retreated to the window box once more, to sulk, Pamela handed him the picture that lay on the table beside the box. It was of a diffident young girl, proudly escorted by her strong hero, everything said in their attitude and expression.

'My parents before they were married. I'm trying to sort a few things out, hoping that some of them can be disposed of, but I never throw old photographs away.'

The policeman in Hunter noted that a search of Mrs Hill's premises could perhaps be justified by the amount of her mother's possessions that it probably contained. 'I should think not. They're historical documents.' He looked again at Pamela's father, young, callow, short and awkward, but St George, defending his maiden from all the dragons she was afraid of.

'That one picture this morning has made me see my parents' whole relationship in a different light. It's silly, really. I've seen it dozens of times before but without looking properly. I've begun to see that my mother's insecurity and helplessness was what my father was attracted to. I'd always thought of him struggling under the double handicap of his disease and my mother's psychological difficulties. He never achieved

126

much in a wordly sense but in her eyes he was indispensable and that was his salvation. Maybe, even, his acceptance of it prevented her recovery or adjustment. I've been promising myself I'll never be judgemental any more.

'Never mind that, though. You want to know who killed her – though I still can't believe that anyone did.' Her mouth hardened. 'If you're right, it could only be someone close, couldn't it?'

There was no help for it. Hunter nodded and announced baldly, 'We've only just realized that you were out of hospital last Monday, Mrs Hill. Could you describe your movements from about one o'clock when your mother was leaving the St Helen's dining-room?' She did so readily, reeling off the list of people who could corroborate her account of the early afternoon, fellow patients, her brother-in-law and Sonia.

'And then?'

'After I'd dropped some rather unsubtle hints, they left me to myself and I fell asleep. Apparently, Sonia rang me when she got back to her flat, but I'm afraid I didn't wake. It was turned six when I roused myself and ate the meal that Sonia had left for me to heat up. After I'd eaten, I started watching a television programme and fell asleep again.'

The cat was glaring balefully at Hunter. He was not an animal lover and refused to meet its eyes, willing it not to approach him. 'Why were you taken back into hospital?'

'Apparently I was incubating a bug, which was why I couldn't stay awake. I woke about midnight, though, in a fair amount of pain and rang the number the hospital had given me. They made arrangements to have me readmitted. After a blast of antibiotics I soon got over it.'

She offered Hunter coffee and retreated to the kitchen. He followed as far as the door to continue the conversation. 'Could you make some comment on your mother's mental capacity? I mean,' he went on, hastily as she drew in an indignant breath, 'was there any confusion, forgetfulness, however temporary? Quite a few of the residents at St Helen's are not so clear minded as they used to be.'

Pamela watched coffee drip through the filter into a glass jug and answered without turning. 'There was nothing whatsoever wrong with Mother's mind. The sort of mentality she had is still around among much younger people, but these days their expectations are addressed not to the men in their lives but to "them". "They" should provide all requirements, meaning variously, the government, the local council, the social services or just their friends and neighbours.

'Stella's like that, a taker. I've been to her house dozens of times, and found someone baby sitting for her, or a friend, "who happened to be a professional decorator", plastering their bedroom wall – though not the walls of Tony's shop. He's fiercely independent. I've never found her out doing an equivalent service for any of them, though she's certainly not without talent.'

'You mean, she chooses useful friends, chums up when she wants something done?'

She shook her head. 'No, she's not so calculating as that. She's just the sort of person who expects other people to solve her problems and that other people seem to like waiting on. I expect I'm jealous.'

'Your sister talked to DC Dean yesterday. She was telling him about the trouble her son had at school.'

Pamela looked surprised that Stella had been forthcoming on such a topic. 'I shouldn't make too much of that. Alistair was never positively dishonest, he just panicked when he was in danger of a reprimand, took another child's dinner money because he was afraid to admit he'd lost his own – you know.' Hunter hadn't known but took careful note. 'I was astonished when he took to designing jewellery. Not only did he not seem interested in any form of art, but he wasn't interested either in what women dressed themselves up in. Still, I didn't like writing essays at school, so I don't suppose anyone expected me to earn a living writing full-length books.'

Hunter took the tray she held out to him and carried it back to the living-room. 'You studied biology, didn't you? How did you come to be a sci-fi writer?'

She drank half her cup of coffee as she considered the question. 'I found I was becoming more interested in how things might have been than how they actually are.' She laughed. 'I developed first a social conscience and then a super ego. I wanted to influence the way people thought and felt more than the way their bodies worked, though I was glad of the knowledge I'd collected along the way. And then I found that writing was an exorcism from all the horrors I'd ever suffered, from my parents, my school, my own personality.'

Hunter smiled, sharing her enthusiasm. 'I suppose a typewriter's like a mirror. What you see when you sit in front of it is yourself.'

'Exactly. I wasn't quite honest with you when you called at the hospital with your clipping from *The Times*. I'm very vulnerable to criticism of my books because more of my true self goes into them than into my relationships with my family and friends. They don't want to hear my pedantic views about big issues like over-population, but, in my novels, I can deal with whole new worlds, species, universes even. And yet, I'm commenting on the problems of life on earth that we touch on in ordinary conversation.'

Hunter had forgotten the case and the ostensible purpose of his visit, having achieved what he now realized was the real one. 'Detective fiction does the same thing in a different way. It deals with a few ordinary people in a circumscribed, earthbound situation, but, if we're thinking writers with bigger aims than large royalties, we're dealing with the same deep questions – about the right dealings of man with his fellows, his surroundings and his Maker, or whatever source of everything you believe in. In your writing you examine such things by making them bigger. I make it all smaller.'

She smiled at him. 'I was beginning to realize you're a writer.'

It was almost midday when Hunter managed to drag himself away from his fascinating literary discussion and back to work. He refused Pamela's invitation to lunch and collected a sandwich from the canteen which he ate at his desk as a penance. Its quality ensured that, as he rinsed away the taste with coffee from the machine in the corridor, he felt completely shriven but still hungry.

His stomach rumbled as he presented himself at the meeting

Browne had scheduled in the early afternoon, and, given first turn to report on his morning, he wondered how to explain his conviction that Pamela Hill was no longer one of their suspects. 'She couldn't have done it because of the way she talks about writing.' Hunter found this ludicrous-sounding argument totally convincing. He understood her new attitude to her mother, triggered off by the photograph and so clearly explained.

He could see, too, how her anger, rising now on her mother's behalf, had made her much more forthcoming about the rest of the family. How was he to explain it to Browne, never mind people like Dean and Mitchell? He mentioned his double trek across town, then summarized the details of Pamela's relapse on Monday and her comments on her family.

'She said Sonia is sharp and sarcastic because, in her circumstances, she can only do work that she doesn't find inspiring, that makes no use of her real talents. She hasn't a lot of time for her sister, though she seems to get on with Fenton quite well. Oh, and there appears to be a nasty little scandal in Alistair's past that I'd like to check out later.' He repeated Pamela's half-hearted defence of her nephew.

Browne made a quick note. 'Get on to his school for details. We'd better check our own records too. We'd have egg on our faces if a relevant criminal record was sitting unnoticed on a hard disc in the computer room. Flick them all through while you're about it. Anything else?'

Hunter hesitated, then took the plunge. 'I didn't get the impression that she wished her mother any harm. She admits to feeling guilty because she found her tiresome and irritating and she's honest enough to agree that she's looking on her mother's life with understanding now because it's completed. She can see the dependence as a tragedy for Mrs Norman instead of just an intrusion on her own life. She feels now that it was presumptuous to place the exploiting of her own talent above her mother's happiness. She feels guilty too for using what she learnt from the relationship in her writing, though I don't see why she should.'

'She's clever enough with words to be able to convince you

that her feelings are all they ought to be.' Hunter wondered whether Dean was right.

'She probably just feels guilty for killing her mother off.' Mitchell had remained silent for a longer time than was customary. 'I'll need more than a sergeant's cultural hunches to cross her off my list.'

'There's only one list,' Browne's tone was curt. 'And I'm in charge of it.'

With an apologetic glance at Hunter, Bellamy volunteered, 'Mrs Hill's next-door neighbour says a taxi picked her up on Monday afternoon.' They all turned to him. 'She was watching out for the family to leave, intending to go in later to see if there was anything she could do. She waited until Sonia drove away, and was just about to go round when this cab arrived and Mrs Hill came out and got into it.'

Hunter felt suddenly cold. He turned over the pages of his notebook and refused to look at Bellamy, but his gaze, like everyone else's was transferred to Browne when the CI made his next announcement. 'Fenton was quite right when he told us that the last time Sotheby's sold a copy of *The Whale* was 1989, but Stevensons dealt with one just short of two years ago, a "very fine" set of copies. That's only one class below mint, so their chap tells me. It was bought, according to their records, by a Michael J. Kelly and offered for sale by an A. E. Fenton.'

Mitchell was first to break the silence. 'Did you check his bank account, sir?'

'Give me time, laddie. I acquired an "authorization of disclosure" for the purpose but now we have this little gem I intend to swap it for a "warrant for seizure of information".' Browne was pleased to see both Mitchell and Carson noting the names of these weighty documents in their books. He turned to Bellamy. 'Somebody's session on the knocker came up with the goods this morning. Would any of you claim to have completed your house to house inquiries?'

Heads were shaken reluctantly before the members of the team trekked back to the various suburbs of Cloughton they had been allotted. The sergeant was let off this chore and sent

131

to set things humming in the incident room. After that he was to sit at Browne's desk and control things until his return. The CI had obviously got itchy feet again!

Hunter felt totally perplexed by Browne's uncharacteristic behaviour, the death of the old woman and the turmoil of his own plans and ideas. Rather hurt too. Why had Browne allotted Dean and not himself to find out where Pamela Hill's Monday taxi had taken her? It could only be because he felt his sergeant was becoming too involved with his witness.

Hunter drew from his capacious jacket pocket the copy of *Stars and Stripes* he had borrowed back from Annette's nephew. He had read it the previous evening – because it pertained to the case? – because Pamela Hill fascinated him? He wasn't sure. Reading the synopsis on the dust jacket, he had not expected to be convinced, but from the second page he had been immersed in the world she had created. He had never, in the past, had much truck with science fiction, had considered it childish or sensational, or, when it became philosophical, offering too sweeping and facile an answer to the world's ills.

This book had avoided the faults he had hitherto found and impressed him. Its criticism of the twentieth century was fierce, the writing simple and sensitive. He contemplated the author's face, gazing back at him from the dust jacket, the eyes clear, the skin lined, unflattered by soft focus. This morning, he had thought he was mentioning his own first novel, unpublished, unoffered to a publisher, in fact, on the spur of the moment, but, looking back now, he knew he had carefully led up to it.

The story had been fiendishly difficult and immensely satisfying to create, written at the end of the previous year whilst he was suffering from glandular fever and, therefore, excluded from the most interesting investigation of his career. Getting the story completed had proved ample compensation. One day, when it was revised and refined to his satisfaction, he would show it to Browne.

'Characters in science fiction,' he had told Pamela Hill, 'have no bounds, physical or mental, except those of their

132

creator's imagination. Police in detective stories have many conflicting requirements. They can't be like real officers because then readers wouldn't be able to identify with them. Men of action like most policemen are don't relax by reading. But they have to have enough in common with real detectives to be recognizable. Most crime writers produce policemen who work according to constabulary rules, but who, in their private lives, reveal themselves as the sort of people who wouldn't be likely to choose the police for a career. It's an uneasy compromise but acceptable as a convention for most readers.

'Having created these remarkable hybrids, the better detective novels then get down to addressing the questions that you struggle with yourself.'

'So you feel awkward,' she'd asked, 'manipulating these creatures you don't believe in?'

He'd shaken his head. 'Surprisingly, they take on a life of their own. They get on with their affairs, inside my head. Then, from time to time, one of them surprises me and I think, "Well, fancy someone like him doing that!" '

She had laughed heartily, clutching her healing stomach muscles and he had felt guilty but euphoric as she had assured him, 'I'm no judge, Sergeant, of whether you'll be published or not, but I can tell you now, you'll never be able to stop writing.' Had she lulled his suspicions by flattering him? He really didn't think so.

Before he had time to convince himself either way, Browne's telephone rang and Mitchell's head appeared round the door. He listened to both to begin with, then concentrated on the telephone voice as he realized the seriousness of the information it was giving him. 'Park yourself, Benny,' he invited briefly as he reached for a pen and scribbled in his notebook, 'and keep your coat on. You're going out again.'

Mitchell perched on a chair arm impatiently as Hunter demanded, 'What time?' and 'What school?' of his unseen caller. The impatience soon evaporated when Hunter gave terse instructions. 'Hepple Lane, Benny, and get things started, will you? Sonia Hill's child has gone missing.' He scribbled on a sheet of paper and handed it over. 'They haven't managed to contact the CI yet, but either he or I will join you pronto.'

By now he was speaking to Mitchell's rear view. The door slammed and he considered his next move. There wasn't much else he could do until Browne and Petty made a few decisions about this new development. As if in answer to his wishful thinking, the door opened and the two senior officers came in together.

'We've heard.' Browne reappropriated his chair as Hunter prepared to impart his news. 'I learnt sweet FA at the bank. No surprisingly large amounts paid into any of Fenton's accounts during the last five years. I didn't bother bringing the details away with me. Who did you send to Sonia Hill's place? Benny? Good. Put us in the picture, will you?'

Hunter swallowed his reprehensible jealousy. 'The girl, Sonia, was doing a full day's work today. There's flu at her school. Mrs Quentin took the boy to nursery school, that one opposite Heath Park. She left him at the door to the cloakroom and assumed that he'd take his things off and go into the playroom place. She went to fetch him at a quarter past three and only realized then that he hadn't been in school.'

'Where's his mother?'

Hunter stood awkwardly, reluctant to sit uninvited in Petty's presence. 'Mrs Quentin rang us immediately from the school. One of the nursery teachers was going to give her a lift then up to Sonia's school. I presume they'll have taken her home to talk to Mitchell.'

'It's a good job,' Petty remarked, complacently from the depths of Browne's better armchair, 'that we were on the ball and followed up Ledgard's suspicions about his grandmother so promptly. It didn't look much of a case but I never like to let a possible trail go cold.'

Browne's eyebrows shot up into his hair and, for the first time since the morning briefing, Hunter smiled.

Chapter Twelve

As they set off to join Mitchell, Browne rightly diagnosed the reason for Hunter's reserved expression. 'Sorry to hand Dean your witness, Jerry, but we've got to get her to admit to a lie and then tell the truth. There's more chance if she isn't embarrassed by having to face the person she lied to.'

'That sounds like Hendon psychology. I was trained in Wakefield.' But Hunter was looking communicative again. 'What do you think we're going to find at Hepple Lane, sir?'

Browne shook his head. 'I can't tell you, except a lot of worried people and a fairly bumptious Benny, sorting them all out with great aplomb.'

'I think,' Hunter remarked, thoughtfully, as they drew up outside the house, 'I'd like to feel Mitchell was in the hunt if it were Fliss who was missing. He's good with kids. One day, he'll probably rear you a rather splendid crop of grand-children.'

Browne smiled when he saw how Mitchell was fulfilling their expectations. A cordon had been drawn round the house to keep out inquisitive neighbours and a uniformed constable stood by the front door, which opened as Mitchell came out to speak to them. 'Superintendent Petty's sent in three uniformed assistants already, sir. I thought it would be all right if Constable Smedley knocked on a few doors in this street for the time being. You can easily get him back if you want him to do something else. WPC James is talking to the women inside. She asked the questions and I took notes.' He handed over his book.

'Which women?' After Hunter's last remark, Browne was

considering the wisdom of leaving his two most ill-assorted men to work here together.

'The boy's mother and the landlady, Mrs Quentin and Mrs Hill. They rang for her and she came in a taxi.'

Hunter made Browne's decision for him by asking, 'It's Nigel who's been talking to these people so far, isn't it? He'll probably have met the child already. Is he joining us? And, sir, Richard is probably wasting his time right now trying to enter Mrs Hill's empty house.'

Browne reviewed his resources. 'Did the neighbour notice which taxi firm supplied Mrs Hill's transport? Get at it from there, then. Let her think we don't know about her little trip for the moment.'

It had grown much colder with approaching dusk and Browne had to blow on his fingers before they would push the buttons of his radio to summon both Dean and Bellamy. 'I'll have a word with Sonia Hill and then leave you and Nigel here, Benny. Keep the WPC here and when Richard comes he can liaise with the PC on the knocker. You and I will go over to the school, Jerry.'

'Thomas's teacher's waiting there, sir. She thought you'd want to talk to her on the premises.'

More urgently, Browne wanted to organize a search of the area where the child was last seen before it got any darker or colder. He went into the house, leaving Hunter to radio for the men he would need and, following the voices he heard, found the living-room.

Two women sat on an old-fashioned button-backed settee, close but not touching each other. Both were immobile and both stared at a point on the opposite wall. The older one was fair and the younger dark but the cast of their features was sufficiently similar for him to identify mother and daughter. The WPC sat on a pouffe in front of them but she was talking to a frail-looking middle-aged woman, who was answering clearly and concisely although she was struggling with her tears.

'I was in the kitchen, getting lunch. We always have it at twelve thirty.'

'So that Thomas is at school in time?'

'Partly. Tom was amusing himself with his cars on the living-room floor but I knew that as soon as my back was turned he'd be at the telephone. He's fascinated by it and it keeps him safely amused. Sonia and I used it when we taught him to recognize numbers. He used to think it worked by magic. At first, when he was left alone with it, he dialled random numbers but that turned out a bit expensive, so we taught him the numbers of several people and how to punch them in. If he becomes a nuisance, people can always hang up.

'We thought of getting the phone wall-mounted when we knew he was playing with it, but I thought he might climb up to it and fall and hurt himself. The novelty wore off after a while and then he only did it occasionally and, anyway, they were all local calls.'

She swallowed, dried her eyes on a wet-looking handkerchief and asked, 'Is all this more important than going out and looking for him?'

Browne came forward. 'It could be. It depends on who he rang and what was said, and, I assure you, arrangements for a thorough search are going ahead right now.' He introduced himself and his rank seemed to reassure Mrs Quentin that the police did have the problem in hand. 'Who did he ring?'

She shook her head. 'I don't know. A neighbour came in to borrow last night's paper and stayed to have a cup of coffee. He might have made several calls whilst I was busy.'

'So, whose numbers did he know? He wasn't old enough to use the directory. He was only four, wasn't he?'

Sonia reeled off a list, tonelessly. 'My mother's, Mrs Shaw's next door, my school office but he was warned only to use that if Barbara had an accident or was taken ill, Alistair's and his friend, Shaun's. Shaun McElroy, that is. They play together at school.'

'I taught him Stella's only yesterday,' Mrs Quentin added. 'He might have tried that because it was a new one.'

A car door slammed outside and Browne caught sight of Bellamy through the window. He suddenly changed his mind about where the DC would be most useful and turned to Sonia. 'WPC James and DC Mitchell are obviously doing all that's

137

necessary here. I'm going to oversee the search round the school whilst there's still a bit of light. DC Bellamy has just arrived and I'm taking him with me because he knows Thomas and Thomas knows him. I won't say "Don't worry" but keep it within bounds. It may be just a fit of disobedience or a bit of an upset with his teacher.'

'He isn't disobedient,' Sonia said in the same expressionless voice.

'All the more reason for him to be afraid to face the music if he usually does as he's told. And he did play tricks with the telephone when he wasn't supposed to.'

He caught Mitchell's eye as he went out, and, leaving the competent Megan James to continue her questions, the DC followed him. 'Have you looked round the house?' Browne wanted to know.

'Not yet, sir. We only got here ten minutes before you.'

'See to it, then. And what about the sixty-four thousand dollar question?'

'The boy's father, you mean?' Browne nodded. 'I got as far as asking if they had any contact. The girl shook her head and the writer woman mouthed "Later". I hoped it was a promise to reveal all if I bided my time. After all, if his father wants him, and has got him, he isn't likely to harm him.'

Browne was confident. 'I'll leave it with you.'

'Sir.' Mitchell was holding out a photograph of the little boy. 'Can we get this Xeroxed?' Browne nodded and climbed into the car. Hunter had the engine already running and the ratchet beneath his seat grated as he pushed it back to accommodate his phenomenal length of leg.

'I was right,' Browne remarked, conversationally, 'about the bumptiousness.'

'And,' Hunter added, graciously, as he settled himself in comfort, 'about the aplomb.'

Pamela Hill edged further into the corner of Mrs Quentin's settee and increased the space between herself and the daughter who sat mute, beside her. She was almost more worried about Sonia than about Thomas. Sonia was behaving just as

Pamela would have predicted in these circumstances. The girl regarded with bitter scorn all those people, including her grandmother, whose inability to cope led them to spill their problems over into other people's lives. When in trouble herself, she bore it in a tight-lipped, self-imposed isolation. Where other people saw a moody and arrogant young woman, Pamela saw a child whose worshipper and mentor had deserted her by dying, curing her of the folly of trusting other people, especially those closest to her.

The control she was wielding now over her speech and behaviour was revealed in the tension of her stiff back and clenched hands. Pamela knew that any physical contact, even if it was accidental, would be unendurable to her, more stressful even than more bad news about Tom. She was glad the older and possibly more paternal officer had left and she prayed that this efficient young DC would be sensitive enough to realize she needed him to keep his manner neutral and official.

She envied all these police officials who could rush about doing things that were useful. The bullet-headed Constable Mitchell was almost bullying Sonia, but he couldn't help her without the information he was demanding. She and Barbara would have to help out when Sonia remained silent.

Mitchell had asked for a physical description of Thomas but it was difficult to think what to say that they couldn't see for themselves in the photograph she had given them. And, after all, the man, Bellamy, had seen him twice. 'The hair on the crown of his head always sticks up,' she offered. 'We lacquered it down so that he'd look tidy in that picture.' What could they say about his temperament? 'He's biddable and friendly.'

'Would he talk to strangers?' Mitchell asked, sharply.

Pamela looked at Barbara and they both nodded. 'Well, yes, he would. He's too young to have learned to be suspicious.'

'Does he like school? What are his hobbies?'

Pamela shook her head impatiently. 'He's too young for hobbies too. He's still just learning to cope with the mechanics of living.'

'He prefers jigsaws to painting,' Sonia suddenly volunteered, 'and football to both.'

Mitchell nodded and scribbled. 'It's silly,' he said, feeling carefully for the best words to couch the question, 'to ask if a four-year-old has enemies, but has he annoyed anyone recently? Have there been any complaints about him?'

Barbara took a turn. 'Some of the family say he's cheeky.'

'And is he?'

For the first time since her arrival, Pamela smiled. 'He's intelligent enough to make penetrating observations and not socially experienced enough to keep them to himself. People laugh at the clarity with which children grasp a concept and express it simply. They dismiss it as a sweeping generalization or as lack of experience. If an adult ever re-achieves this ability to cut through social subterfuge and see things as they really are, he's called a philosopher and is reputed to have a great mind.'

Mitchell had turned from Pamela, obviously deciding that she'd stopped being a grandmother and gone into writer mode. He addressed Sonia directly. 'What did you dress Thomas in this morning?'

'He dresses himself!'

Mitchell ignored Mrs Quentin and kept his eyes on Sonia. She seemed, Pamela observed, capable of coping with answers that merely required factual lists. 'Blue denim trousers, a red sweatshirt with a Bart Simpson cartoon on the front, dark blue shoes with bright red laces . . .'

'He's just learned to tie them.' Mitchell frowned more ferociously at this further interruption and, chidden, Mrs Quentin subsided. Sonia, having stopped speaking, remained silent. Mrs Quentin pulled herself together, offered to feed the assembled company and, to Pamela's relief, departed to the kitchen. Mitchell continued to contemplate Sonia serenely and, after a few seconds, his patience was rewarded.

'He had a badge on his sweater, a round blue one that said "I am 5". Shaun gave it to him and he was most pleased with it. He said it would make everybody think he was a big boy.' A further wait produced nothing more.

Pamela was puzzled by some of the police activity she was watching. A search of Thomas's room seemed logical enough, but why the bathroom? And why on earth the soiled washing, including the load already in the machine? She could think of no reason, either, for the cross-questioning of Barbara Quentin about her family, habits and friends, or the details of Tom's evening meal and bedtime routine when he wasn't here to go through it.

The refusal to allow them to use the telephone made sense. Obviously the police wanted the line left clear for messages from their colleagues. Maybe even from a kidnapper. Though they were not a rich family, they could have given someone the impression that they were well off. Barbara's house was a biggish and well-maintained one in a prosperous area, and perhaps some people thought writers were well paid.

Pamela longed for someone with whom she was free to discuss the suspicions that were teeming through her head. Tom could have been taken by someone who had lost her own child. He was an appealing infant, certainly. Her imagination began to run riot. She saw him successively lost and frightened in a dark street, unconscious and unidentified in a hospital bed. No, surely these people would already have checked that. Knocked down by a hit and run driver, then, badly hurt in a ditch, or . . . She firmly refused to let herself believe that anyone would harm him deliberately.

Sonia was not stupid. She would have considered all these possibilities and then some more. However must she feel?

Suddenly, her daughter answered this unspoken question. 'I don't feel anything,' she told the seemingly phlegmatic Mitchell, her expressionless monotone vanishing and her voice rising in near hysteria. 'Why don't I feel anything? There's something wrong with me!' She stood up and looked about her wildly. 'There's something very wrong with me!'

Mitchell nodded, calmly. 'Yes, there is. You're in shock.' He turned to Pamela who had come forward and ventured to put an arm round her daughter's rigid shoulders. 'Can you give us her GP's number?' The call was made and as they awaited the doctor's arrival, the food on Mrs Quentin's table congealed and the room grew progressively darker.

At eight o'clock that evening the team gathered in Browne's office for yet another conference. This time there was no need for Browne to stir them up. Eleven hours ago, they had been investigating the death of an old woman, not particularly attractive and mourned fairly perfunctorily even by her close family. Now, a child was missing, small, appealing, suffering from the disadvantage of having no father and known personally to one of them. Each of them would work unrelentingly till either he dropped or the boy was found.

As chief inspector, his task must be to co-ordinate their efforts, and ensure that the suggestions of the less forceful and possibly more practical were given a fair consideration. 'What possibilities should we be considering? Jennie?'

WDC Smith was ready. 'I think, sir, we'd better try to work out whether there's a connection between Thomas's disappearance and Mrs Norman's murder.'

'Fair enough. What connection do you think there might be?'

'It's obvious. The same person . . .' Dean was silenced by Browne's iciest glance.

'The same person,' Jennie continued, hastily, 'who benefited from the old woman's death might have needed to be rid of Thomas, maybe because of something he knew.'

'Like what?' Dean was pushing his luck.

Before Browne could administer a verbal rebuke, Mitchell answered the question. 'His grandmother said he didn't miss much and he was sometimes in bother for saying things that upset people. Have the telephone people let us know who he rang this morning?'

Browne shook his head. 'We're waiting to hear from them. You think he said something then that sealed his fate?'

As they considered what Thomas could have known, Jennie cut in, indignantly, 'Let's not assume the worst yet. He might just be lost. Or he might have been abducted by some disturbed woman who wanted him for some reason of her own. A nursery school would be the obvious place to pick up a small kid.'

'Surely, in this day and age,' Bellamy observed, 'the school would be sufficiently security conscious to look out for that sort of thing.'

'In theory they would,' Mitchell granted him, remembering his nieces and nephews, 'but, in the hassle of wiping runny noses and stopping them fighting and making sure they didn't lose their gloves, whoever was supposed to be looking out could easily be distracted.'

'Maybe,' Jennie suggested, hopefully, 'he just wandered away to look at something – maybe an interesting car – and then just got lost.'

Mitchell was doubtful. 'He doesn't seem to be shy. He'd have asked someone.'

'Maybe the wrong someone.'

There was a depressed silence, broken by Hunter, the only member of the team with young children of his own. 'It's a long shot that two members of the same immediate family have been done away with by two entirely separate and individual killers.'

'It's too early,' Jennie insisted, hoping she sounded more convinced than she felt, 'to assume that he's dead. Maybe it's just a bit of attention seeking. After all, his only parent is a working mother.'

'Not at his age,' chorused Mitchell and Hunter, and, even in these fraught circumstances, a smile went round at this unaccustomed agreement. 'Suppose he's been taken for what someone can make out of it,' Hunter went on, 'not quite independent of the Evelyn Norman case, but because of the publicity. It's been briefly reported and people have heard of Mrs Hill. She's comfortably off and people expect writers to be rich.'

The team liked this more optimistic theory and hastened to support it.

'Mrs Quentin's house is in good nick and in a good area.'

'And the *Clarion* mentioned the Fentons. Most people round here know that Alistair's worth a bob or two.'

'We're keeping the line clear,' Browne assured them. 'If you're right, Jerry, we'll be hearing from someone before long.'

Carson, uncomfortably perched on the window sill, as befitted the youngest officer present, was hatching his own theory. 'I think we ought to look at the other parent.'

'We will,' Browne told him, grimly, 'as soon as we know who he is. Did Pamela Hill reveal all, Benny?'

Mitchell looked up from his notebook. 'I left it with Megan, sir, WPC James. Mrs Hill decided she'd spend the night with her daughter, but she needed to go back home to feed her cat and pick up the pills the hospital gave her and her night clothes and so on. I thought it wasn't quite the moment for heavy handling but I briefed Megan to ask her whilst she was driving her over. You know, something on the lines of: "This is the best way you can help us to help your daughter." She hadn't come in yet last time I checked.' Browne nodded.

'We haven't found out yet where she went swanning off to in her taxi on Monday,' Dean reminded them. 'And where were all the rest of them earlier this afternoon?'

'The family, you mean? All going about their lawful business, according to them. Fenton was serving in his shop with hardly a customer to prove it. His wife was shopping in the market, so we shan't get much corroboration of that. Then she went to her doctor's surgery, "about her leg", Fenton said. If the session was an early one, we might be able to eliminate her.' Browne referred briefly to the notes he had been given only minutes before the meeting and had hardly had time to skim through himself. 'Alistair Fenton hasn't been tracked down yet, and I think we'd better find out something about Sykes too. He's at least acquainted with Sonia Hill.'

'He's been helping her to sell some of her work through his contacts,' Bellamy offered. 'And,' he added, suddenly remembering, 'preventing Alistair from incorporating her into the firm.'

'Mrs Hill was writing at home when she was sent for. Sonia usually works just mornings but she was asked to do as many afternoons as she could manage this week because of staff illness. She opted for Tuesday and today.'

'Fair enough, Benny, but someone had better go up there and check it out. Can you look up the head's address and see

144

to it later tonight?' Mitchell nodded and subsided.

Hunter, who had so far remained in his chair, now left it for his customary prowl round the office. Carson, his hindquarters numb from the hardness of the window sill and the draught from the ill-fitting frame, debated the wisdom of appropriating Hunter's seat and decided to risk it. 'You've had one session with Alistair Fenton, haven't you?' he asked Bellamy. 'What's he like?'

Bellamy wrinkled his nose. 'The sort of fellow who'd train slow race horses, and then back them – if he could be bothered!'

Possibly inspired by his walk round one corner of the crowded office, Hunter suggested that an exhaustive search of the Cloughton pubs would not be unfruitful if Alistair's evidence became vital.

'If you're volunteering, I've better things for you to do,' Browne told him with mock severity. 'I know Superintendent Petty has been quite generous. We've three extra DCs as from tomorrow and they've allowed us all the uniformed men we asked for to patrol the streets and take the photograph round the houses, but you can forget an authorized pub crawl. We've got road blocks on the main routes to Manchester, Leeds, Bradford and Huddersfield but there are plenty of byways to all four places. The other nursery parents are all phoning each other. Mrs McElroy, mother of Thomas's friend, Shaun, is co-ordinating that. She'll contact us if anyone has relevant information.'

'What about the people at Thomas's school?'

Hunter stopped prowling to answer and realized that Carson was in his chair. 'Would you jump in my grave as quickly?'

Carson was not intimidated. 'No, sir, I'd get my stripes by finding out who put you there. Head teachers don't have to ring up to find out why their pupils are absent, do they?'

'No, but she knows that if she'd said something, we could have started looking two hours earlier when it was still well light. She suggested that someone talked to young Shaun.' Browne looked apologetic. 'Can you do that as well, Benny? You should have the right touch with all those nieces and nephews to practise on.'

Jennie was surprised. 'Is your sister married? I thought she lived with your parents.'

Mitchell grinned. 'Siobhan does. I've got two more – and two brothers.' Jennie blinked. She had visited at the Mitchells' house. Six children reared in that tiny place? It went a long way to explain Mitchell's obsessive tidiness. It must have been the only way to survive.

'Will you go right now, Benny? With luck the lad won't be in bed yet and I've nothing else of paramount importance to say here.' Mitchell took the slip of paper Browne handed him and departed.

Hunter, slipping into his seat for the remainder of the meeting, felt an intense and personal anxiety about this little boy he had never seen. He could hardly believe that he had spent a great part of the afternoon at Browne's desk, half toying with the idea of quitting the police at some future point to become a full-time writer. Certainly, he was not the man of action that Mitchell was – or Dean, or Browne himself – but he realized now that he was his own kind of detective. Writing, for him, was just an absorbing and vastly satisfying hobby.

Right now, he wanted only to search for and find this child, relieve the catatonic mother, the distressed grandmother and the distraught Mrs Quentin from whose immediate custody he had vanished. Hunter smiled to himself as he realized that Pamela Hill had become for him not the literary mentor he'd been trying to make her but the anxious close relative of a missing boy.

Chapter Thirteen

On Friday morning too, Mitchell was first to arrive in Browne's office, anxious to report and be busy again and impatient with everyone else for being merely on time. Browne assured him that the searchers and dogs were out again now that it was light and told him that the road blocks had produced nothing.

The CI suddenly realized that, the previous day, Mitchell had been on the case solidly from eight o'clock in the morning till after ten at night, eating and drinking on the wing. Ever since he had been drafted to the section, Browne had admired the keen young DC's determination, and had pushed him, knowing that his work always had first priority in his life. Virginia had gone back to Oxford now, of course, but it dawned on him for the first time, that soon, the family that Mitchell's zeal for truth and justice caused him to neglect was going to consist of his own daughter and grandchild.

By the time the rest of the team showed up, Mitchell's impatience had made him feverish. Browne let him make his report. Shaun had been asleep in bed by the time he had arrived at the McElroys' house. The child's mother, still stationed at the telephone, receiving and logging calls from other parents, decided that the importance of any information he might divulge justified waking him. 'Obviously,' she told Mitchell, 'I've asked him myself what happened at lunchtime. He just says he saw Thomas and he hadn't hung his coat up yet. If you think you can get any more out of him you're welcome to try.'

It had not proved to be a fruitful interview. Shaun had been fractious, tearful and confused. 'I fixed to go again this morning, sir.' Browne nodded and amended Mitchell's action sheet.

'Sonia's headmistress is a Mrs Costello,' Mitchell went on. 'She spoke quite well of her on the whole, though she was not very happy about her coming to school in weird and wonderful clothes that she's designed and made herself. In the beginning, she took Sonia on as a favour to a social-worker friend whose caseload Sonia was part of, because of the pregnancy and because she saw the education authority's psychologist when her father died.'

Mitchell recalled Mrs Costello's smug expression as she recounted this little bit of social work of her own. 'She wasn't much use in the office at all, Constable, when she first came, but Miss Thompson was getting towards retiring age, so, for a trial month, they shared the job. The girl was quick and after those four weeks she more or less took over.'

It had been getting late and Mitchell had elected to opt out of asking questions, sit back in his chair, drink the coffee she had offered and let her run on. 'Schools have to manage their own budgets now, you know – and the authority seems to think we can make our allowance go further than they did themselves. It sounds a lot when you hear how much a year we're given, but when you have to break it down and make it cover everything . . . More coffee? Yes, I always buy this brand.

'We've managed several days this week by having Sonia in charge in my office whilst I've been covering for my colleague in her classroom. It's cheaper to pay Sonia extra by the hour than to employ a supply teacher. And I enjoy it. I never went into teaching to become an administrator but it's the only way up, you see. There's no promotion in the classroom. Isn't it silly?'

Mitchell thought he agreed that it was.

'Sonia copes with everything that might happen in my office and, although it's bending the rules a little, she copes quite well with a class if it's absolutely imperative that I deal personally with a visitor or a phone call.' Mitchell had pinched himself awake and asked a question.

148

'Duties? Well, she opens the post and sorts it. She's in the office during assembly for the phone. Then she answers the routine letters without reference to me, although I always check before I sign them. There's never a mistake. She keeps the weekly accounts, meals money, school bank, YPO bills and so on. A professional accountant checks it over termly but there's never any bother. She's not above brewing the staff tea at break time, or dealing with children's minor injuries and ailments. She's not always too sympathetic, especially if they make a fuss, but she's calm and practical.

'Often she finishes a morning by helping another member of staff in a classroom because she gets through everything faster than Miss Thompson did. I can hardly reward her speed and efficiency by cutting down her hours, can I?'

'She sounds an absolute paragon. She enjoys her work?' Mitchell had asked, determined to slide in a contribution to this compulsive filling of the silence.

'Oh, I didn't say that. As a matter of fact, I think she hates it.'

'So you don't think it would have been too difficult,' Dean asked, 'for her to have left school whilst Mrs Costello was teaching?'

Mitchell shrugged. 'She'd have been taking a risk. You surely don't think . . . ?'

'Frankly, no.' Browne smiled. 'But I don't fancy the flak we might get if Superintendent Petty finds out that we haven't done a thorough check on the only suspect for Mrs Norman's murder who is young and pretty.' He looked at his watch. 'I've filled in your sheets. We'll be better employed out and about this morning than sitting talking here.' He was beginning to give them out when Hunter gave a loud exclamation. 'Just found the solution to everything all on your own, have you, Jerry?'

Hunter shook his head. 'What's Alistair Fenton's second name?'

'Edward, the same as his father's.'

'So we have another A. E. Fenton.'

'Who's supposed to have had a substantial win on the pools about two years ago.'

149

'And didn't want his family to know anything about it.'

'Whose father says he got interested in rare books some time ago and asked how you'd go about putting them up for auction.'

Reluctant though he was to interrupt Hunter's and Mitchell's antiphonal chant, Browne felt impelled to ask, 'That's not in the file! When did you talk to Anthony Fenton?'

Mitchell reddened slightly. 'On my day off on Wednesday, sir.'

There was a ten-second silence whilst Browne got his anger under control. 'What do you suggest I do to you, Mitchell, that will teach you not to try to do my job for me?'

Mitchell bit his lip. 'Anthony Fenton's already done it, sir. He charged me thirty-five quid for that book on marine biology that was my excuse for going into the shop. He realized it was an unofficial quizzing I'd given him and it was his price for not dropping me in it.'

'Well,' Hunter suggested, 'now the CI's found you out, you might as well go and sell it back to him.'

In the uproarious laughter, Mitchell's shout was the loudest. Browne began again to distribute the action sheets. Then the telephone rang.

Sergeant Paul Taylor stood on the muddy towpath, allowing himself for just a few seconds to appreciate the March sunshine, fitful and fleeting, but magnified when it appeared by its reflection on the surface of the canal in front of him, the wet roofs behind him and the puddles round his feet. Until yesterday, his plan for his day off had included a stool and a rod and line, but a child was missing and, although he was exactly where he had intended to be at this moment, his occupation was not the pleasant one he had been anticipating.

The team of searchers he had volunteered to oversee consisted of a motley collection of neighbours and friends of the child's family and a few colleagues, some of them officially off duty like himself. He had divided the area and the men assigned to him methodically and, through a screen of black branches, he could see most of them, bright in their anoraks, caps and scarves, their backs bent as they poked and grubbed diligently where he had directed.

It was a grim task that they had been set, but it had at least distracted everyone from yet more unfunny jokes about snakes. He had reserved for himself a row of dilapidated buildings where he had played as a small boy, in spite of, or possibly because of, the warnings from his parents, his teachers and the police that to do so was extremely dangerous. He had to go under the railway bridge to reach it, across a section of the towpath that was cobbled. Some of the small rounded stones had sunk where the path had subsided and the puddles here were minor ponds, although, for the moment, the rain had stopped.

A joiner and small builder had taken over the disused warehouse alongside and, to pass under the bridge, Sergeant Taylor had to squeeze between his large lorry and its waiting load of planks and window frames, leaning precariously against the wall. Long grass and saplings on the railway embankment showered him with drops of water.

The buildings he was making for were a row of cottages once built for the local mill workers and now awaiting demolition. They consisted of three low-ceilinged storeys, the ground-floor windows boarded up. The boards had, in many cases, been torn down again, either by the wind or by the district's youth in search of adventure or a headquarters from which to organize one. Tiny areas, just eight feet by three, outside the front doors made back yards, once jealously guarded by their tenants, minute but their own space.

Old stone sinks that had once served in the kitchens, but which had been replaced as civilization encroached by porcelain ones, remained in the yards where later tenants had used them as plant containers. There were plant pots too, many of them broken, and a few of the original dustbins, though most of these had been appropriated by householders near by, including Taylor's father, as rain butts or containers for compost. Some of the fall pipes and drainpipes were still quite serviceable, he noticed.

Taylor inspected the yards carefully, climbing from one to

another over low walls where lichens grew, supporting one another's existence, half hidden by tendrils of ivy. Nothing in the yards. He'd better begin on the houses themselves.

He saw to his relief that, in the first cottage at least, he wouldn't have to risk the bedroom floors. From gaps in the roof, light filtered down to the wooden floorboards of the living-room, which were themselves little more than rows of mouldy sticks. Suddenly, he was transported back eighteen years. A half-rotten, peeling shutter was reared against one wall, still boldly emblazoned with his initials, PRT, amateurishly executed in red brush strokes. It was the claim he had made for this particular room as headquarters for his own gang. He smiled at his memories of the den they had made in this very spot, the scraps of ill-assorted food they'd smuggled here.

One night, they had all sneaked out here from home with sleeping bags, and returned only two hours later, their tails between their legs. Not that they'd been conscience stricken, and certainly not afraid. It had just been that, in the blackness of the night, all the fun had evaporated. The sleeping bags had become cold and wet, and, though the boys had consumed the day's full complement of food, they had been hungry. Sleeping here had suddenly seemed a stupid thing to do.

They had all made their ignominious way home to their own beds, undetected, except for fat Colin, who could never do anything properly. At least that time, though, he hadn't got the rest of them into trouble. Taylor decided to come back when he wasn't busy and take the shutter home. He'd cut out the bit with the daubed initials, dry it out and hang it on his wall. He grasped the shutter to test its weight, kicking aside the debris round the bottom.

The floor it rested on gave way without warning and Taylor stepped back quickly to avoid an unplanned dip in the water in the flooded cellar. He flashed a torch into the hole he had made and froze as its beam picked out a small hand and a sodden red-ribbed cuff.

Browne signalled to his team to remain where they were as

he noted down Taylor's instructions. 'Those derelict houses, sir, just beside Masons' builders, near the railway bridge between the river and the canal . . .' Certain that he could find it, he replaced the receiver and turned back to his men. 'Sit down again. They've found him.' His tone said it all and none of them asked hopeful questions. He repeated Taylor's news for their benefit, then set off for Mill Bank Cottages, taking with him Hunter and, after some hesitation, Dean.

On the town side of the row, two disused warehouses had been converted, one into the offices of a canal boat company and the other into a thriving pub. Browne parked outside the Tiller and Tipple and the three officers walked along a track that led under a road bridge towards the towpath. As they entered its shadow, Browne registered the smell of damp earth and the sound of traffic thundering overhead. The wind rippled the surface of the water and the wavelets caught the light and made moving patterns on the underside of the bridge.

Emerging on the far side, he felt surrounded by water. To his right, the river, which had run parallel to the canal for a hundred yards or so, now turned and spilled over a weir. The sun suddenly reappeared through a substantial gap in the clouds and the whole scruffy industrial scene glittered.

Browne gave thanks for the small miracle before concentrating grimly on the reason for his presence here. He could see Taylor, swathed in luminous yellow waterproofs, waiting to show them the exact position of the body, and hurried to join him. When Taylor indicated the collapsed section of floor, the hand he had seen was no longer visible. The water was moving and the cellar below seemed to be flooded to within a foot or so of what had been its ceiling.

'Have you called your searchers off?' Browne asked.

The young sergeant looked worried. 'I blew my whistle to collect them up, sir, and ticked off all the names on my list, so I'm sure no one's still out looking. Most of the volunteers went down to the Tiller to get something to warm them up but they'll wait there a while to see if you need them for anything else.'

'To go on looking if this isn't the right child, you mean?'

Browne glared at Dean, who fell silent.

'Us coppers, on and off duty, hung around here.' He waved his arm to where his colleagues stood in a tight group at the far end of the terrace. Browne promptly employed them in taping off the area in readiness for the SOCO who were doubtless on their way. Then he allowed even the on-duty officers one warming tot and a half-hour reprieve.

Taylor took Browne to the back of the house and indicated the steps down to the cellar. 'You haven't wasted much time getting your bearings,' he commented, approvingly.

Taylor grinned. 'I'm afraid I mucked around here often a year or two ago. It's deteriorated a lot since then, although it wasn't exactly safe even then. They put me through to the Super himself when I got in touch, sir. He's sending the frogmen and the SOCO and he said he'd bring Dr Ledgard with him.'

Browne, who knew all this, nodded and returned to the front door. 'We'll leave the interior to the specialists, I think, and have a look outside. Do you know if the cellars are separate or connected, Paul?'

'They used to be separate, sir, but I don't know what's fallen down or what vandalism there's been. It's pretty certain that no one got to this cellar from one of the others since all last week's rain, though.'

Browne and Hunter made a cursory tour of the other four cottages. Inside they were dim, their ceilings bulging and their floorboards rotten, but tattered remnants of wallpaper remained in place and there were oddments of disintegrating furniture. It was a place to entrance a child, but no four-year-old would have come to it by himself from a school three miles away.

Returning to the yard at the first house they noted that the brambles growing over a collapsed section of wall had been recently broken and trampled. Both the front and back doors had at some time been forced open, but it was obvious that neither of them had shifted for some considerable time. In their present position they allowed ample room for a child and reasonable space for a slim adult to slip through either of them.

154

There were signs of entry by the window and, surprisingly, the sash still allowed it to be raised and lowered, but the footprints in the mud were small and Browne was not so old as not to remember when it had been more fun to climb through a window than walk through a door.

'There's a doll's pram parked out at the back,' Taylor volunteered. 'Classy job, sprung like a baby's. There's no doll in it but some clean blankets that look hand-sewn.' Browne made a note, then raised his eyes and rested them on the rising, scrubby hillside.

When Superintendent Petty arrived a few moments later, he had Mitchell in his car. Browne expected the DC's manner to reflect his triumph at having managed to reach the scene of all the activity, but his future son-in-law seemed uncharacteristically subdued, and Browne remembered that this, whether or not the body Taylor had found proved to be Thomas Hill's, would be the first child's death that Mitchell had come up against professionally.

More vehicles drew up behind Petty's and disgorged the various experts whose services they required. Deprived at the moment of a body to pronounce upon, Dr Ledgard chatted quietly to Hunter as they watched the frogmen quickly organize their equipment and begin their operation. In a very short time a shout from one of them preceded his reappearance carrying a small, limp form which he laid on the plastic sheet that Ledgard had placed ready for it.

The skin where it was visible on the hands and face was sodden and wrinkled, but the child was recognizable to all of them as the one they were looking for. The face was round, the hair dark and the picture on the sweatshirt was unmistakably Bart Simpson. The officers stood in a silent semicircle round him and Browne could see that Mitchell was quietly weeping. He was neither faint nor sickened, quite capable of carrying out instantly any task his superior officers might require of him, but unashamed of his grief or its expression.

Dean turned from the tiny corpse to stare at Mitchell and for once, Browne let his dislike of the DC surface. 'Get yourself over to that row of houses and start knocking,' he snapped at him. With a scowl, Dean obeyed, marching, head high and neck reddened to the terrace behind Mill Bank. The houses were similar in construction to those by the canal but in slightly better condition and obviously inhabited, scruffily curtained, their yards full of junk. Browne sent Mitchell in the opposite direction, to a pair of houses well back from the towpath that looked clean and well maintained. 'Ask about the doll's pram. Its owner might have seen something.'

There were various tyre marks on the path where it widened in front of Masons' workshop and the cottages. Mason had had his lorries out first thing this morning and they had almost certainly obliterated any useful tracks from yesterday. Nevertheless, Browne set a keen-looking uniformed constable to waste his time examining it. Then he turned to Ledgard who was rising from his examination of the body and coming to meet him.

'Anything?'

'A contusion on the left temple.'

'Did he drown?'

Ledgard shrugged. 'I need to look at the lungs.'

'Nothing else?'

'Yes.' Ledgard's voice was tight and Browne could see that he was very angry. 'Something you've always wanted to hear me say. I'm going to do the PM right now. This little mite was four years old! Coming?'

Chapter Fourteen

Only seldom did Browne find himself at the mortuary twice in a week. More jonquils, their buds further open, seemed as unfitting a decoration for it as they had on Tuesday, although the forsythia had appropriately withered to a brittle brown.

The pathos of the small body had increased as it lay, taking up only half the space on the ridged white slab. Ledgard lost no time in providing them both with protective clothing and getting to work. 'Immersion in cold water causes cutis anserina – gooseflesh to you. The cold contracts the erector pilae muscles. The head sinks low in the water and therefore the blood gravitates towards the head and neck. You get decomposition first in the face and neck, though there's none here yet, of course. Heat is lost twice as fast in water, but decomposition is retarded . . .'

Browne's discomfort grew with this unwanted torrent of verbal detail. 'There's no lividity till the body's at rest. The vitreous humour K rises steadily in twelve to seventy-two hours, though there's a slight retardation in water. We'll have to allow for that.' He reached into gurgling depths in the miniature chest. 'There's water deep in the principal bronchii that's pushed the residual air beyond it and caused ballooning of the lungs, see?'

Not wishing to, Browne averted his eyes. The dreadful commentary was unrelenting. 'The vascular bed of the lungs is compressed. It's left no room for dilatation of the vessels. That's why there are no petechiae. You can see marked congestion and cyanosis reflected in the right side of the heart so the principal veins have become distended with dark blood.'

157

It occurred to Browne that this verbalizing of the techniques of his task was Ledgard's way of coping with his feelings, comparable with Mitchell's tears. He switched off mentally from the macabre commentary which had been virtually incomprehensible to him and, without making a conscious choice, began to think about Virginia.

Suddenly, he became aware of the real reason why he felt so angry about the pregnancy. It had nothing to do with the interruption of his daughter's education. He was quick and intelligent himself and had never felt held back by not having official qualifications. In present times, a degree was no passport to employment and success, anyway. Nor had he ever thought that Benny would neglect the responsibility he had incurred. The tears had surprised him but he knew the lad's instinctive and dependable loyalty to all the other members of his family.

What had made him furious was Benny's appropriation of Virginia's first loyalty before he himself was ready to relinquish it. He had expected more than twenty years of coming first in his daughter's life, together with Hannah, of course. Her becoming a parent herself had robbed him of that precious remnant of Ginny's childhood. She was still his daughter, certainly, but, primarily now she was this infant's mother and Mitchell's future wife. Why, he wondered, had all these things become clear to him now when the scene before his eyes was so horribly riveting? He supposed it had left his subconscious mind totally free to work everything out for him. Now he had identified his dragon he could fight it. Suddenly, he felt immensely cheered.

'Cooling will have been about three degrees Fahrenheit an hour for the first twelve hours,' said Ledgard, and Browne became aware of the inappropriateness of his raised spirits. He stored them away for future consideration and tried to persuade Ledgard to part with some information he could understand.

Hunter, left in charge pending Browne's return from the post-mortem, decided that what Mitchell needed was the company of another child, alive and well. 'The McElroy boy for you, Benny. Be firm with him. We need everything he can tell us.' He made his manner almost peremptory and avoided Taylor's blunder. Mitchell had shaken off the sympathetic hand placed on his shoulder and spoken so rudely to Taylor that he knew that in the near future he would have to apologize.

There was no such pussyfooting from Shaun. 'Thomas is dead and he's still got my badge!'

Mitchell noted the mother's startled expression. 'Who told you that?'

Shaun shook his head. 'No one but I heard Mrs Blackwood saying he must be. Will he still wear it, even though he's dead?'

Mitchell gave the question serious consideration. 'I should think so. He'll be five in August, even though he's dead. He'll be very glad to have it and I'll buy you another one.'

'Today?'

Mitchell shrugged. 'I'm a bit busy today.' He fished in his pocket and produced fifty pence with a glance at Mrs McElroy to check that it was enough. 'Here you are. You can go with your mother and buy it yourself. Who put the badge on Thomas's jumper?'

'I did, and I got it the right way up. It was upside-down to Thomas when he looked at it, but I put it so it was the right way up for other people to see. I let him wear it because he saved all his black jelly babies for me.' He picked up the fifty-pence piece that Mitchell had put on the table, examined it and slipped it into his pocket.

'Why didn't you and Thomas go into the classroom together?'

'Thomas said he had to go to the lavatory.'

'And you didn't wait for him?'

The look Shaun gave Mitchell was admonitory. 'It's rude to stand listening when someone's peeing!'

Mitchell grinned. In his youth and in his house, it had often been unavoidable. 'Didn't you wonder where he was when he didn't come in later?'

'I forgot about him.'

'How was that?'

Shaun's face expressed bewilderment at the silly things grown-ups wanted to know. 'I don't know. I was doing a blue picture and then it was the Postman Pat viddybo.'

Mitchell produced a forty-piece jigsaw puzzle and continued to chat to the child as they put it together but nothing else transpired that seemed to him immediately relevant. When Shaun was dispatched to play in his bedroom, Mrs McElroy produced coffee. 'I didn't think he'd be so callous,' she remarked, apologetically as she passed Mitchell's cup.

'He isn't,' Mitchell assured her. 'He doesn't realize what death means. He imagines Thomas in some sort of nearby room that, for the moment, he can't go into himself.'

She shrugged. 'Who's to say that he's wrong? Which of us does know what death means?'

By early afternoon, Browne's team was gathered yet again in his office, most of them suffering from indigestion after a hastily snatched lunch. 'This afternoon's plan is very simple,' he announced. 'Just saturation questioning of anyone who had anything to do with the child, the school people, all the family, friends, neighbours, doctor and anyone else we can think of.'

Before they departed, he gave them a brief summary of Ledgard's conclusions so far. 'The body had been in the water more than twelve hours. There was a bang on the head, sufficient to stun, but death was by drowning.'

Dean asked, 'Could either the blow or the drowning have been an accident?'

Browne shook his head. 'Ledgard's evidence doesn't rule it out, but that stretch of the canal is four miles from the school. Someone has to have driven him there.' He referred again to the rough notes Ledgard had given him. 'The stomach contained canal water swallowed during the struggle. The poor kid might not even have been properly unconscious when he was pushed down the steps. There was froth coming out of his mouth and nostrils as some of you saw. Ledgard said it was inhaled water and mucus, a classic sign of drowning.'

'We're looking for a callous coward, aren't we?' They all looked at Mitchell. 'Well, in both cases the victim was fatally injured and left to die after a period of time. Having botched the job, the killer buzzes off to save his own skin.'

'Neither death was quick and clean,' Browne agreed. 'Jerry, I want you and Benny to go back and talk to the three women in Hepple Lane. Get them to tell you everything about the child they can think of. Nothing is too trivial. Richard and Jennie can do exactly the same at the school, both with the children and the staff. Nigel and Robin, will you follow up those phone numbers? Except Mrs Shaw. She's in Hepple Lane so Benny can call on his way to number twelve. Don't mention the child. Just ask what calls they received between ten thirty and twelve thirty yesterday.'

Carson looked puzzled. 'Can't BT help us? Mrs Quentin said she had itemized bills.'

'Well, yes and no. I got the data protection form, provided the reasons for our nosiness and got the Super to sign it with a cross but their computers don't perform the same miracles as ours. It's going to take them two days to find and run their unbilled usage program. Even then, any calls using less than ten units don't get logged so those young Thomas made may not show anyway.'

'What are you going to do?' Only Mitchell would have asked.

'Check on your theory and Jerry's that Fenton junior helped himself to *The Whale* and financed his business with it. Don't envy me. You'd be surprised what muck bank managers drink and still call it coffee.' He grabbed his raincoat from behind the door and ushered everyone out.

Mitchell and Hunter spoke little on their journey to Hepple Lane. The hail crashing on the car roof as they drove produced a tinny cacophony which would have drowned any discussion of the case and from time to time a sudden stronger gust blew the vehicle over towards the centre of the road. Three doors down from number twelve was as near as Mitchell could park. He slammed and locked the door and pulled up his anorak hood. 'Hell's teeth! I'm glad we're not out searching in this.'

Hunter opened the gate and stepped on to the path where a

thick privet hedge afforded a degree of shelter from the wind if not from the wet. He contemplated the annihilation of the crocuses that edged the pavement and seemed to have strayed on to Mrs Quentin's lawn. The garden was by no means unkempt but it was perhaps the most untidy in the lane. Hunter thought it was perhaps the only one not the responsibility of a paid gardener and wondered which of the two women tended it. A white-painted cast-iron urn on a pedestal had dead and blackened foliage hanging from it, but, round it, neatly pruned roses were showing their first leaves.

Mrs Quentin let him in and he deliberately turned away from the tricycle parked tidily in the niche at the bottom of the stairs. Pamela, she told him, as she showed him into the sitting-room, had just returned from identifying her grandson's body officially. 'Sonia felt she couldn't manage it but now, I think, she wishes she'd been. It would have been a last little service to him and seeing his little body wouldn't have been worse than imagining it lying there.'

Hunter had not met the elegantly dressed blonde woman in the armchair by the fire. 'My sister, Stella.' Pamela Hill waved an arm in her direction. Hunter introduced himself and communicated Browne's request for all the information they could produce on any aspect of Thomas's brief life.

When Stella Fenton spoke, however, it was merely to justify her presence. It seemed to be a summing-up of a longer account that Hunter had missed. 'Whatever the school thinks, I'm sure my place is here with my relatives at this sad time.' To arrive among them, however, seemed to be the full extent of the obligation she felt. She sat back against the cushions, poking at her thigh from time to time.

Pamela tried to co-operate with Hunter's request. 'I'm not quite sure what you want and we told you most of it yesterday. Thomas was very well co-ordinated physically. He reached all the baby landmarks ahead of schedule – crawling, walking, climbing. He throws and catches a ball well' – hurriedly adjusting her tense – 'promised to be good at sport. He was very observant too. He seldom missed anything, wasn't easy to fool.'

162

'He wasn't a messy child, or clumsy,' Mrs Quentin put in. 'I suppose that's part of what Pam was saying. He didn't spill food or drop things. He didn't sit about quietly though, or like sitting on my knee to have a story read to him. He preferred chasing about.'

'He could be quite impertinent on occasions.' Stella's contribution was met with stony silence except for the squeak of Hunter's pencil and it stemmed the promising flow of details that had been filling in the police picture of this second victim.

The doorbell rang again and Mrs Quentin admitted Mitchell, fetching him a towel to mop his streaming hair. 'The child rang Mrs Shaw yesterday,' he told Hunter, 'and chatted to her for a couple of minutes. He said he had a secret. Unfortunately, she agreed that he should keep it and didn't ask what it was.' Hunter's gesture invited an explanation from the family but no one could oblige him.

'He loved secrets,' Sonia said.

'He did, didn't he? He could hardly contain himself at Christmas with so many of them to . . .' Mrs Quentin stopped suddenly.

Mitchell turned to her urgently. 'You've remembered what it was?'

She shook her head. 'No, but there's something else. I fetched him home from school on Monday and we passed St Helen's House on the bus. He was looking out of the top window when it stopped outside. He said he could see a special yellow car. He said he'd had a ride in it but he gave me one of his old-fashioned looks and I knew he hadn't. He wouldn't tell me whose it was. As we said he liked having secrets and he was fascinated by cars.' All eyes were on Mrs Quentin, Sonia's enormous in a face which Mitchell thought had lost flesh since the previous day.

'Who's got a yellow one?'

They all looked at Stella, who eventually said, 'Well, Alistair has, a J-registered MR2. So what? There are almost as many yellow cars on the road as there are red ones.'

Barbara Quentin asked, 'Sergeant, is there anything you can tell us . . . I mean, did he . . . ?'

163

Pamela rescued her. 'We'd like to know how he died, Sergeant, and whether there was any sexual interference. Whatever you can tell us won't be worse than some of the things we're imagining.'

Hunter gave them brief details. Suddenly, tears were streaming down Sonia's face. Mitchell saw that Pamela's relief exceeded even her pity. She sat on the chair arm and held her daughter's hand as Sonia sobbed. 'I dreamed about it last night when I finally got to sleep. I . . .'

The telephone in the hall rang and was answered by one of the two constables who had shared the task now for twenty-four hours. Sonia's voice rose. 'All this phoning and it's mostly from people who never bothered with him when he was alive.'

'It's not only your grief.' Pamela's words admonished but her tone coaxed. 'Everyone has a right to be horrified. And those patient officers are saving you from all the hassle of the media. Surely you're pleased to know how many people loved him.'

Sonia was not to be consoled. 'All this din and milling scores of people, in and out of the flat! There's no place to be alone, that's mine.'

Pamela sighed and glanced first at her watch and then at Mrs Quentin. 'I'll have to go and see to the cat again, or ring and ask my neighbour to do it.'

Sonia sniffed and scrubbed her eyes. 'I'd like you to go back home now, and everyone else too. I don't want to be rude and I'm grateful for everyone's help but I've got to learn to be without Tom. But first, I want to make a picture of him. I want to begin it straight away.' She left the room and they heard her footsteps going upstairs to her own flat.

Pamela stood up. 'Do you need me for anything else, Sergeant?'

Hunter stood up. 'Not just at this moment, Mrs Hill.'

She quietly fetched her coat and slipped it on. 'Can you give me a lift, Stella?'

Stella shook her head. 'I need a word with these gentlemen.'

Mitchell pricked up his ears but Hunter appeared not much interested. 'You can speak to Constable Mitchell. I'll see you home, Mrs Hill.' They went out together.

Mrs Quentin disappeared tactfully as Mitchell turned enquiringly to the blonde woman who had remained in her chair.

'Do you imagine your investigation will last much longer, Constable? All this publicity won't be very good for my husband's business, or my son's.'

'All publicity is good publicity and our investigation will go on until it's finished.'

'Is there a connection between the two deaths, do you think?'

'Who knows?'

'Are you quite sure my mother was killed? Isn't her death much more likely to be a tragic accident? Mother had been sadly failing towards the end.'

' . . . She was sadly failing to convince me,' Mitchell told Browne, some time later, 'of anything but her anxiety to protect her son.'

Chapter Fifteen

The afternoon downpour abated sufficiently long for Jennie Smith to dash from the nursery school car park to its bright and stimulating entrance hall with her new hairdo unscathed. She wrinkled her nose at the smell of drying clothes, then paused for a moment to admire a striking collage on the wall. It was large, some four feet by six, and featured stylized underwater creatures and plants. The creatures were all made of brightly coloured felt, the plants of crêpe paper, and the water was represented by an overlay of tiny strips of silk and satin in shades of grey, streamers of cellophane in blue and green and strips of aluminium foil.

Dean forced the door shut against the wind and came to join her. 'Cripes! That's advanced artwork for nursery kids.'

'Do you think Sonia did it?'

Dean shrugged. 'It's a thought.'

Hearing their voices, a middle-aged woman in twin-set and pearls put her head round a door that had been left ajar. 'I was listening out for you.' She indicated hangers for their dripping outer clothing, then ushered them into her office. Jennie encouraged her first to talk about herself. 'I'm not a qualified teacher. I just run the school as a business. My own children are all getting on with their own lives now, which is very right and proper, and my husband is a busy lawyer who can't discuss his clients' cases. This place does more for me than just provide extra income. It's a way of staying involved.'

Unqualified she may have been, but, after only a few minutes, Jennie decided that, unless they were unusually excellent, the teachers she employed would not match her concern for, interest in or understanding of the children in her charge. She had never met the small boy whose death they were investigating but Mrs Threadgold's observation and analysis of him brought him to life for her, figuratively at least. She had obviously been fond of him. ' . . . He was very mature for four and his mother in some ways is rather immature – although that's unfair. She is only twenty. I tend to forget that most of the other parents are at least five years older. In any case, perhaps maturity isn't quite the right word. Being an artist gives her a different scale of values or set of priorities from most people.

'But Thomas hasn't suffered. Plenty of older members of the family kept an eye on him and he quickly learned to do for himself a lot of things that other children have done for them. Quite simple things like tying his shoelaces, and some quite complicated ones, like remembering what he's supposed to bring to school and delivering accurate messages.'

Jennie knew she was making a good job of the interview, but was surprised that Dean had acknowledged it by sitting well back, taking unobtrusive notes and not interrupting. Mrs Threadgold's conversation revealed an intimate knowledge of the families of her charges. Never descending to gossip, she revealed impressions detected by her sensitive interest.

She moved on to practical matters. 'Numbers are down today and quite a few of the mothers of the children who are present have elected to stay on till they go home.'

Jennie smiled. 'With all that help you'll be having an easy afternoon, then.'

Mrs Threadgold shook her head. 'No, it's made things quite difficult. The children aren't sure whose authority they're under. The intelligent ones are taking advantage and playing one side off against the other. The weather's exacerbating the situation. Cats and children always become wild and unreasonable when it's very windy.' Jennie and Dean both laughed but Mrs Threadgold did not. 'Oh, I'm quite serious. They rush round driven by a restlessness they don't understand. I've noticed it often.'

'But today, under the circumstances . . .'

She shook her head. 'The parents are upset, and the staff, of course, but the children aren't, not really. To them, "Thomas is dead" means "Thomas isn't here just now". They have to accept so much that's inexplicable to them that death is just part of all the rest of it. By the time they understand that Thomas really isn't coming back, they'll be used to the idea.

'Shaun is one of the children who's absent today. His mother is attributing to him the shock and grief she would feel if her own close friend had died.' Jennie smiled, remembering Mitchell's account of his conversation with Shaun. Mrs Threadgold described him as a small, timid, elfin child, older than Thomas. 'Thomas was stouter, both mentally and physically. He fought most of Shaun's battles for him. Being without him will be better for Shaun's development.'

'Are you saying the little Hill boy was a bit of a bully?'

'Not at all. It was just that Shaun hid behind him, did everything he suggested.'

Jennie felt a little puzzled. From Mitchell's description the child had sounded reasonably forthcoming, even a little precocious. Perhaps he was by Mitchell's standards. He could be timid and yet still have a middle-class *savoir-faire* that was lacking in Mitchell's small relations.

Dean put away his notebook and they accepted Mrs Threadgold's invitation to go into the classroom and speak to the children. 'I'm sure you'll have the sense not to interrogate them but to chat to them as you play with them.'

They nodded, accepting this polite warning. The teacher in charge was finishing a story, the children sitting cross-legged on a carpet in front of her. She showed them the final picture, then they got up and returned to the tables placed about the large room, where bricks, crayons, clay and various puzzles were set out. The tots who were not chattering cheerfully were quarrelling about the toys and the two officers realized that Mrs Threadgold had been right; none of them was thinking about Thomas.

Jennie lost herself amongst the children and Dean strolled across to the teacher who was replacing the story book on a shelf. 'You'll be the policeman,' she informed him. Glad of this assurance of his identity, he let her chatter on. 'Mrs

168

Threadgold said she wasn't going to introduce you formally with the children listening but she told us what you wanted. I can tell you quite a lot about Thomas. For a start, he wasn't very keen on sitting still at story time. He'd sneak back to the tables and do a jigsaw if I didn't watch him . . .' Examples of Thomas's artwork were produced and thick wallets of snapshots of him with other children, engaged in various activities. 'I'm the more or less official photographer. It's always been a hobby of mine.'

As the commentary droned on, Dean almost envied Jennie as she sat helping a stolid-looking child to thread brightly painted cotton reels on to a long boot lace. He noticed a model shop set up in a corner, constructed of wooden blocks and stocked with empty packets, sealed with Sellotape. Dean said a quick prayer and the Almighty rescued him from the inveterate photographer by allowing one of the parents to catch sight of pictures of her own child.

Taking his cue from Jennie, he went to sit beside an infant who was busily drawing circles on a sheet of paper. 'That's good.' He pulled the paper closer to get a better look. 'Are they bubbles?'

The small girl looked more scornful than upset. 'They're mouseholes.'

'Where are the mice?'

Now she pitied him. 'Inside the holes, of course.'

Dean shrugged. Where else?

The child had no wish to be disobliging. Carefully, she selected a green crayon and sketched with it a balloon shape, larger than any of the mouseholes. She added a wavering line at one end and quite recognizable whiskers at the other. 'He can't get in because he's too fat.'

She handed Dean the crayon, hopefully, and he shot Jennie a triumphant glance. Mitchell wasn't the only one who had the right touch with children. 'I'll draw a cat to chase your mice.'

The child promptly burst into floods of tears. Dean retired, offended, and Jennie came to the rescue, handing the small girl a tissue. 'Did Thomas like drawing pictures, Helena?' Helena sniffed and nodded.

Mrs Threadgold spoke to Dean out of the side of her mouth.

'He'd have been keener if his mother hadn't expected him to show promise of being as good as herself. Did you see the collage she gave us out in the entrance hall?'

A dispute over a model train suddenly escalated and the toy became a weapon. Dean and Jennie escaped during the stern lecture that ensued. Dean had not resented Jennie's success with Helena. After all, they'd met before. 'Good job you knew that kid who was howling.'

Jennie looked startled. 'Never seen her before.'

'But you knew . . .'

'They all had name tapes on their jumpers.'

Dean made for the car. Not to worry. He was good at frightening things out of people.

Everyone reported to Browne's office at six thirty as requested. Browne looked round at their red noses and grey faces. He smelt their wet clothes and noted that both Dean and Carson were sneezing. Holding out his hands for their written reports, he piled them, unread, on his desk. 'Enough's enough.'

They looked at him hopefully. 'You've each got thirty seconds to put the rest of us in the picture, then you're free till tomorrow morning to do what you like. I expect that, like Jerry and me, you'll go to the pub but I recommend Richard and Robin at least to give serious consideration to an early night.'

The reports were snappy and none exceeded the time limit Browne had allowed. No one ventured a question to hold things up and their departure was swift and silent. Each of them dreaded making the remark that might have changed the CI's mind.

'Afraid a complete night off doesn't apply to us, Jerry.' Hunter, who had supposed as much, was philosophical. 'We won't get smashed but I intend to have rather more than a token pint, so no cars. We'll go to the Shorn Lamb which is the nearest decent pub to my place. Hannah has already offered to drive you home if you walk back with me.'

'It's the silly season, is it?' Browne looked blank. 'You said the other day that coffee was for routine inquiries and ale was for producing wild ideas when sensible ones are getting us nowhere. You've justified the booze-up. I suppose you can't make out a brilliant case for charging it up to expenses?'

Browne grinned and waved Hunter to his armchair as each of them reached for a file from the pile on the desk. By eight o'clock they had familiarized themselves with the state of the case and installed themselves in the snug at Browne's local. Hunter found it cheerful and comfortable and honestly modern. It was lit by undisguised electric bulbs and no attempt had been made to convince the customers that the plastered ceiling was supported by beams.

The arrangements were convenient for their purpose. Along one wall, small tables stood in a series of bay windows. Sitting at one, you could conduct a private conversation, but, facing into the room, you could still feel yourself part of what was going on. Hunter sat on the upholstered bench that ran round an empty bay. Browne considered joining him but then pulled up a stool. 'If I've something to lean my back against, I'll go to sleep. Besides, when I fall off this, you'll know that if you buy me any more beer you'll be holding up the investigation.'

Hunter wondered if this was a hint that he was in the chair, but Browne got up to stand the first round as was his custom. As Hunter waited, two men came in, one with flaxen hair and Scandinavian good looks, the other dark, smaller and slighter. The fair man handed a bank note to his companion, then settled himself at a table for two in the opposite corner from their alcove. The dark man joined Browne at the bar.

Hunter's hackles rose. There had been something about the way the money had been offered and accepted. The manner of the man at the bar had reminded Hunter of a child waiting for ice-cream money from a parent. Why should one young man be subsidizing another? Hunter rebuked his own disapproval. Perhaps, it was the fair man's turn to pay, but, in that case, why wasn't he at the bar? He wasn't disabled. Perhaps the dark man was out of work – but giving him money for drink was surely more humiliating for him than just placing a glass in front of him.

Hunter wondered why it was necessary for him to analyse

171

this relationship. The two blokes had only come in for an innocent drink. Maybe he was the prude that the rest of the team gave him the doubtful credit for being. Maybe they were right to think he was obsessed. The man at the bar turned to catch the eye of his friend and gave him a sweet smile. Hunter clenched his fists. There wasn't much doubt now. He turned away, consciously relaxed his fingers and endeavoured to concentrate on the brimming glass he was being handed.

Browne gave a contented sigh. 'Let's just enjoy this one. We'll get down to business with the second. Tell me what Tim and Fliss are getting up to these days.'

Hunter grinned. 'Fliss is busy making maximum capital out of her birthday. After the fiasco of a party that we had last year to which she invited practically the whole of her class, we suggested that this time she should ask just two or three friends to tea and we'd take them to Leeds to see *Coppelia*. She jumped at that idea but now she's trying to twist Annette's arm to organize a party as well.'

'And Tim?'

Hunter shrugged. 'He's all right, passed Grade Four on his oboe, can't wait for the cricket season.' His voice lacked the fondness and pride it usually held when he talked about his children and Browne realized that the sergeant's attention was held by something out of his own view across the room.

'What are you staring at?'

Hunter's face was grim. 'They're adults, sure enough, and they're most certainly consenting, but since when has the snug in the Shorn Lamb been "in private"?'

Browne managed a casual-seeming glance at the two men who were now exhibiting a rather obvious degree of enthusiasm for each other's company. He drew in his breath sharply and answered Hunter's enquiring expression in an undertone. 'The taller, fair one is Alistair Fenton. I saw him when he came to the station to speak to Nigel.'

Hunter cheered up. 'Good. Are we going to have a word with them?'

Browne shook his head. 'No, I said we were going to enjoy our first glass.' He chuckled at Hunter's frustration. 'When we do talk to him, it won't be to take him to task about his sexual habits. Still, perhaps if we could manage to drift within earshot of the loving couple it won't spoil the taste of your beer too much.'

'Is the other one his business partner?'

Browne looked again. 'No. I haven't met him but Bellamy said Sykes is a tall thin chap with red hair.' He got up, glass in hand, and strolled over to examine a half-completed diagram that recorded the results of the games so far played in an area darts tournament. He spoke over his shoulder as Hunter followed him, raising his voice very slightly. 'When I was a nipper, I used to look for my dad's name on here, and now I'm looking for my lad's. It makes you think.'

Hunter spluttered into his beer. Browne's father was a retired steel worker who lived in Sheffield and always had and Alex, his son, was at university in Durham. The two officers glued their eyes to the bright green chart, both grateful for their keen hearing. Though much of the two young men's conversation was trivial it was not altogether disappointing. It became clear that Alistair Fenton had made himself responsible for the dark man's domestic arrangements which, in several respects, were found wanting. Fenton was apologetic, and conciliatory, the other petty and ungrateful.

'I just can't manage it yet, Carl.'

'You've got all the mod cons at your own place!'

Fenton sounded almost tearful. 'But I have to. Tish knows how much goes into my account. He expects to see me spending some of it.'

'You're ashamed of me. If you weren't you'd take me to live there.' He pushed back his chair and left in prima donna fashion, leaving his coat draped over a chair. Fenton slipped into his own before grabbing it and hastening after him in just the manner Carl had intended.

Hunter made as if to follow. 'Aren't we picking them up?'

'Not yet.' Browne drained his glass. 'We know where to find the Viking hunk and, as long as he's getting his bread buttered, the other one won't be far away.' He pushed the glass into Hunter's hand. 'Go and do your stuff with those and then we've got work to do.'

He shook his head sadly at Hunter's retreating figure.

173

Having discovered that Alistair Fenton was homosexual would perhaps not quite convince his sergeant that he was also a killer. Nevertheless, if he were proved to be so, the fact would give Hunter great satisfaction. He would consider it entirely fitting. A good many of Browne's questions concerning Fenton had been answered by the scrap of conversation they had overheard. The bank manager had revealed, as the team had confidently expected, that Fenton's current bank account had been credited twenty-two months ago with Mr Kelly's cheque for twenty-six thousand, five hundred pounds. This sum had almost immediately been transferred to a business account in the name of Alistair Fenton Designs with himself and Stanley Sykes as joint signatories.

The business account had grown with what must have been gratifying speed and twelve months ago it had begun to pay each month an equal sum, generous but not extravagant, into the personal accounts of the two partners. Sykes' account was now very healthy but Browne had been surprised to find that Fenton's was overdrawn almost to the maximum amount that the bank would allow to one in his circumstances. Now they knew where all the money had gone. Unless . . . There was always the possibility that the contrasting state of the two bank accounts represented a spot of blackmail, based on the relationship with Carl or some shady dealing in Alistair's inglorious past that they hadn't dug up yet.

Browne wondered how much Stella Fenton knew or suspected about her son's activities and his financial situation, and how far she was prepared to protect him. To the point of disposing of her mother? Mitchell had been prepared to float the idea. But, if he was right, where did Thomas come into it? What had the little boy learned that had sealed his fate when he revealed it in an innocent telephone call?

Richard and Jennie seemed not to have made much headway at the school. Several people admitted to having seen Mrs Quentin and Thomas arrive and some remembered that they'd spoken to them. Browne was puzzled. Even though the teacher had never enquired for him, was it possible that the children had been so lost in their afternoon activities that not one of them had wondered about him? Browne supposed that it was. Small children had their priorities constantly overridden for reasons quite beyond their comprehension. Some grown-up, they had assumed, had had other plans for Thomas. And, unfortunately, their assumption had been right.

For another two hours, the two officers sorted through the pieces of information at their disposal. Towards eleven, they called a halt and set out for Browne's home, thankful that the rain had stopped and each privately hoping that his degree of inebriation was not apparent to the other in his gait or manner.

'Early start tomorrow?' Hunter enquired after they had both successfully survived the head-spinning effects of sudden cold fresh air on an intoxicated brain. 'What's on the agenda?'

'Well, since Carson's traced Mrs Hill's taxi driver, I think it's time to ask her why she hasn't told us about her trip to Southlands Drive on Monday, especially as it skirts one side of St Helen's House. And I suppose I'd better make you happy by bringing Alistair Fenton in. There's certainly a fair amount we need to discuss with him.'

He yawned extensively. 'It's no good, Jerry. I can't think any more tonight. We're pretty second-rate coppers compared with Rory Alleyn and Adam Dalgliesh. I haven't had much time to spend with them recently but I can distinctly remember an occasion when each of them worked right through the night, got clobbered on the head and still was in a state the next morning to run rings round his subordinates. I only feel as though I've had a bang on the head!'

Hunter gave the comparison the consideration his CI expected for it. 'They didn't drink on the job, sir,' he said after some seconds, 'or, if they did, no one told Miss Marsh or Ms James about it.'

Chapter Sixteen

At Saturday morning's briefing, Browne and Hunter inspected one another for signs of a hangover. Finding none and having sent the other officers about their business, Browne asked Hunter to collect a car and bring it to the front door.

Hunter was approving. 'Are we going to pick him up?'

'Who, Fenton? No, we're going to see Mrs Hill, see if we can shake her up a bit.'

'Shake her?'

Browne nodded. 'She's altogether too calm and collected. We'll pull rank and see if, just for once, we can get her to say more than she means to.'

'You should take Petty instead of me then.'

'I didn't say we'd put the frighteners on her!'

Hunter laughed and went downstairs to collect a key. Two unexpected phone calls, one fairly lengthy, meant a fifteen-minute wait for Hunter. He spent it jotting down an idea for a new book that had occurred to him as he drove Fliss to school. This was not a usual part of his daily routine and he had observed as he parked a good twenty yards away, the nearest he could get, and walked with her to her classroom door, that a good many more parents had been awakened to an awareness of their children's vulnerability by the death of Thomas Hill.

Browne appeared and was apologetic. Hunter, having unburdened himself of his new plot, was forgiving. By now the rush to work was over and the journey to Pamela Hill's house was easy. Everyone's children, they hoped, were safely at school, their accompanying mothers had returned and morning shoppers were still waiting at home to see if the weather would improve. Mrs Hill's suburban road was deserted. The pavement on her side was edged with a row of blossoming cherry trees. Browne contemplated them through the slanting rain, gaudy but dejected, like a chorus line giving the performance of its life to an empty house.

He dismissed his fancy and followed Hunter along a path through a garden vandalized by a week of wind and hail. Pamela Hill was not surprised to see them. 'I know what you've come for. I gave DC Mitchell the impression that I would talk about Thomas's father, but I did that on the spur of the moment to prevent him from upsetting Sonia any further. I credited him with less sensitivity than he proved to have. Since I'm not sure but only suspect, I've decided after all to say nothing. I can only tell you that the person I sometimes think it might be would have no motive whatsoever for harming Thomas. As far as I know, he's never even seen him.'

She had delivered this obviously prepared statement as they all stood just inside the hall by the front door, but, when the two officers showed no signs of departing, she led the way to the sitting-room and invited them to make themselves comfortable. As Browne immersed himself in the photographs of European castles in the book lying on the coffee-table, Hunter supposed he was to take over. He refused the proffered chair and paced the room, avoiding various piles of books and papers. 'What we've come to ask, primarily,' he began, 'is why you got into a taxi at three twenty-five on Monday afternoon and travelled to an address in Southlands Drive which is less than fifty yards from St Helen's House. And, having gone there, we'd like to know why you didn't tell us about it.'

She nodded as though he had told her something rather than asked it. 'I'd better tell you the whole story. I'm glad you're the one who's asking.' She walked over to the window and stood with her back to them both, looking out. 'My husband died as the delayed result of an accident on a building site. It paralysed him from the waist down. We'd always had a very good physical relationship and I found it very frustrating when it was – er . . . discontinued. So, I had an extra-marital relationship, an affair, if you like.'

Browne had the impression that she had anticipated having to tell this story and prepared this speech too.

'You're going to demand names and numbers, aren't you? Well, he didn't do much that he needs to be ashamed of so I might as well give them. He's Owen Davies and you have his present address from your helpful taxi driver. He was more committed to me than I was to him. For me, it was just a physical release, that and the offer of the company of somebody who wasn't seriously clinically depressed.'

She turned from the window and they saw that the self-possession that Browne had wanted to disturb was destroyed. 'Sonia found out. In the space of just a few months the father she idolized was first physically wrecked, then psychologically damaged and finally betrayed by her mother.'

'So she was getting back at you?'

'Possibly. I'd prefer that explanation. I fear, though, that she may have been forced into the relationship that produced Tom as the price for the man keeping his mouth shut. She didn't hold back from telling me exactly what she thought of me but she was terrified of anyone else knowing in case her father got to hear.'

Hunter was horrified. 'You mean your . . . the man you're telling us about was also sleeping with Sonia?'

She half smiled as though drawing comfort from the thought that there might be a possibility worse than what she believed to be the true state of affairs. 'I think Sonia was seduced by Owen's son, Nevin. Owen is amusing company, quick and intelligent and quite handsome even now, but he's weak and lazy. His wife left him years ago and neither of them was much concerned for their boy.

'I was very sorry for Nevin, but he's a nasty piece of goods. At the time, Sonia insisted that she couldn't name the father, that there were several possibilities. If she said that to protect her child from Nevin's claims, it was a waste of her reputation. He certainly wasn't interested in Thomas – but posing as the dissolute daughter was one of her ways of punishing me. I

178

don't think she was believed even by the people who would have liked to believe the worst.'

Browne wondered if this was a reference to her sister.

'Obviously I owed it to Sonia to offer her and Thomas a home and I would have done, even though, when I began writing seriously, I found him a great distraction. Barbara was our salvation. Sonia wanted to leave home. We'd patched up our relationship and she'd begun to understand both my temptation and my very great regret. She still thought, though, that after a respectable interval, I might take up with Owen again. So did he.'

'And eventually, you did?'

She shook her head. 'No, but he hangs around and can't understand that whatever it was I needed I get now by writing. I could never bring myself to tell him that I'd just been using him during a stressful period in my own development. It's only partly self-preservation. It wouldn't do much for his self-esteem, would it?'

'So, what happened on Monday?'

She sat down, grey faced. Hunter was alarmed, remembering that she had been out of hospital less than three days and that in the last week her mother and her grandson had both been killed. 'I had plenty of time to think during my stay in hospital – for the first time in years. I decided that I had to be brutally honest with Owen and make a clean break. I could have written to him, I suppose, but I would have found that too easy. Making myself face him was a sort of penance.'

She turned exclusively to Hunter. 'So, a fine person I am to write books about aliens who come and expose human defilement, greed and stupidity. Or perhaps I'm the best person. I certainly know a lot about it.'

Hunter said, soberly, 'We neither of us exclude ourselves from the criticisms we level at humanity in general.'

She turned to Browne. 'Have you read your sergeant's book, Chief Inspector?'

Hunter squirmed and she immediately apologized. 'I didn't mean to embarrass you. I was trying to change the subject. I wanted a break from wondering how many of the terrible events of this week have been triggered off by my heedless selfishness.'

The rain had stopped again when they walked out to the car. 'That was all very interesting and probably all true.' Hunter took the wheel and moved off along the wet road. 'But it doesn't mean she couldn't have called in at St Helen's and disposed of her mother. Where now?'

Browne wagged his head reprovingly. 'Don't try to put me off. What's the subject of this master work?'

Hunter grinned. 'I thought we'd agreed long ago that there was only one literary genre worthy of our consideration.'

Browne tried to clear the inside of the windscreen to the detriment of a clean handkerchief. 'I trust I'm not going to lose my invaluable sergeant because he's defected to his fictional counterparts.'

A serious enquiry had been implied. Hunter gave an honest answer. 'I flirted with the idea but I decided the force needed people like me to counterbalance people like Benny.'

Browne fished for the peppermints he had left in the glove compartment. 'I'm obviously not giving you enough to do. OK, let's pick up the handsome Viking.'

Sykes was working at his dining-room table. He had an office downstairs that had been intended as the place where he would produce his drawings, lavishly equipped now, in their prosperity, with adjustable drawing boards and a myriad technical gimmicks. Sykes however preferred the more homely surroundings of his flat, where he could stop and drink coffee whilst conflicting ideas fought their own battle in his imagination until one emerged triumphant.

He paused now, enjoying the pleasure he always derived from the soothing austerity of the room. The walls were flat painted plaster, each hung with only one picture. The couch, constructed to last and inherited from his father, had been re-covered in plain cream linen. Its back was draped with his favourite of Sonia's tapestries, the room's only significant area of colour, vibrant with the hues of exotic birds.

In an hour or so he was scheduled to lunch with Alistair and discuss how far they could fulfil the following year's requirements of various up-market chain stores in the nearby towns. He shuddered at the thought of the dual onslaught of Alistair's cooking and his 'designer' decorations. Until recently, Alistair's hospitality had run to meals in various trendy restaurants. He showed little aptitude for or enjoyment of home cooking now he had taken it up and Sykes supposed and hoped that the phase would soon pass.

Where the hell was Alistair, anyway? Why hadn't he been here when the police came pounding on the door? He must realize that with all this trouble going on in his family they'd be bound to want to talk to him. To be missing whenever they called was asking them to become suspicious. He sighed, considered the drawing in front of him, and added another minute line. Please God, Alistair would be sober when he did condescend to turn up. He was getting a bit too fond of the hard stuff these days.

He put his pen down, firmly. The design was finished. If he elaborated it further he'd spoil it. He looked at it wistfully. Terry, downstairs in the workshop, was waiting for it, but Sykes had an impulse to lock it in his filing cabinet till Terry and his mate had gone home, or, better still, to give both of them the rest of the morning, and thereby the weekend off. Then he himself could translate the precisely penned lines to the materials they were planned for – though, as a craftsman, there was no skill in his own fingers that was lacking in theirs. What did he think he could do for this particular piece that they couldn't?

He smiled to himself, remembering a time when his raw materials had not always been the purest and had sometimes proved recalcitrant. He had welcomed the difficulty, making a virtue of necessity, letting his imagination work on a small flaw until he had incorporated it into the piece. Those were his real achievements, when he worked with the interesting idiosyncrasies of a particular lump of rock. The designs he did now were too theoretical. He was imposing himself on the gems instead of letting them speak to him.

181

He sighed and rang down for Terry to come and fetch the finished drawing. Usually he took it himself but, today, he couldn't bear to see Terry and young Carl doing the work he longed to do himself. He'd become a victim of his own success.

Of course, he could branch out in other ways. He certainly wasn't short of ideas, but he was restricted under the present arrangements by whether or not they had commercial potential. Nowadays, he wasted most of his time. He was merely going through the academic process of producing rings, brooches and earrings just slightly different from those he had sold already. One rich customer had an equally rich friend who wanted something 'just like it' but just sufficiently different for it to be 'still exclusive'. What fools they were, but he was the biggest fool for pandering to them. They left him no space, no chance for his imagination to run free any more amongst his chosen materials.

He'd had the ghost of a new idea whilst he was talking to that policeman the other day. He'd liked him – Bellamy, wasn't it? He hadn't shared his own vision but he had looked around him and seen things and commented on them honestly. What about making whole pictures? Much smaller, of course, but a bit like Sonia's collages, only using stones and metal. He knew what subject he'd start on. He'd been reading that book of Sonia's mother's that he'd borrowed from the library. He had no wish just to illustrate Mrs Hill's description. It had been of the moon – its own moon – rising over a planet, and odd phrases had struck chords in his own brain, had begun the painful process of imaginative creation.

He'd read of turbulent water and tiny islands, and, suddenly, he had seen them in terms of filigree silver, gold wire, amethysts, lots of lapis, of course, and bits of garnet and coral. And an opal, exactly the right opal, for the luminous moon. Perhaps some crystal for the breakers. No! Crystal wasn't right. Too flashy. He wanted to make something full of luminosity and rich, subdued gleaming. He might have to incorporate some dull glass if he was planning a piece of any size. In fact, it would make a useful background. There was a lot you could do with glass.

His mind played with some of the possibilities now. He wasn't sure about it yet. He wasn't going to tell Alistair about any of it though. Alistair would tell all their customers that he was 'branching out', and, before he knew where he was, he'd have orders for his new, even more exclusive 'limited edition miniatures'.

The doorbell rang. He took up his drawing and handed it to Terry, waiting outside. He closed the door and wandered into the kitchen to make coffee, still thinking hard. In their business, the work of the real artist had been lost. He had become a 'designer' and downstairs, they employed two 'skilled craftsmen'. Being an artist wasn't quite the same as either but it incorporated both. His work was suffering because he didn't handle his materials any more. He no longer had time to play with the little coloured pebbles until he'd seen all their possibilities.

He decided that, this very morning, he would contact his old supplier and ask for a cheap bagful of the bits and pieces he used to make do with before Alistair won all his money. He got them for peanuts because they were 'flawed'. What a description when they only bore the marks of processes mightier than those of any machine in any workshop. They'd acquired their faults from the Great Creator. He laughed at himself as he finished his coffee, realizing how sentimental and self-important he'd become. Nevertheless, he knew now the direction his work should follow in the next few months. He'd made a decision and he was happy again, in one department of his life, at least.

There would be no business side to this new project. Of that he was determined. He welcomed and fell into the old familiar concentration in which he doodled, sketched and jotted semiconsciously. When the sound of a car brought him out of his trance, some time later, he found the basic design of his proposed picture already mapped out on the paper in front of him, needing only a little refinement, some delicious planning of fine detail which he'd leave to be dictated by his materials as he used to. Promising himself an hour inspecting the equipment in the workroom in the afternoon when Terry and Carl had gone home, he strolled to the window and looked out.

Oh, God, Alistair had been drinking. From the way he was fumbling with his car lock, he must be at least tipsy. Thank goodness his precious car seemed to be undented. Why on earth, Sykes asked himself, couldn't he get on with his own life and work, uninvolved with all the mess and confusion this relationship brought him? Why the hell did he have to love Alistair?

Chapter Seventeen

Sykes went out on to the shared landing as Alistair stumbled up the stairs. 'My kettle's on. You'd better come in and have some black coffee and we'd better forget lunch. The police want to see you again. They were here this morning, wanting to know about your car and whether you took it out on Thursday afternoon. Did you?'

Alistair shrugged. 'They won't believe I can't remember. I'll tell them I was with you.'

Sykes shook his head. 'You can't. I was working here when they came looking for you. What on earth are you doing with yourself lately? It's a month or more since I've been able to trace you except when you come back unexpectedly. Where were you on Thursday, anyway?'

'Does it matter?'

'Not to me,' Sykes said, untruthfully, 'but it will to that cop, Bellamy, and his cronies.'

Alistair settled in Sykes's kitchen rocking chair and accepted a mug of coffee. 'Are they coming back, then?'

'They didn't say so, but if you've any sense you'll go to them and tell them whatever they want to know.'

Alistair rocked himself and avoided Sykes's eyes. 'I don't feel well. I might go later on.'

Sykes's patience was fast running out. 'You won't feel any different till you stop pouring alcohol down your throat faster than your system can process it. Go now!'

Alistair pouted, childishly. 'You're getting really boring. Did you finish the design for Mrs Crossley's pendant?'

'Terry's got it. Why do you ask? Is she getting impatient?'

185

Alistair shrugged. 'She was just asking how it's coming along.'

Sykes asked, genuinely wanting to know, 'Don't you feel stupid when someone wants to discuss a design with you and you don't know the first thing about it?' Receiving no answer, he pushed on, 'Don't you think it's about time we dropped this silly charade?'

Alistair giggled. 'I just plead my artistic temperament. You, the artist, haven't got one, but the one I've invented sends the ladies wild. It's our best advertisement.'

Sykes was angry. 'No it isn't, it's ridiculous. One of these days you'll see one of my pieces round a dolly-bird's neck and fail to recognize it. Then you'll come unstuck.'

Alistair went on rocking and smiling. 'No, I won't. I'll just say the only reality for me is the design I'm actually engaged on. All else is nothing!' He struck a theatrical pose, then dropped back in the chair. 'Anyway, I don't have anything to do with dolly-birds.'

Sykes refilled Alistair's mug, then wandered back to the window. 'Drink that, and then, if you don't get down to the station, I won't design any more jewellery at all.'

'What on earth do you mean?' Alistair jerked forward, the prospect going a fair way towards sobering him.

Sykes drew back behind the curtains. 'There isn't time to explain now, and you won't have to go. Your visitors are back again. You'd better go and let them in.'

Irritated by having to make yet another visit to pick up Alistair Fenton, Hunter had not been much mollified by what they had managed to get out of him. He had freely admitted receiving a phone call from Thomas Hill on Thursday morning.

'He was trying to cadge a ride in your new car?'

He'd nodded, sullenly. 'What's wrong with that? The kid was crazy about sports cars. No harm in giving him a spin.'

'You took him?'

He'd shaken his head, quickly. 'Didn't get much chance, did I? But I would have done.'

'Did you tell him to keep it a secret?'

'What?' Fenton had looked startled and then worried.

'He told Mrs Shaw he had a secret,' Browne had explained, patiently. 'Would that have been it?'

'It might have been. He was crazy about secrets too.'

'Did you talk about keeping the car ride a secret?'

He'd shrugged. 'We might have done.'

Suddenly inspired, Hunter had asked, 'Was he so keen because the car was new? How long had you had it?'

Fenton had been proud of his car, happy to talk about it. 'Just over a week. It's the T-bar version. It's got an acoustic control induction system, tilt-adjustable steering-wheel – and an eight-speaker stereo . . .'

'When had Thomas seen it?'

The question stemmed Fenton's fanatical torrent of technical details and his answer was offhand. 'I didn't know he had. He told me he'd seen it on Monday afternoon from the bus . . .' He'd stopped in confusion and Browne had finished his sentence for him.

' . . . when it passed St Helen's House whilst you were "visiting" your grandmother.'

'It's one thing to have our man and another to prove he's guilty.' Hunter was prowling round Browne's office whilst they reviewed the situation. 'What's he doing now?'

'Cooling his heels in an interview room with a uniformed constable and drinking coffee.'

'If it's from the canteen, it might bring him to heel all on its own, but, seriously, if Carl Sanderson agrees that they were together all Thursday we'll have to let him go after thirty-six hours.'

'Unless the lab strikes lucky with the car. He said that Thomas had never been in it so any trace of him will clinch things.' Browne grinned. 'He was so anxious to describe all its virtues, you'd have thought he'd have been more pleased that we want to examine it in detail.'

Hunter paused in his perambulations and sat down. 'Who's gone to see Sanderson?'

Browne grinned more widely. 'Richard. I want Sanderson

scared. Nigel's gone back to Sykes with a different set of questions. Most of the others are on the knocker again.'

'But can't we hold him longer for Mrs Norman? He told us a pack of lies about last Monday and now he's admitted he was at St Helen's at the right time, more or less. Did we manage to pin the medics down to a more precise time for the injection?'

Browne shook his head. 'Just a lot of ifs and buts about the amount of the drug, the amount of food Mrs Norman had eaten, her individual metabolism and so on. It boiled down again to the fact that she was alive when Debbie put her to bed at about four o'clock and she was dead when Dr Pedlar certified her so at about half-past nine. Then there's all the stuff in various people's statements about when radiators went on and off. Don't forget what a hot-house an old people's home is.'

Hunter looked glum. 'I suppose if the inquiry goes on long enough, we might find they all lied to us and they all called at St Helen's.'

'That's certainly what his brief will say.'

'He's called one?'

Browne shook his head. 'Not yet. He's still listening to Fowler being sympathetic.'

Hunter chuckled. 'I've heard Dave Fowler doing his spiel before. "In every enquiry we have to inconvenience so many quite blameless people. But I'm sure you understand that justice has to be seen to be done." ' His assumption of Fowler's fatherly manner and south Midlands accent was clever.

'Fenton Junior didn't strike me as being the most intelligent suspect in the case. I intend to keep him talking to someone as long as we have him. He's quite liable to give himself away further, and, if he knows anything to anyone else's discredit, he's likely to drop them in it.'

Browne's telephone rang. After a moment, he handed it over to his sergeant. 'For you.'

Hunter listened and then covered the mouthpiece. 'Our GP is downstairs, mine and Annette's. He wants some advice without making an official report.'

'You've put him up to it, haven't you? Anything to get out of going through this lot yet again.'

Taking this as permission, Hunter made for the door. 'Never mind. I saw Benny coming in whilst I was admiring your view. He can help you and when I ask for coffee for Dr Haigh and me I'll send a couple of cups up here.'

He was not sure whether his session with Denis Haigh would be more or less tedious than his CI's with the already much studied case file. Haigh had overseen in his medical capacity the birth and rearing of both Hunter's children and the sergeant knew that he would not have come today on a matter that was not sufficiently serious to interest them. He knew too, however, that Haigh was near retiring now, that his younger partners considered his ideas somewhat old fashioned and that, out of genuine concern for him, they made sure his case load was light. He was likely to make the most of his problem and to take his time explaining it.

Haigh stirred sugar into his coffee with enthusiasm. 'Lethal substances, so they tell me, both sugar and caffeine. Banned the caffeine three times over this morning, one case of palpitations, one of insomnia and one chronic anxiety. Afraid I don't practise what I preach nowadays. Please yourself when you get to my age.' Hunter hoped the doctor's aversion to personal pronouns was not going to make his evidence too confusing and wondered why he was being glared at.

'Ought to keep off it yourself with your temperament and stress of occupation. Still, must admit you're looking a lot better than I expected considering the sorry state you got yourself into over Christmas.'

Hunter smiled sycophantically. 'I'm as good as new, thanks to the expert care I received. It seems you have a problem yourself?'

Haigh looked offended. 'Been talking to my partners? Convinced you that I'm failing, have they? Wishful thinking, that's all it is. Never better! Bit slower, maybe, but nothing that my experience doesn't compensate for.'

'You look in the pink,' Hunter assured him, 'but haven't you brought me a problem?'

Haigh dropped his irascible senior-partner pose and became serious. 'I'm not sure what I should do about it. You see, it depends on an impression, a memory, and I haven't kept the evidence, not knowing I'd need it.'

Hunter realized that Haigh had become considerably less clearly articulate even since they had met in Haigh's professional capacity three months ago. Perhaps his partners were right. 'Could you go back to the beginning?'

The doctor nodded and tried harder. 'I was setting out with my wife to visit relatives and on the way we were to deliver a prescription to an elderly patient. Save him coming out in this inclement weather.' Hunter, long suffering, waited. 'Great gust of wind removed my hat and blew the prescription out of my hand. Both hat and scrip landed in a puddle. Thought to myself, how odd. Same thing happened to what-d'you-call-it a couple of weeks ago.' He shrugged. 'Suppose it's not strange at all, really. With the weather we've been having for the last fortnight, the surprising thing is that half the prescriptions we've written didn't end up the same way.'

Hunter knew that to interrupt with another question would delay the climax of the tale still further. He restrained himself by shading in alternate sections of a complicated pattern he'd drawn in his notebook.

'Put my foot on it quickly and fished it out. Passing schoolboy rescued my hat. Wasn't any use any more – the prescription, I mean. Everything I'd written was just a pale blue wash. See!' He fished in his pocket and thrust the damp piece of paper at Hunter. It was as described. Only the patient's name and address remained, written in the top right-hand corner in his receptionist's childish, backward-sloping but very legible hand.

Haigh allowed Hunter a few seconds to examine it and then explained, 'The name and address survived because Susan uses one of those nasty, cheap-jack biro things. Suddenly thought to myself, "That's funny," though it wasn't really funny at all. It was a serious matter.'

'You're telling me the same thing happened to someone else?'

'That's right, or so I was told. Patient came into my consulting room and asked about innoculations required for entry to Mexico. Had to go and look it up in the back office. Must have appropriated a blank prescrption form whilst I was gone. Must be more careful in future. Anyway, as I was saying, patient came with the same story. Prescription fished out of a pocket before going into the chemist's. Completely washed out when it came out of the puddle. Sounded quite plausible. The spoiled prescription was handed back to me so I wrote another without a qualm.'

'So why are you worried now?'

'Because I'm sure now that the form that was brought back to me was completely washed out, even the patient's name and address which should have been written in Susan's nasty black biro and should have still been there.'

Hunter saw the light, at last. 'So you're prescribing for an addict who's trying to get extra supplies by forging a prescription, then washing out his amateur efforts and getting you to write another genuine one? What drugs are involved?'

Haigh shook his head, looking puzzled. 'It wasn't that sort of drug. It was for syringes and ampoules of insulin.'

Browne had invited Mitchell into his office for a further study of the house to house reports and the pair sat sustained by the contents of two large mugs as they read, studied and occasionally conferred. The current silence had lasted half an hour when Mitchell suddenly sat up with an exclamation. 'Fool!' He struck his forehead with the heel of his hand in case Browne thought the castigation was aimed at him.

Browne waited for an explanation but Mitchell merely asked, 'Is it all right if I use this phone?' Browne nodded permission and his DC dialled urgently and identified himself. 'It's about Shaun's badge.'

Browne listened as the voice on the other end of the line, presumably Mrs McElroy's, quacked. Mitchell's questions were terse. 'When did he get it?' More quacking. 'He told me he put it on Thomas's jumper. When exactly did he do that?' He thanked her, replaced the receiver and faced Browne excitedly.

'Shaun gave his badge to Thomas the afternoon he died.

191

That's what I'd understood him to mean but it was worth checking. He'd only got it on his birthday the day before. That evening no one knew where Thomas was. According to the family, everyone thought he'd been at school all afternoon. Mrs Quentin left him in the cloakroom and went home, Sonia was at school all day, all the others were about their legitimate business. But, when we asked what he was wearing, Sonia said he had the badge on his sweater. How did she know?'

Suddenly there was a rap on the door and Hunter came in without waiting for an invitation. 'Barbara Quentin is diabetic,' he announced. 'Dr Haigh says Sonia usually collected her medication for her. She forged a prescription for insulin!'

With Mitchell at the wheel, the three officers lopped two minutes off the time it usually took to drive to Hepple Lane. They found Barbara Quentin there, looking bewildered. 'Sonia's left. I've just got back and found a note in the kitchen and Sonia and all her belongings are gone. She just says she can't stay here now without Thomas. That's understandable, I suppose. Everything's here to remind her . . .'

'The note,' Browne demanded. She made as if to hand it to him but instinct made him cut in front of her and handle it with tweezers. 'Not,' he remarked to Hunter, 'that it's likely to be a forgery, or to have any prints but Sonia's and Mrs Quentin's, but we'd better go through the motions.' He turned to Mrs Quentin. 'You weren't expecting this? She hadn't said anything?'

She shook her head. 'I hope she hasn't done anything silly. Shall I ring Pam?'

The officers conferred briefly whilst she stood watching and trying to make some sense out of the situation. 'What has someone got against this family? I'm sure the letter's in Sonia's writing but maybe someone forced her to write it. I can see that living here now is painful for her but I wouldn't have expected her to go off like this without any discussion. Pam brought her up to have better manners.'

Hunter wondered how she would judge their own manners as they departed without ceremony having instructed her to ring the station immediately if Sonia herself or anyone else should contact her on the subject of the girl's disappearance.

'The mother?' Browne's eyebrows rose interrogatively. Hunter was undecided. Mitchell shook his head. 'No, the boyfriend.'

Chapter Eighteen

Sonia drew away from the traffic lights and turned right along-side the park. Everything had just about fitted into the car. She had managed to get her own clothes into just a couple of suitcases, except for those awful garments she'd had to wear for school to satisfy Mrs Costello. She wasn't going to need any of them again. Tish wouldn't expect her to waste her time at school any more. Most of what she'd earned she'd had to spend on her rent and the expenses for Thomas.

She would decide later what to do about all his things. Mum and Barbara had provided a good many of them, so she couldn't really claim them, but she didn't mind. It was as well not to have anything to go back for. She realized she was exceeding the speed limit and braked till the needle moved back to thirty. No one had the right to stop her moving house but there was no need to attract unwelcome attention by break-ing the law. In any case, it was developing into quite a beautiful afternoon. The Hepple Lane crocuses were over but the sun was shining and the daffodils on the steep bank that edged the park had buds like yellow cigars.

She wasn't concentrating on the scenery, though. She'd be able to finish her tapestry underwater scene in a week or so if she didn't have to go to school any more. The small one she'd done for the nursery had been a useful planning exercise. She'd realized as she worked at it that she had found a theme that suited her but she was using the wrong materials. What she had produced was fine for the children, but using wool to suggest wet surfaces was much more challenging. That long bare wall in Tish's hall would be just the place for it; no distractions and the light was exactly right.

194

She drove through the gateway, frowning at the intertwined initials, AFD, chiselled into one of the stone posts. That would have to be changed. As she put the car in neutral, she turned and gave the folded hessian an approving glance before she climbed out. It took up the whole of the back seat and spread out to cover the two suitcases on the floor in front of it. It was a good job the rest of her pieces were on a smaller scale and had fitted into the boot. She rang the doorbell.

Sykes, surrounded by 2H pencils and sheets of paper, was not pleased to be interrupted but he made himself smile when he saw who his visitor was. He felt uncomfortable and the false smile intensified his discomfort. 'How are you, Sonia?' What did one say to someone whose small son had just been murdered? Not that she looked in much need of the comforting phrases he was finding it difficult to frame.

She was looking about her at the front of the house. 'I shall have to do something about this unattractive area. You've made an effort with a couple of bushes, and, of course, business premises need car parking space, but it's a bit gloomy, not much of an advertisement.'

So, she wasn't ready to talk about the tragedy yet. He was not sure that this evasion was good for her but it made things easier for him. He stood back to let her in.

'Some window boxes at least and something on top of the wall that borders the street.'

'Yes, you're probably right. Alistair isn't here. He's down at the police station. God knows what he's telling them. You don't think he's really mixed up in this business in some way, do you?' He realized that he was talking to her as though she were not involved herself and ground to a halt in some embarrassment.

Sonia chattered on. 'My mother might not be a hundred per cent in favour of the new arrangements. Not that she's in any position to stand in judgement over anyone else but it always makes things pleasanter if there aren't family feuds to cope with, especially if Alistair's going to go on sharing the building for a bit. Though that shouldn't go on for too long. He doesn't contribute anything and the company can't go on subsidizing him and lover boy for ever.'

She perched on a hall chair and examined the plain wall opposite, measuring it with her eyes. 'Sometimes, I wonder if he really thinks you don't know about him and Carl, that he's gay, I mean. And he's quite convinced that you believe his story about the football pools.' She removed her coat and hung it on the hall stand, then sat on the corner of the telephone table to inspect the wall from a different angle. 'I could kick myself for suggesting anything about Gran's wretched book to Alistair. I could have found out all I needed to know from Tony without involving him and I'd certainly have had more sense than to put it up for auction in my own name. Still, I was only eighteen at the time. Perhaps I wouldn't have carried it off so well then as I know I could now.'

She smiled at him, having reached a decision. 'That wall's got to be the place for my under-sea tapestry. I shall make a positive showcase of this flat.' Her voice flattened. 'And there's no brat now to disturb your work. It was hard doing that for you. I took him down to those ruined cottages along by the canal. He'd found the spare syringes at the back of my drawer. Called them rockets. He wanted to ask Barbara if he could have some more to play at landing on the moon.

'I showed him the steps going down to the flooded cellar. I told him if he ever mentioned the rockets to anyone I'd push him down there and leave him. He thought I was joking.' Her hands gripped the edge of the table, white-knuckled and her voice rose in pitch though not in volume, so that she spoke in a strange high whisper. 'I pushed him forward towards the water to scare him a bit and, suddenly, he wasn't there any more. I couldn't pull him out. I couldn't see him, or even hear anything except water lapping the steps and some other children yelling over by the next row of houses.'

Her face was an expressionless mask as she sat silent for several seconds. Then she resumed in the flat tone. 'That's where Nevin took me. That's where he was conceived. If he had to die, it was the right place.'

Sykes's brain seemed to have broken in half. One part was tape-recording all that Sonia was saying, the other still grappling with the first of her horrifying revelations. 'Are you telling me that Alistair's not faithful to me, that he's got somebody else?'

Now, Sonia was brought up short. 'Someone else? Else? Don't be ridiculous, Tish. You aren't one of them!'

'I love Alistair. Surely you realized. Why else should I let him stay here?'

'But I love you.' At last the tears came. 'I've loved you ever since you first spoke to me. You love me too. You must.'

Sykes rose but had to reach for the back of a kitchen chair to steady himself. He spoke slowly and carefully, as though it were a physical effort to move his tongue and lips. 'I must make it quite clear to you that there is no place for you in either my personal or my artistic life. Yes, I am "one of them", a homosexual. I'm looking for neither a wife nor another business partner.'

He drew a long breath and there was silence of several seconds as each of them realized the chilling implications of the other's words. Sykes was the first to recover at least some of his self-possession. 'You aren't well, Sonia. Come into the kitchen and I'll make you some tea.'

She followed him obediently and watched him as, mind racing, he went through the motions of brewing tea. Had she just confessed to killing first her grandmother and then her son, and told him it was all for him? His mind rejected the question and raised another that he could cope with. 'One sugar and a dash of milk. That's right, isn't it? There's a packet of digestive biscuits in the cupboard behind you.'

He noticed, amazed, that the hand that passed her the cup was rock steady. What pretext could he find for shutting her in here whilst he phoned the police? She was sipping her tea and watching him over the rim of her cup. There was no key to the kitchen door and the main doors downstairs were unlocked front and back. 'If you're going to stay for a while, I'll bring some of your things in from the car.'

She shook her head, half smiling. 'There's no hurry.'

'Fair enough, but while you finish your tea, I'll start clearing my workroom a bit. I've got the sofa bed in there now.' He did not add that it also contained his telephone extension. She nodded and was rearranging the objects on the table as she allowed him to pass her.

He collected his belongings together a little more noisily than necessary, having pulled the door as nearly as possible shut without risking alerting her to the sound of the latch. He picked up the receiver, dialled and spoke. He had given his name but not his address when he felt the jab in the back of his neck and registered the hissing words. 'If I'm not having you, that little rat Alistair isn't either.'

What had she picked up? He kept several potential weapons in his table drawer. Raising his arm in automatic self-defence, he felt another prick on the inside of his elbow joint. He stayed conscious just long enough to register Browne's ring of his doorbell and the pounding of Mitchell's feet on the stairs.

Browne was not surprised to receive Mitchell's phone call. Deciding that speed was of the essence, they had dispensed with an ambulance and loaded the prostrate Sykes into the back of the car. The constable had enjoyed the delights, rare for him these days, of a journey to the Royal Infirmary with siren blaring and lights blazing.

'Sykes is going to be OK. They wouldn't let me see him but he's conscious and lucid. Presumably he'll give evidence but I imagine we've got enough without him. She's probably said enough to convict herself.'

'Fishing, Benny?'

'Yes, sir.'

'You'd better come and do it in my study with a glass in your hand.'

Needing no second invitation, Mitchell had presented himself within the half-hour, conscious of the privilege that was being extended to him. Though quite familiar with the rest of the house, he had penetrated only once before into the minute room under the stairs that Browne called his study. A dining chair had been squeezed in for him and Mitchell settled on it as comfortably as he could, regarding Hunter with mock concern. 'Is there room for a yard and a half of legs in that corner?'

198

'Watch it,' Browne warned him, 'you're not my acting sergeant this time. Still, you had a fair amount to do with nailing the lid on this case so we thought you had a right to know what we've got inside.'

Browne supplied him with a full glass and Hunter satisfied his curiosity. 'Jennie was off duty so we sent for Megan James again after you'd gone. She knew Sonia and she'd coped very well with her on Thursday. Sonia immediately went into catatonic mode again.'

Mitchell nodded. 'Do you think she's insane, clinically, I mean?'

Browne took a long swig at his glass and raised his shoulders in an exaggerated shrug. 'That, thank Heaven, isn't for us to decide. At least she's not denying everything and, with luck, in the morning she'll sign what Megan took down. She couldn't tell us enough.'

'There's no one so bitter as a woman scorned,' Hunter put in sententiously, 'for that particular reason. According to her, none of it was her fault. If Sykes had liked children I think she would have made a more serious effort to save the child when he fell into the water – if he did fall. We only have her word for it. Thomas had heard his mother telling Mrs Quentin that she'd be alone in the office that day so he risked ringing her. She grasped the opportunity to give him instructions to hide in a lavatory cubicle and then meet her behind the school. She had money to pay into the bank as her excuse if anyone saw her or if she was missed at school. And she considered she was doing the whole family a favour when she disposed of her grandmother.'

'What made her think Sykes was keen on her?' Mitchell was puzzled. 'He can't have given her any encouragement.'

'She first met him at a craft exhibition where he showed a great admiration for her work.' Browne collected their glasses for refilling. 'I gather she saw him as some sort of a father figure as well as husband material – a sponsor of her talent except that he hadn't got any money. She fixed that for him, unwisely involving her cousin. Alistair had done whatever she told him since the days when she did his homework for him to keep him out of trouble at school. She bailed him out of various scrapes at home too, according to her mother. Oh!'

'Something wrong?'

'Yes, the beer's running out. I'll just nip down the cellar and replenish supplies.'

The telephone rang as he opened the door. He answered it as he passed, calling over his shoulder, 'Benny! From Oxford. Ginny for you. Move yourself. If I know her, she'll only have one fifty-pence piece.' As he descended to the depths below his living-room he could hear Mitchell proposing dates for a possible visit to Oxford.

On the way back, his arms full, he kicked at the study door to be let in, noting that the conversation between the young people seemed less amicable. Benny was beginning to sound positively irate. Hunter, having opened the door, was obligingly relieving Browne of half his load when Mitchell, oblivious of them both, lost his temper completely. 'Best thing for everyone be damned! I've heard enough of that. I can feel completely redundant and our son can be born illegitimate just to allow you to prove that you can function perfectly well without me. Just so that we'll know, when you do take us on, the favours are all on one side . . . !'

By the time Browne's arms were free to shut the door there was little point in doing so. A less astute detective than Hunter would have been in full possession of the truth. The receiver banged down and the doorway was filled with twelve stones of furious fiancé. 'Thank you for your hospitality. I think I'd better go.'

As Hunter tried to work out in which direction it was safe to look, Browne deliberately caught his eye and grinned. 'To save you inventing sudden illness or baby-sitting problems, how about if I kick you out too? Come again when the atmosphere's more conducive to social chat.' Hunter departed thankfully.

Browne put two dirty glasses back on the tray and refilled his own. Before it was empty, the telephone rang again. Smiling to himself, he took his beer into the hall. 'Is Benny still there?' his daughter's voice demanded.

'No, he's on his way home, giving his car engine the hell he'd like to give you, judging by the way he shot off down the drive. Is it anything I can help with?' He waited for her put-down.

'Well, you can offer an opinion. By the way, Dad, can you afford a wedding?' She sounded quite diffident.

'We'll have a whip round at the station if I run a bit short.'

'I don't think a big white affair would be quite the thing but I wondered what Benny would think about cream.'

'You'd better ask him yourself. Personally, I think it would make him look bloody silly.' Not very witty, he had to admit, but better than getting too heavy. He had sense enough to know that the moment of capitulation was not the time for congratulations. He trusted Benny to know it too.

Sergeant Paul Taylor's appearance in court had been briefer than he'd expected. The OTL driver he'd booked had been satisfactorily heavily fined and his licence suitably endorsed. He'd take Jennie for an early evening drink when she came off shift in a few minutes. She wouldn't be expecting him but Bennett was on the desk and he never minded delivering messages. Taylor hung his key on the board, then strolled across to leave his note.

In front of Bennett on the shiny wooden counter were two neatly lettered cards. From one of them, the letters of his own name, as those of familiar words will, jumped out at him. He turned the card round to read it the right way up. *And when Paul had gathered a bundle of sticks and laid them on the fire, there came a viper out of the heat and fastened on his hand*. Acts 28.3.

Taylor grinned. 'The snake turned up yesterday, still in the car. We think it got between the back seat frame and the boot lining. I'd been wondering why the joker had stopped. Have you found out who was doing it, then?'

The grin was not returned. 'I always knew who it was. It was me. I was going to put up a text that seemed to make an ironic comment on the affair every day until it was sorted out. It tickled me that I was the one picked to watch the board. I worded my negative reports to the CI very carefully. It didn't seem very amusing any more though, once the little boy went missing, so I didn't put the others up. Drop them in the bin for me on your way out, will you?' He pushed the remaining card towards Taylor. *Pray unto the Lord,* the sergeant read, *that he take away the serpents from us.*